GREY PIGEON
and other stories

Neelum Saran Gour

PENGUIN BOOKS
An imprint of Penguin Random House

PENGUIN BOOKS

USA | Canada | UK | Ireland | Australia
New Zealand | India | South Africa | China | Singapore

Penguin Books is part of the Penguin Random House group of companies
whose addresses can be found at global.penguinrandomhouse.com

Published by Penguin Random House India Pvt. Ltd
4th Floor, Capital Tower 1, MG Road,
Gurugram 122 002, Haryana, India

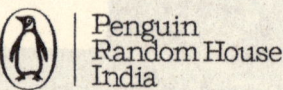

First published by Penguin Books India (P) Ltd 1993
This edition published by Penguin Random House India Pvt. Ltd 2019

ISBN 9780143449034

Typeset in Palatino by dTech Services Pvt. Ltd.New Delhi

Printed at Repro India Limited

www.penguin.co.in

This is a legitimate digitally printed version of the book and therefore might not
have certain extra finishing on the cover.

PENGUIN BOOKS
GREY PIGEON AND OTHER STORIES

Neelum Saran Gour is the author of *Winter Companions and Other Stories*, *Speaking of 62*, *Virtual Realities*, *Sikandar Chowk Park* and *Song Without End and Other Stories*, all published by Penguin. She has published a postcolonial parody of Charles Dickens, Arthur Conan Doyle and P.G. Wodehouse; translated her work into Hindustani in *Baasath Ki Baatein*, published by Penguin-Yatra (now reprinted by Prabhat Publications); written a critical study of Raja Rao entitled *Raja Rao's Metaphysical Trilogy*; and edited a pictorial volume on the history and culture of her city, Allahabad, called *Allahabad: Where The Rivers Meet*, published by Marg Publications. Her recent work includes *Three Rivers and a Tree: The Story of Allahabad University*, published by Rupa and Company; *Allahabad Aria: Stories about Allahabad*, published by Rupa; and *Invisible Ink*, published by HarperCollins. *Requiem in Raga Janki*, winner of the 2018 Hindu Fiction Prize, a fictional biography of the famous singer Janki Bai Ilahabadi, is her latest novel, published by Penguin Random House.

Her work has appeared in several anthologies and journals and she has been an active book reviewer for the *Times Literary Supplement*, *The Indian Review of Books*, *The Book Review* and *Biblio*. She has also written humour columns for the Allahabad page of the *Hindustan Times*.

Her work has appeared in numerous international and national publications which include *Desert in Bloom* (Pencraft); *Growing Up As a Woman Writer* (Sahitya Akademi and Sage Publications); *Fear Factor* (Picador India and Picador Australia); *Only Connect* (Brass Monkey, Australia, and released in an Indian edition by Rupa); *The Creative Process: Seven Essays*, edited by Jasbir Jain; *Indian English and Vernacular Literature*, edited by Makarand Paranjape and G.J.V. Prasad; and *Learning Non-violence*, edited by Gangeya Mukherji (Oxford University Press). Her forthcoming works include essays in a volume on Rudyard Kipling, published by The Indian Institute of Advanced Study, Shimla, and the Kipling Society, UK, and on Raja Rao, published by Routledge.

She is a professor of English at the University of Allahabad. For more information about her, visit: www.neelumsarangour.com.

To Sudhanshu,

who knows the story of each story
that I write.

Contents

Contents

Acknowledgements

I must mention my debt to the journal *Al-Risala* for quotations from the Quran for the story 'Goddess of Clay'; to P. E. Roberts's *History of British India* for sections of historical detail for 'Notes and Chapters'; and to the 12 April 1865 issue of the *Pioneer* for certain references in 'Coming of Age'.

A NEW YEAR'S PARTY

They called him Uncle Scrooge. Not that he was a miser or had ever displayed any special proofs of callousness but his widower status, his solitary spartan ways and his accounting job somehow tempted the literati of the neighbourhood to draw some rash parallels. Especially in the Christmas season.

True, he worked on Sundays and all holidays including Christmas but that was because there was little else to occupy himself with. This Christmas Eve was no different.

Geoffrey Fernandes, old Geoff, worked until dusk fell and when the lights began to shine outside his fourth-floor windows, he decided to call it a day. On this day the stenographer, the two clerks and his partner had taken the second half off and the responsibility of closing the windows, switching off the lights and locking up was his. Pocketing the keys, he creaked down the old wooden staircase, sixty-four moaning steps and emerged upon Metcalfe Street.

A Calcuttan Christmas was a sight in itself, reflected he, walking down Chowringhee. An English dish with Portuguese sauce upon a Bengali bill of fare! The shades of night cast a generous covering over the city's many destitutes and if a street-light fell upon a haggard, half-naked woman or if a thin claw was thrust beggar-wise under one's nose, it only lent a certain Dickensian aura to the place. This was the city of the Fagins and the Dawkins and the Nancys of God's unchanging world, thought old Geoff. And he, poor old Scrooge, nasty old Scrooge, locked up in himself.

It was also the city of the Doras and the Rosas! The air was aswirl with the gold dust of galaxies of little giggling electric bulbs, opening and closing, winking, racing to left, racing to right, falling flat, a little wink here, a little blur, dip, blush and twinkle there, all

1

a vast chorus in a hilarious musical comedy of light. Now a slow minuet and now a roaring rumba. Gold dust, river mist, tinsel and gloss, the very streets gift-wrapped in crackling tissue, tied up in little leaping festoons and scallops of streamers, looped and twisted and knotted and dangling with rainbow baubles, and a syrupy, confectionery smell everywhere! Gracious, thought old Geoff, what a long line at Flury's! The Bengali does not bother much about his bread but he loves cake. Witness the rows of piled-up plum cakes, five rupees a piece, sixteen rupees a piece and twenty rupees a piece, all spread out or towering in little cocoa hillocks upon cloth spread upon the pavement. The giddy doors of restaurants swing open, swing shut. Their ceilings are hung with tinsel stars, gauze demons, cardboard moons, crazy puppets. And a laughing, lewd, husky music, all asleep and astaggering, floats out and teeters down the street. Old fat men wearing paper caps, claiming to be Mickey Mouse or Superman, blowing straw whistles, fox-trotting without partners, or taking swigs out of bottles. And, tonight's carol singers already upon street corners, sitting upon rickshaws, tuning up with a few delightful, unholy lyrics, the ethnic dholaks athump, the fiddles shrilling higher and higher, the harmoniums trickling and snorting in unheeding mutiny down the scale, and naughty voices croaking naughty, crazy words with expressions of soulful piety! Crowds of applauding jokers, drunks, dancers, teeny-boppers.

Geoff turns into New Market to buy a few flowers. A couple of long-stalked tuberoses, smelling of paradise and a romp in a monsoon garden and a sleep in a wreath-strewn grave. A scent which brought in memories of the future and hopes of the past. A tuberose for the vase, a bottle of Army rum and a token plum cake—that's Christmas for me. Finally, a long trudge up the stairs to his apartment on Kyd Street, the unfailing crash against the bicycles in the dark corridor, the unlocking of a door and the click of an electric switch. A buoyant, bouncy voice is heartying up the room. A lady smiles winningly and music strikes up. Calcutta television gives Geoff Fernandes dozens of joyous companions upon this evening of evenings. He drinks his way slowly and purposefully down the bottle. Ants hear of cake crumbs and descend in their hundreds to carry away the loot.

There is still the most important ceremony to perform, the two letters to write to the only two persons in the world he cared to invite on New Year's Eve. My dear Alphonse, he scribbled. My dear Sheena . . . . .

They never, never dropped in together. How could they? Their trains arrived at different hours of the evening. Hers came in at 8.45 and she being a flighty, bubbling creature who loved to dawdle before shop-windows, day-dreaming, was ever late. His came in at 3.00 so he was usually already in before Geoff returned from office, laden with his parcels.

The key was in a crack above the mailbox. Old Alphonse knew exactly where it was and he knew how to make himself comfortable in the old apartment. After all, hadn't he lived in it for years and years before Geoff took over?

What point was there in coming home early?—was Geoff's argument. After all, the old guy would be fast asleep after his journey and absolutely at home.

Planning the eats was the tricky thing. No sweets. The old one was diabetic, the young one probably on her perennial diet. Nuts? But what about his teeth? Slices of off-season pineapples, cookies, wafers, cheeselings, mince-pies and grilled chicken off a cart. Fine, fresh rolls and tins of cheese, tins of soup, slices of salami and ham. He had that bottle of Johnny Walker tucked away for some such glorious day. But what a lot of packets and only two arms to load them on. Well, he'd done his best for them—they were hard to please, those two, but surely they'd see at a glance how much thought and money and affection had gone into the feast. So he reflected, struggling up the dark, old stairs, carefully balancing his way lest a single item fall.

The lights were on in the apartment and what a comforting feeling that was—to feel that somebody was already there in that chilly, empty home before him. He pushed open the door.

There was his battered old over-nighter on the floor but where on earth was he?

'Alphonse!' cried Geoff. 'Where are you, Alphonse?'

A low grunt from the loo set his mind at rest. The old fellow's bowels were a problem—always had been. They roared, rumbled and revolted at all hours.

He dumped the parcels upon the table. The checked tablecloth was already laid, the TV going full blast. A rumpled cushion upon the rocking-chair, ash upon the threadbare rug—Alphonse had smoked and slept, leaving these marks of his presence. Geoff sank slowly down into the armchair, savouring the soft assurance of another unseen human presence here with him and here before him. It was comforting not to stride into a void. 'Oh, there you are, Alphonse!' cried he, rising to his feet as the old figure came shuffling out, holding himself aslant, taking the short, sudden steps of a very old man.

'Happy New Year, Alphonse!' he cried warmly. 'Er—ring out the old, ring in the new, you know, Alphonse, old chap!'

The old man grunted and shot him a sharp, accusing look. His faded grey eyes could pierce holes through one's skin, thought Geoff.

'Not so soon, dash it, Geoff!' came the baritone protest. 'It's four hours to go.' He lowered himself slowly down the rocking-chair.

'Always in a hurry to ring out the old—eh?' He shrugged cynically.

Geoff laughed uproariously. 'Ha-ha-ha indeed! Touchy, Alphonse?'

The old man waved an invisible fly aside. His eyes went round the room, warming upon old bric-a-brac, puzzling over new books, peering at pictures.

'There, Alphonse, that's you.' Geoff pointed at the yellow monochrome upon the wall above the mock mantelpiece. 'Remember yourself?'

'Hmm,' responded his guest. 'You still have it here?'

'You're decorative, you know. Add quality and atmosphere. I'd cherish that portrait even if I didn't know you from Adam. As it is, I'm fond of that fluffed cravat and those collar-studs and that air of supercilious gravity, Alphonse. There's aristocracy in 'em all.'

'They weren't bad,' conceded Alphonse. 'What's that you got on the wall?'

Geoff scanned the far end of the room. That? Don't you remember? It's an old print of yours—a Rembrandt called *The Philosopher*. Used to lie about in your files. So I decided to salvage it and put it in a respectable frame. The fellow did a good job. Like it?'

'Um,' assented Alphonse. 'You've had them chairs polished.'

'Same old things,' informed Geoff. 'The upholstery was all gone. I had them done up. How d'you find 'em?'

'Terrible,' snorted Alphonse, closing his eyes upon a satisfying inhalation of pipe.

'And that . . . that object?' He opened his eyes and pointed at a yellow fibre-glass garden chair Geoffrey had picked up at an auction.

'That's a washable chair, Alphonse,' explained Geoff.

'A washable. . . chair!' The old man's eyes shone with merriment. 'How very extraordinary! A washable chair!' His shoulders shook with convulsive laughter. 'How very strange! A washable chair, to be sure!'

Geoffrey was beginning to find this senile humour trying.

'What's strange?' asked he testily.

'Why should one wash . . . a chair? Ho, ho, ho!' went the old guy and collapsed in spasms of wheezing laughter. Geoffrey shrugged, rose and strode to the sideboard and stopped short all of a sudden.

'What's that now?' asked he in wonder.

'For you, lad,' answered the merry old man. 'And a Happy New Year to be sure.'

'A Dom Perignon! 1952!—It's terribly good of you, Alphonse.'

'Don't mention it,' wheezed the guest. 'Ring in the new, my lad.' He pointed a threatening finger at Geoffrey's face— 'but never, never ring out the old.'

Geoffrey laughed. 'I never do, I never do, Alphonse. It can't be done.'

'I'm afraid,' he went on, unlocking a cabinet, '—that I haven't anything equally splendid for you.' He extracted a small packet from the recesses of the cabinet and slapped it heartily upon the peg-table beside the rocking-chair.

'What is it then?' queried the guest.

'Something you like,' said Geoff affectionately. 'A whole book of crossword puzzles. Keep you busy all evening. And a detective novel to set your wits racing. Keep you busy all night. Remember last year?'

A gleeful grin cracked across the guest's face.

'Just so,' said he. 'Quite so.'

Those crossword puzzles would almost all be worked out in a couple of hours, Geoff knew. Some of the tougher ones would be left for Geoff to work out. That detective story would tease the old man out of all thought and speech and he would pester Geoff for his opinion and his own detective devices until next morning. The old man slept badly—his sleeping was done in the afternoons.

'Oh, by the way, I have last year's crosswords all worked out for you. Took me some time, you can bet. Some still remain to be solved. But Sheena is clever . . . .'

'Sheena?' The old man sniffed. 'That young lady is to be here again?'

Geoffrey nodded. 'Charming, isn't she?' he asked. 'She'll help us work out what remains of that puzzle book. May be she'll tell you who murdered Alfred Fletcher on the night of 21 November.'

'That,' said the old man, '—is a silly young piece.'

'But you can't deny she's enchanting and full of fun and ideas and she has answers for everything.'

He looked at his watch. 'She should be here now. I don't know where she's got to.'

He went and stood by the window. Down below, the Number 59 tram shuttled past, clanging all its bells, rattling upon its guttural track. A nippy south wind stole in, wet from the Bay of Bengal. Taxies scurried about in 31 December frenzy. Rickshaw pullers still raced, hot-foot, bearing little old Chinese ladies in pyjamas and jackets and puckered parchment faces. The shops began pulling down their shutters.

'Relax, Alphonse,' Geoff called over his shoulder. 'How 'bout those crosswords now? Or wait. Let's open up that Johnny Walker. The night is young, as they say. She'll be here soon. Bound to be.'

Nine-thirty and still no sign of her. The party couldn't begin without her and here was this old fellow getting restive. Geoffrey clicked impatiently, glass in hand at the window. She was the limit. She loved making them wait. It was one of her little ways.

'Sorry, Alphonse,' he muttered, apologetic. 'I guess we'll just have to do without her. You carry on with those puzzles—I'll go warm up the soup. Let me fix you another drink.'

'A silly young piece.' He heard Alphonse grumble into his beard. All the same it was all too obvious that Alphonse, like him, Geoffrey, was impatiently waiting for the giddy girl to arrive. The anxious look he threw at the door, the start when footsteps sounded on the stairs, all bespoke suppressed anticipation and restless suspense.

He carried in the soup tureen from the kitchenette and set it centrally down upon the chequered tablecloth. He undid the packets of wafers, spread butter and cheese on rolls, arranged pineapple slices upon a plate and the festive chicken upon another, brought in more dishes, bowls, spoons . . . . That was when a door banged shut, down below, a cab started, a bell shrilled and presently a flurry of high-heeled shoes clattered up the stairs and a strong whiff of cologne swept in with the breeze.

Alphonse dropped his book upon his lap. Geoffrey dropped the spoons upon the table.

'She's here!' he cried, excitedly. The old man nodded joyfully and the door burst open.

'Oh, Geoff, old boy!' cried her high, childlike voice. 'How unforgiveable of me, I do declare! I've kept you guys waiting.' She flung her bag upon the settee, pirouetted round and hugged Geoff, stared in mock astonishment at Alphonse, reflected and pecked him on the cheek.

'Sorry, old bear,' she cooed. 'I didn't mean to be so late but . . . anyway, its fun to have folks waiting for you, isn't it? I love doing it. Fancy having a life in which nobody's waiting for you. And this . . . this Neanderthal man? Whoever's he? Oh, oh, it's Alphonse. My, isn't he old! I took him for your prehistoric orangutan.' She tinkled out her kiddish, outrageous giggle. And Alphonse always so sensitive to her words, or didn't she know that? 'Peanuts, baboon?'

Alphonse was white with sudden rage. 'I imperfectly comprehend your import, young lady,' said he stiffly in his best Oxonian accent.

'Oh come, Alphonse, drop that courtly air. Anyone would imagine you're a stuffy old earl that the taxidermist has filled up with rotten straw!'

'I insist,' said Alphonse gruffly, '—on a proper observance of form. I am considerably older than you, lady, and I take strong exception to your language.'

'Why, what's wrong with him?' cried she, stung. 'I haven't been here five minutes and there he goes again. What you need, sir, is a string of good, contemporary, soul-stirring profanities and I've a mind to let you have 'em and gratis.'

'Sheena, please,' begged Geoff.

'Is this propah? Is this right?' she mocked.

'I do believe you're mad, both of you. You're like oil and water. Can't mix. I call you here and the moment you set eyes upon one another, you fly at one another's throats!'

'But this . . .' he flung his arms out despairingly, 'is my party. I'm going into the kitchen. Kindly let peace be restored by the time I return.'

They sat, opposite one another in perfect harmony, smiling amiably when Geoff returned, carrying the glasses. Suddenly the comedy of it struck him.

'Sorry, old girl.' He smiled. 'I guess you just got us both het up with waiting. We're old chaps, you know, and prolonged tension, stress . . . .'

'And I . . . ' she put an arm round Alphonse's shoulders, 'got het up with guilt. Stress . . .' she smiled winningly into Alphonse's disgruntled face— 'is right.'

'Anyway,' said he, popping the Perignon, 'whatever have the two of you been saying to one another to re-establish such peace?'

'Nothing,' barked Alphonse.

'Nothing.' Sheena giggled. 'We're at war.' She laughed amusedly. 'We don't have anything to say to one another, Geoff. It's you we wish to speak to.'

She'd hit the nail on the head, he speculated. Whatever could those two ever find to say to one another? Absolutely nothing. She so young, so impetuous, he so old and so temperamental. It was he that loved them, wanted them to meet, interact, enrich him with their presence. They were important to him. But, it was unlikely that outside the dim circuit of his room, they would ever meet elsewhere. And their coming together like this solely for his pleasure quite overcame him. If they'd only get along better, there could be such an identity of attitudes between them. But they were stubborn as mules. We three, he reflected, ought never to part. We must hang together. Consider our eyes, our noses, our stubborn chins. Consider our flying rages, our inveterate, compulsive solitudes. Remember our names, our homes. We are of a piece, alone in the world. Why then can they never agree? Why must I always negotiate between them, the patient, pettifogging pacifist? Why must I look forward to these meetings?

'What's for dinner? I could eat a horse!' she exclaimed.

'Shocking,' muttered Alphonse audibly.

She looked him up and down.

'All your favourites.' Geoff hastened to step in. 'And no extra calories, I assure you. Anyway, you're thin as a rake.'

'Much too thin,' said Alphonse dismissively.

Sheena looked as though she would burst.

'What beautiful champagne!' She sighed, choosing to ignore him.

'Dom Perignon,' said Alphonse, addressing the cabinet. '1952. Long before you were born.'

'It's Alphonse's New Year gift to me,' explained Geoff.

Sheena looked contrite. 'Oh, dear,' she said pitifully. 'And I haven't anything for you. You'll say I haven't any manners.'

'Nobody said you had, my dear,' said Alphonse sweetly.

She stabbed him with a killing look. 'But, Geoff, remember, even if I've got nothing for you today, I'll surely get you something next year. And . . . and, Geoff, when you're old, and ill and dying, I'll be by your bedside, mopping up your spittle and closing your eyes and laying you out straight and nice and arranging the wreaths . . . .'

'Ugh!' cried Geoff. 'Will you please stop it!'

Her eyes were large and grave.

'I mean it all, Geoff, honest.'

The little perisher, she had him all in a sweat!

'Alphonse and I have some crossword puzzles here that we could not quite work out to our satisfaction,' said Geoff, changing the subject. 'Alphonse thinks you're clever, Sheena. Don't go by his frowning face. But he's got this deep faith in you. "Only she," said he, "can work these out for us." And what Alphonse said, so say I.'

'Well, may be I can,' she replied playfully, taking a sip. 'And may be I can't. But I can try.'

And thank God for that, thought Geoff, relieved. Get her busy and keep her wilful little nose out of mischief. There's no knowing what she'll say or do next. Still, there's no getting away from the fact that where she turns up, anything may happen. Too flighty, too fanciful and too ambiguous altogether. She's got this little streak of cruelty too, the little beast. Loves coming up with the sly, the hurtful, the raw-nerve observation. But then, when you're least expecting civility from her, she'll stun you with her absolute tact and good sense. Mad girl, he thought affectionately. Now, Alphonse—he went on, sinking deeper into reverie—is reliable. He's solid and square. You don't like him completely but you know where you are with him. He's got this tough-nut gruffiness and stuffiness but a single remark from you can bring mist to his eyes and a quiver to his voice. He won't reveal all his secrets to you but he's by and large forgiving; and where he's not, he'll freely agree with you when you set out to prove your point. There's sound stuff in the old guy and I wish it were possible to have him here with me for good—but it can't be done and more's the pity.

Geoff looked long and fondly at the yellow-tinted portrait on the wall.

'Who's that gargoyle?' broke in her sharp young busybody voice.

'Mind your ps and qs, young Sheena. That's Alphonse as a young man.'

She uttered a little squeal and gazed at the picture with glee.

'Golly!' she cried, her eyes like saucers.

There's mischief brewing in that vile young brain or my name's not Geoff Fernandes, thought Geoffrey apprehensively.

'Portrait of the Artist as a young Ghoul? Ugh.' She took a deep breath. 'I marvel that you can sleep alone in this room, Geoff, with that . . . that thing looking at you all the time. I mean, I don't want to hurt your feelings, Alphonse, you're sweet and all the rest, but I think your present complexion and figure is a great improvement upon your past. The roses may have fled from the cheeks and the lilies from the brow but at least you no longer give one the creeps.' She tittered maliciously.

'You,' rejoined Alphonse calmly, rising to the occasion, '—are no oil painting yourself.'

'Oh, I'm sure I'm not,' she said modestly. 'But I hope soon to be.'

'And that reminds me, Sheena,' interrupted Geoff hastily, before Alphonse opened fire, '—when am I to get that photograph of yours? D'you know, when you aren't in front of me, I have trouble remembering your face.'

'You'll have to wait.' She waved an affected hand. 'Till I'm much prettier. I'll send you a blow-up of mine.'

'Gather ye rosebuds while ye may . . .' began Alphonse's wheezing cackle.

'Oh, help!' cried Sheena, rolling her eyes heavenwards.

'And why haven't I a picture of yours?' she demanded, flirtatious, wrathful.

'I . . . I haven't a proper snap yet,' stammered Geoff, confused. 'I don't photograph well—most unphotogenic, you know—I mean there're many snaps of me but I don't think I look like any of 'em. They're—how d'you put it? —they aren't true to the real me, the . . . essential me.'

'Rubbish!' she declared. 'You're a jolly sight more presentable than that . . . that moth-eaten earl there with that . . . that feather-duster of a beard . . . !'

'Oh, hell, Sheena, must you now?' protested Geoff feebly. I'll never have these two together here again. What a rotten idea!

To his immense surprise, he opened his eyes to behold Alphonse convulsed with spasmodic gusts, which he realized was Alphonse's version of a boisterous laugh.

'Ho! Ho! Ho! Ich! Ich! Ich!' went Alphonse. 'Feather-duster! Oh ho ho ho! Feather-duster indeed! Feather-duster, to be sure. I insist . . .' he turned to Geoff, '. . . on toasting this young lady. I'm proud of her. Young lady . . .' His beetling brows shrank in awesome concentration as he fixed his piercing gaze on Sheena's pouting face. 'Young lady, I'm proud of you and no mistake. I'm proud of your spirit, I'm proud of your speech and I'm proud of your splendid presence of mind. I drink to your health, madam.'

And the Perignon went gurgling down the thin alley of his throat and a drop or two ran down his chin and wet his old beard.

'Why, did I say something wrong?' asked Sheena, bewildered, turning to Geoff.

'He likes you after all, that's all, my dear,' said Geoff. '—and I absolutely join him in this toast. To the New Year and to our own Sheena! For she's a jolly good fellow!' cried he with a flourish and gulp, singing out the last words with abandon.

He wished he could snap all three of them together. What a great photograph it would make, old Alphonse, himself and Sheena. But then, how on earth could he himself get into that photograph? One couldn't shove oneself into the group and without him there in the middle, ordering it all, what would be the point? And, an outsider in their midst, brought in solely to execute the mechanics of camera-operation, would somehow break the spell of their three interlocked presences. It was upon a happy note of singing and toasting that they sat down to dinner.

'Mmmm,' murmured she, biting into the pineapple. 'This is splendid.'

'Not bad at all,' wheezed Alphonse, spooning up.

'You've done yourself proud, Geoff,' exclaimed she. 'Candles too!'

'All in your honour, milady,' said Geoff gallantly. 'This night,' intoned he, getting sentimental, '—is no ordinary one for me. May I make bold to tell you, young Sheena, that you look absolutely stunning in that crimson blouse.'

'This one?' She noticed it absently. 'Why, don't you remember it? It's one of Hannah's. You sent it across.'

Geoff peered at it in amazement.

'Well, well, well,' said he. 'You don't say so? Now that you mention it, I do remember it on Hannah when she was young. But you've done something to it, haven't you?'

'Oh, I've added a pair of fancy epaulettes and styled it a bit.'

'Most becoming. Perfectly charming, my dear,' said Alphonse with a courtly little bow.

'And now,' pronounced Geoff when the meal was over, 'will someone kindly tell Alphonse and me who killed Alfred Fletcher?'

'Alfred who?' She laughed. 'I thought you guys had puzzles for me to work out and now this.' She went on after a little pause. 'What d'you expect of me? Who d'you think I am?'

'The hope of our future!' cried Geoff, tipsy and roaring with laughter.

'I'd much rather draw you some pictures,' she said, sinking down on the sofa. 'I'm rather good at lightning sketches—or don't you know?' She looked from Geoff to Alphonse and back at Geoff. 'Ha! Suppose I gave you Alphonse's nose and beard and suppose I gave him your chin and your eyes—what fun?'

'How very extraordinary now,' exclaimed Alphonse, staring at her over the rim of his glasses.

'What?' asked Geoff.

'I too,' said Alphonse, '—loved to sketch and let me tell you, young lady, that which you have just described was one of my favoured pastimes. Interchanging noses and eyes and expressions. It was very, very adventurous.'

Sheena was interested. 'It sure is. You don't mean to say that it isn't my original copyright? You did it before me?'

Alphonse nodded happily, rocking very hard upon his chair.

'I sure am impressed,' she said.

'Oh, Alphonse is a man for all seasons,' said Geoff. 'You've got to know him better, Sheena, to realize how clever and deep and inspired he is.'

'Tut! Tut!' clicked Alphonse bashfully.

It was upon that instant that a loud bang outside the door arrested Geoff's attention. Bang, bang, bang, bang! It was followed by a salvo of blasts; motor horns began simultaneously beeping, fireworks exploding. Sky-rockets zoomed off in iridescent tangents, bloomed into giant flowers that broke in the upper air and rained burning petals upon the city. Outside the dark windowpanes, showers of smashed golden dragons cascaded in the dark air. Geoff rushed to the window. Balloons soared, puffed up, swayed and swung aslant away into the night and a burst of riotous clapping and singing shot out of the TV screen.

Happy New Year! And Happy New Year! And Happy New Year again—they chanted. Standing, beating time upon the rug, Geoffrey Fernandes found himself smiling tipsily and clapping to the music, wishing himself a Happy New Year again and again and again. That's what one waited for—this moment of the trapped present, this make-believe zero-time, this instant of pause between two calendars of time, a carnival of gilt glory, this tutored fling of music and this lissom excess swaying upon the screen to lend your old bones its own illusion. They did not say anything like 'Peace on earth and goodwill to all men'. The world had grown up. But after half an hour of intensive merriment, the compère flashed into view, smiling beatifically as in a vision of indescribable cheer. 'Goodbye and good luck,' she bade him personally. 'And keep smiling.'

It wasn't necessary to utter any farewells. Geoff Fernandes knew that he had thrown a successful party and got away with it. And to throw a successful party when one is all alone of an evening and all alone in the world—well, almost—is no mean feat. To throw a successful party with nobody attending save an old grandad, dead and gone for forty years and more, and a flighty young fantasy of a granddaughter, unborn still and unlikely ever to be born, was, by God, no minor feat. There was no one else that Geoff Fernandes cared to entertain now save past or possible people. Five rich fulsome years in the beginning of one's life spent with the one; and maybe five possible years at the end of one's existence with the other—nobody knew how many significant beings passed one another by in time and could never meet save in him. To get them to meet and be his guests, be it only once, was old Geoffrey's wayward dream. And he'd carried it off, he happily knew, this tipsy New Year's Eve.

THE TASTE OF ALMONDS

The late Nizam of Hyderabad, it was said, relished burfi made from the milk of cows that had been fed on a special diet of pistachios.

It was a scale of splendour that Nawab Jamaluddin Naqvi, senior baron-in-residence of Sher Kothi, Khoa Mohal, Kanpur, had not been able to match. All the same he had, in his youthful days, devised some modestly comparable approximations.

The decades had robbed Nawab Saab's memory of all redundant details, personal or public, as his progeny had deprived him of the freedom of movement deemed injurious to his well-being. It was just as well, for Nawab Jamal Saab senior's intelligence was now rendered altogether impervious to most demanding subjects. Only the very remote past shone in his eyes with the sharp clarity of a world recognized. That Sher Kothi was now a ramshackle, mouldering structure, moss-covered, vermin-infested, rafters rotten, and the roots of the peepuls rending asunder the old stone pavings, made no impression upon his consciousness. And that Khoa Mohal, once the extensive property of Nawab Saab's forbears, was now a filthy labyrinth of dingy alleys, slushy, smelly and inhabited by poor vendors, shop-assistants, baker's boys, poor tailors, shoemakers and embroiderers, mattered little to him.

Half a century's close consort with Allah (five interviews a day) and for the last two decades a stern leash upon the errant Iranian blood had refined Nawab Saab's spirit and bent his back. But as age advanced and the cornices and balustrades of his sprawling Saracenic homestead crumbled and gave way, as the world receded in clarity and the very birds wheeled away in ever-fading circles into the sooty sky, the pangs of the palate arose with vengeful spite to torment and to mortify. And the palate, Nawab Saab sorrowfully realized, may not be mocked.

Not for him the strong savours of the common gourmand, all nutmeg and saffron, burning paprika or pungent cardamom. Nawab Saab's savours, like his sensibility, were more sophisticated. To him there came insistently, like the voice of Satan in the Garden, the tender scent of pomegranate, memories of lost Quandahar, cashewnut in cream in ivory bowls and ah! most tantalizing, visions of almond blossom, almond burfi, sweet, delectable almond paste beneath its mantle of shining foil, moon-cool and fulfilling as a draught of spring-water from a rivulet of paradise!

To waken of a summer's morning, obsessed with the feasts of the past and to discover the door of the court unbolted was a happy agreement of circumstances worthy only of Allah's foresight. One intuition alone sustained him. Somewhere down the way, to right and then to right again, beyond the mosque and the tentmaker's, was Nadeem, faithful retainer, sweet sycophant, Nadeem, prince of the palate, sweetmeat wizard, artist par excellence!

So, into the entrails of a hectic teeming bazaar wandered Nawab Saab for an hour and more, asking: 'May the offence be excused, noble sir, but be this the lane wherein Nadeem Khan, the sweetmeat seller, holds residence?'

It was a quest unrewarded. Nobody in that crowded, noisy bazaar had heard of Nadeem Khan. The blazing sun made Nawab Saab's brow sweat and made his ragged kurta and checked lungi cling to the clammy skin. The dust and slush soiled his old *nagras* where the embroidered peacocks once reposed. Noise, rancid gutters, horse's hoofs and bicycle bells made havoc of his confidence. And a multitude of preposterous shop-signs, each more grotesque than the last, confounded his befogged wits. It was a crazy, teasing world. He paused before a stall and read with difficulty (the language of his own time being Persian or a civilized Urdu), the Hindi alphabets: *'Hul-chul* Chaat' and above it the pious sentiment: 'This too shall pass.' To the best of his knowledge and belief, *'hul-chul'* meant 'hurly-burly', confusion; and why the shop-owner should designate his shop 'confusion' was beyond his comprehension, and what confusion should have in common with the observation that all is ephemeral challenged his powers beyond their scope. He shook his head, mystified, and went on. There was another entitled *'Badnaam* lassi' or 'Whipped curd of ill-fame', surely an extraordinary style of advertisement, where he was offered two choices, an Amitabh Bachchan glass, to wit, a nine-inch tall glass, or a Mukri glass, that is, a five-inch glass, allusions which were lost on Nawab Saab's intelligence and did nothing to further his grasp of contemporary things. Declining, he hastened on, only to be arrested by the caption: 'Sold by son but guaranteed by father' over a cart and beneath, in golden letters the name '*Hahakar* Kulfi' or 'Uproar Kulfi'. This was Kanpur's mad, boisterous folk culture and it only made Nawab Saab's confusion worse confounded. 'Nadeem, Nadeem,' he muttered to himself, his eyes scanning the bewildering names, sweeping over the wares, darting into the interiors.

And it was at the end of an alley, upon a dingy plank over a drain, that his search was crowned with partial success. A sweetmeat shop, though not Nadeem's, and plying a brisk trade judging by the crowd, almost as numerous as the flies, and above, the piquant sign: 'Welcome and Be Cheated. Asad Mukhtar—Sweetmeat Seller.'

The array of colourful sweetmeats laid out on open trays or piled in symmetrical pyramids upon platters or still sizzling in large iron cauldrons of boiling oil, would not, in their appearance and colour scheme, have met with Nawab Saab's approval. But hunger having given him an open mind and the crowd of customers having afforded him ease of access, he professed himself willing to give Asad Mukhtar, sweetmeat seller's talents a fair chance.

He was not impressed. There were pedas choked with sugar, smashed-pearl laddoos which stuck to the teeth or dry gram-flour laddoos which grated against the tongue. Squares of cottage cheese paste as cottage cheese had no business to be; jalebis too viscous of syrup and too soggy of skin. It will be evident, by reason of Nawab Saab's growing disgust, that he had already given Asad Mukhtar's skills more than a fair chance when at last some milk-cauldron-scrapings set in trays brought to the discerning palate a faint, long lost intimation of the past. And it was precisely at this moment that all hell broke loose.

'Hey, grandsire! What's that you're doing, grey-beard? I saw you, I did, you mangy mongrel!'

His bent back prevented Nawab Saab from drawing himself up to his former height but his eye was austere and his voice admonishing.

'Your pedas are inedible, noble sir,' said he. 'Less of the sugar and more of the milk. Your laddoos have no trace of chopped raisins or walnuts or cashewnuts. And you must not expect me to believe that the medium you use to fry your jalebis in is the best Khurja ghee. There is no silver foil on your burfies, but this I concede, your *khurchan* is passable . . . .'

'Ah-ha-ha-ha!' roared the excitable young man, at a loss for words. 'Oh, God above, he robs me in broad daylight, pays not a paisa, tries everything, helps himself, then spits on my skill!'

A crowd had gathered. Nawab Saab's runaway rhetoric had drawn the masses but his talk of cashewnuts and pure ghee in this humble pocket of Kanpur had provoked their merriment. Clearly in this nautanki there was a clown to hoot and the Kanpur crowd knows a good nautanki when it sees one. There was immense laughter, many sallies.

'Khurja ghee!' roared one. 'You oil your beard with it, do you, old timer?'

'I get my retainers to massage my calves with it, sir,' was Nawab Saab's unruffled reply. A shocked silence fell at the felon's smooth daredevilry. At his age and with a back as bent as that and a prayer-mark as large as a rupee coin on his forehead too!

'What I am looking for is some good old-fashioned malai-gillories. Real cream and almonds.' Nawab Saab sought the crowd's assistance. 'Can any of you gentlemen tell me where those can be had?'

'I'll give you malai-gillories!' shouted the young man, at the end of his patience. 'Were it not for your bent back, grandsire, your beard would pay for your booty!'

Nawab Jamal Saab stared at the rash young serf, incredulous. His eyes were irascible, his voice dangerous as he intoned the following words:

'Do you know who it is that stands before you? You are addressing Nawab Jamaluddin Naqvi, owner of this estate, this bazaar and a quarter of this city.'

Look on my presence, ye scullions and tremble—his voice suggested.

'What is more, for your inadequacies at your art, I shall have your shop closed down, your vessels confiscated and your back dealt twenty lashes at the very earliest, sir.' His voice was icy in contempt. 'Your place shall be taken by Nadeem Khan, when I can find him, Nadeem Khan, the finest chef in all Kanpur and Unnao and Etawah as well!'

The young man froze where he stood and his face went pale, his fury forgotten.

'Nadeem Khan has been dead these thirty years, sir,' said he slowly. 'He was my maternal grandfather.'

'Nadeem Khan dead? How? When? Why wasn't I told? Ah, Nadeem, Nadeem!' The old man's grief was pitiful to behold. His red eyes filled and his voice was shrill. He sank down upon a wooden bench. 'Ah, Nadeem, my friend. And where can I get my gillories now, answer me?' He sniffed like a child. 'There are no almond gillories left in the world. And no friends like you. Quality is gone and fineness too. Ah, the world is too poor now, O Nadeem.'

Some men from the crowd came forward and put their arms about his bowed shoulders and knelt before his form. And one said: 'Ah, do not weep, old master. For those that are gone belong to Him now, says the Book, and presumptuous are we to claim them for our own.' And another whispered: 'Hush, do you know who this is? It's the old Nawab of Sher Kothi, the senile one, the one who's kept locked up.'

A wave of compassion swept over the crowd. Such things do happen. How did he get out? Never mind, he doesn't remember his way about. Almonds and walnuts, was it, grandad? To crush beneath teeth you lost a quarter-century ago? 'For shame, Asad. Salaam him, Asad. Go on, where's your Islamic civility, man? Render unto the old masters the things that were theirs, if only in charade, Mian!'

And Asad came down from his wooden platform, his ladle and boiling cauldron forgotten, and kneeling in the dust, bowed low and salaamed the old one. And said: 'Huzoor, your wish is my command. There, there, now. Gillories it shall be, though with my last paisa. Almond gillories, be sure now and no mistake, old master.'

His brother Khursheed brought a charpoy for the Nawab to sit on and the shoemaker next door appeared instantly with a fan. 'Be seated, master, be seated,' urged many gentle voices.

Nawab Saab's tears were dry now and he was in his element. This courtesy of fawning and feting he knew and understood. Speech breaks from his lips in an irrepressible wave.

'At my behest,' he is telling the crowd'. —a seer of almond paste was boiled in three seers of sweetened milk in an earthen pot perched upon a slow-burning wood fire. From dawn till dusk it thickened, the cream removed repeatedly, flattened on a platter and chilled over blocks of ice. And when cool, stuffed with cardamom and chips of almonds, twisted cunningly betel-wise, sprinkled with the essence of rose, and folded in foil of silver . . .'

'So shall it be and exactly so, old master,' whispered the old seamstress in the burqa. 'Rest thy poor bones awhile on this charpoy and we, thy slaves shall do the rest.'

So Nawab Saab yawned and the excitement of the morning having imposed a heaviness on the limbs and a drowsiness upon the eyes, stretched himself, yawned again, sleepily murmured God's name and went to sleep.

And how, they asked of one another, can we poor folk get almonds for him? Almonds sell at two hundred rupees a kilo. And Khurja ghee is hard to come by for the likes of us. Milk for it alone shall cost fifty rupees and more. And no man here but makes a petty sum too small to fill his belly or clothe his own. The poor cannot afford to pay such largesse nor enact such scenes of munificence. Yes, they said, the world for us has become too poor, for was not once this filthy lane a flourishing hive of merchants and do but observe it now.

But there were others that urged: silence, I beg you, consider this old one here. If there is one that is poorer far than we, yonder does he lie and may the Prophet pardon my presumption. To him do we owe that two-and-a-half per cent rather than the ne'er-do-well mendicants that come abegging at our doors.

And then there transpired a most wonderful gesture, yes, even in that dingy lane. Seamstress, tailor, shoemaker, baker-boy, rickshaw-puller, fruit vendor, holy man and gram woman, barber and butcher, all came forth and said: 'Asad, my lad, take this and use it. It's all I can spare today, may God not shame me for my poverty, but it's what I give you for him that lies there . . . .' So they came, many more than one may think possible, cultured and fine as only the very poor can sometimes be.

And so Asad sent Khursheed to buy more milk and the seamstress volunteered to buy the almonds and the tailor and vendor brought wood for the fire and the curd-man supplied the earthen pot. Nawab Saab slept upon his charpoy, the mosquitoes gently fanned away from his ancient limbs by Asad's young wife.

And as the work went on, they stole looks at him and whispered about him. A very holy man he was, they said. A Haji. That was when he was younger, said another. He had the permitted four wives but the only snag in his serenity was that the four devout ladies were given to bickering and spitefulness all day and try as he might he could not maintain equality and accord betwixt them. My father told me all about it as a child. So Nawab Saab grew disenchanted with his women. They say that he fell headlong in love with a nautch girl but when he announced his decision to marry her, a storm broke out. Such moral indignation there was, such turbulent discourses from the Book. All that Nawab Saab said was: 'Why, what difference betwixt four women and five?' But public opinion prevailed and so Nawab Saab renounced his nautch girl, sadder and wiser, and loved no more.

Everyone laughed throwing indulgent glances at the charpoy. 'Hush, for shame!'—reprimanded the tailor. 'A Mussalman must not gossip nor deride another. Scandal-mongering is haraam, *so* hold your tongues.' But someone else had news to impart. The young nawab, his grandson, has a bicycle shop on Meston Road and locks up the old one personally before he leaves. An old maid cooks and sweeps. The young Nawab's father was a great cockfighter and the young one is an accomplished kite-flyer and wins all the bouts. This old one wanders about when he can and is brought home by kindly passers-by.

It was many hours later and well into the dusk when Nawab Saab was woken up with the gentle plea: 'Huzoor, awake. Your almond gillories are ready.'

Sitting on his charpoy, Nawab Saab wiped his mouth, cleaned his beard and dried his eyes.

'That was good,' sighed he, a man content.

Asad, the sweetmeat-seller bowed. Hasan, the tailor, bowed. The grocer, the bangle-seller, the seamstress, the barber, the butcher, the tea-shop owner, everyone bowed low and said: 'The honour is ours, old master.' And a few smiled but a few faltered.

'We regret, old master, that your honour had to wait long for the gillories to be ready,' apologized Asad.

'Ah, no,' murmured Nawab Saab.' I quite enjoyed my slumber on this charpoy. I dreamt of almonds . . .' He chuckled mischievously and looked round for laughter. Everyone laughed politely.

Nawab Saab took off his battered cap and handed it regally to Asad. 'Take that, my man,' he pronounced with solemnity. 'That is a royal cap in recognition of your services. I regret that I do not have any gold on me today, but that cap is far more precious. Show it anywhere on my estates and take anything you want in my name.' Nawab Saab grew sententious. 'Take anything from the world, I tell myself, my men, but pay for it. Take first and pay later, or pay first and take thereafter but pay you must, now or in jahannum.' He swelled with importance. 'Only we, who came as conquerors, took and paid nought, but that was our privilege.'

The shades of night had fallen upon the old blackened balustrades when Nawab Jamaluddin Naqvi, seated royally upon a rickshaw drawn by Mehtab the puller and escorted by a flock of his loyal subjects, was conducted to his residential quarters in Sher Kothi, his palate at peace and his pride most appeased.

And Asad put the cap reverently upon a ledge in his shop for even with his unpolished sense he knew what it signified. Like the coins of the old water carrier in our history books who was exalted to kingship for three brief days and who insisted on striking leathern coins cut out of his water-bag for the citizens to use, be it only for three days, the cap stood for the richness of some delusions and gestures, a gift from the poor to the poor, where all are poor before God.

PORTABLE PROPERTY

The house on Shilpara Road had long lain vacant and Subir Sanyal, its owner, had despaired of finding a suitable tenant. The main road whips itself round the ancient banyan tree, beneath which a vermilion god reclines, past the straggling market and the carpenters' shop and the kerosene depot.

One man turns into Shilpara lane on the right and asks for S. Sanyal at the first house. So a tenant at long last—the neighbourhood was agog.

A bachelor, yes, confirmed fat Sunanda Sanyal noisily across the yard from her balcony. Unattached? Indeed, yes, and he needs lots of space for his things. Rich, that means. The women exchanged meaningful looks. In the shoddy, suburban lane curiosity simmered and came to a boil.

That evening a truck roared into Shilpara lane, loaded high, bringing everybody to their windows and balconies. It rolled carefully down the unpaved lane, bumping over the small drains, turning and backing with much cautioning and calling of instructions from the two labourers who had leapt off.

The bachelor emerged from the front seat and the neighbourhood experienced a severe disappointment. For, Rajni Kant Swamy was an unprepossessing man. Bald and slight and a little squirrel-faced, with the gentle, worried eyes of the confirmed gentleman anxious not to offend or incommode. He was dressed in a dapper little bush-shirt that would have fitted a schoolboy. He stood, casting embarrassed and confused glances at the open windows and full balconies pronouncing judgement upon him as he alighted. Sunanda Sanyal beamed broadly, her strange pidgin Hindi words colliding helplessly with floods of excited Bengali as she opened the door and stood in welcome. Poor Sunanda, they all said; no husband to quarrel with, no children to break her windows or scribble on her walls, nothing, absolutely nothing, to encourage her favourite amusement. And he wasn't even young or good-looking. She'd die of sheer boredom, poor woman.

It took about an hour to unload the truck. O Mother!—they exclaimed in the balconies, what a mountain of luggage there was. Junk of all types—empty birdcages, faded lampshades, an old radio, a couple of divans, some old wooden chairs, many tables of varying shapes and sizes, a hi-fi set, an oven, a fridge, a battered gramophone, a great many bookcases and trunks and cabinets, even a vacuum cleaner. Whatever would a lonely old bachelor be needing so many things for?

'There's scarcely any place left to plant one's two feet in'. Sunanda Sanyal communicated to the neighbours the following day. 'For that petite little man, fine, he could live comfortably in a rabbit's burrow. But I, with my majestic body, oh no! The place is positively claustrophobic! But,' —she went on to say— 'he's a perfect gentleman. Why, he couldn't say boo to a goose!'

Rajni Kant Swamy spent a long and deeply enjoyable weekend setting up house all by himself, putting the bookcases in the corner there and the cabinets beside the window and then the cabinets in the corner there and the bookcases beside the window, shifting and shuffling until he was completely satisfied. The battered standard lamp with the faded camel-skin shade (all the way from Afghanistan it had come) went to the far end of the room. It brought back a sudden, overpoweringly vivid image of Siddiqui reciting a couplet on the cold lawn in Secunderabad, bowing in gracious acknowledgement of the applause. The fridge went just behind the door and the oven beside it. The vacuum cleaner, a genuine Hoover, went into the cupboard. The racks went all along the walls, bearing his father's wheezy old radio, his grandfather's chiming clock and the gramophone with its stack of heavy old lac disks. His own hi-fi he arranged carefully on a cabinet. An occasional brass table from Moradabad, intricately carved wooden peg tables from Saharanpur with the dust of the decades caked in the fissures of their floral motifs. Two slim coffee tables fitted somehow in the space left unoccupied. The high-backed chairs stood like ancient eyeless idols with limbs of black. Turning a corner, he sent a shaky rack clattering loudly to the floor.

Oh dear, he thought, lovingly caressing the rack with one hand and rubbing his grazed shin with the other. What a terrible jungle of furniture!

From place to place, on the move every three years, he had hauled this cumbersome load of things, like a large, unmanageable family, he, alone, the silent human patriarch to this motley tribe of objects.

He emerged on his veranda on his way to the tap in the yard to fetch a drink of water and immediately found himself trapped in the icy, ironical gaze of the two girls on the terrace opposite. Blushing deeply, he rushed back, almost stumbling over a chair and upsetting his tumbler of water. Crossing the room, he flung open a window only to find a man staring intently at him above his paper from his rocking chair. 'Dear me!'—he exclaimed—for he had had a Macaulayan education and said 'Dear me' and 'Bless my soul' occasionally. He shut the window nervously. There was nowhere to hide from prying eyes. It was then that the doorbell rang, loud, demanding.

He opened the door and his jaw dropped. For Durga Das-Gupta was a tall, handsome woman, big-boned, a Bengali goddess of war. Each feature was bold and clean, a cleft chin, large lips, finely cut, a massive knot of hair and rich eyes outlined in kohl. Her husky voice, loud and twanging and deeply musical, seemed to snap out battle orders. She strode in.

'Pardon me, Mr Swamy—is that the name?'

He bowed and squirmed with pleasure, welcoming her in.

'How good of you to come,' he muttered.

'I live in the house opposite,' she explained. 'The ground floor,' she added brusquely. 'The fact is, Mr Swamy, there's a strange man come to repair the plumbing and I feel somewhat apprehensive. If you could . . . if you would just stand by . . .'

The words registered slowly. He was being asked to step into the role of a protector to this magnificent creature. He simpered in pure delight, squaring up.

'Oh, certainly,' he gushed.

They went down the stairs together. She might have been an imperious arch-duchess. Her feet rang royally on the stairs, her saree flew round her like a purple cloak. Walking at her heels he almost felt a humble page-boy.

A schoolteacher nearing forty like himself, he concluded. He stood, feebly engaged in taking in the bookshelves, the plain, ascetic furniture, the piles of exercise-books on the solitary office table, the red and blue pencils. When the mechanic left she insisted on escorting him back to his flat. To be honest, he was not too keen. It struck him that he had nothing edible in the house worth offering to a guest apart from a packet of salted biscuits.

With trembling hands, he put the kettle on the stove, adding milk and sugar to the water. She seated herself on one of the high-backed chairs and cast her regal gaze round the room like a queen surveying her subjects, taking in the confused assortment of furniture and shoddy bric-a-brac. She raised a quizzical eyebrow in bemused query. He felt the powerful command of her personality and felt impelled to explain.

'The rubbish of many years,' he said with a timid, self-deprecating laugh.

'So I observe. Were I living here I would remove these two carved tables and get rid of those silly wicker tables,' she declared without preamble and with the signal finality of the irate queen expressing her right royal displeasure and banishing a couple of unsatisfactory subjects to the farthest corner of her realm.

He understood her point. 'True,' he murmured in approval, his voice sounding just a trifle timorous.

A familiar odour of burnt milk assailed his nostrils. He beat a sudden and ignominious retreat to the kitchen. 'Oh dear!' he sighed in despair. The milk trickled down in a snaky trail, he looked around agitatedly for something to mop it up with, found an old shirt on the peg in the veranda, tried to slop up the mess, made a still greater mess, and stood still in total distress.

'I never,' declared she, '—make tea in this absurd way.'

The queen had reached the tribal pockets of her realm and gently but firmly wished to teach her barbarian subject the essentials of civilized living.

He fussed over her tea, apologized in confusion for his soggy biscuits, gave an uncontrollable giggle and hated himself savagely for it.

'How come,' she wished to know, '—that out of all this miscellany of things the only subjects you have failed to acquire are a wife and children?'

He stood in the audience chamber, cowering beneath her

steadfast gaze. She raised the chipped tea cup like a jewelled goblet to her fine, carved lips.

'Well,' murmured he, his voice sounding unnecessarily shrill and unsteady. 'Marriage is somewhat different from buying a wicker table.' He tried to follow it up with what was intended as a full, hearty laugh but what seemed more like a tuneless cackle. He pulled himself up sternly. How ridiculous he was getting.

She eyed him gravely before passing sentence. 'Not so very different,' she said critically. 'There is a market. You choose among many specimens one which pleases you, or'—here she grimaced '—one which is merely useful. The exchange is made. You carry it across your threshold and use it for a number of years. When you tire of it you push it into the spare room and get yourself another. Or you die, leaving it forgotten in your room. And . . .' —her eyes flashed, bright with venom— 'there is a great variety to choose from—centre tables, side tables, occasional tables . . .'

'Multiplication tables!' he piped up suddenly, tuning into the idiocy of the conversation. There was something inexorable and devilish about this discursive woman.

'Also multiplication tables,' said she in dry deprecation. 'I perceive that you have a happy sense of word-play.'

'But how materialistic you are!' he added meekly, emboldened.

'Not at all,' she replied analytically. 'Your Plato—I notice that you have books related to him on your shelves—would place his fine original table somewhere outside our poor little mental caves. I daresay it wouldn't be exactly a material table. How can you be sure where matter begins?'

A damned metaphysician!—he exclaimed to himself in wonder, his mind quite boggled by the eccentric high-seriousness in her voice.

'Thank you ever so much,' he gushed at the door, quite overwhelmed by her towering stature and her magnificent presence. 'Please do come again. I did so much enjoy our little table talk.' And she flashed him an intense, piercing smile.

Back in his room with the door bolted securely against the world, he almost swooned with joy and admiration. Durga Das-Gupta. Middle-aged. Spinster and schoolteacher. Freelance cynic and metaphysician. She seemed to him the epitome of ideal womanhood. Like the goddess Durga on her lion, ten-armed, with jewelled weapons, deadly and dangerous, and utterly, utterly gorgeous.

Rajni Kant Swamy spent the next two days in sheer euphoria. 'Were I living here . . .' she had said, and, 'you have failed to acquire a wife and family.' A new, impossible, breath-taking idea shaped itself diffidently in his mind.

The following weekend when the doorbell rang, Rajni Kant Swamy flew to open the door. To his utter disappointment it was not the ravishing lady but a tall, grinning stranger.

'Enter Ajit Das-Gupta,' declared the apparition theatrically to the dumbfounded Rajni Kant, striding magisterially in. 'You have the pleasure of addressing Ajit Das-Gupta, the Shilpara Road sage. Yes, how right you are. I am, to put it briefly, my sister's brother.'

Rajni Kant Swamy murmured uncertainly in welcome and subjected his guest to a mildly dubious scrutiny. Ajit Das-Gupta swung long legs over the rim of his chair and pressed a much beringed hand earnestly over his rakish wind-cheater. A Chaplinesque moustache sprouted on his upper lip and he had brilliant black pupils that raced with his speech. The garrulous, leisured, archetypal Calcuttan.

'In Shilpara Lane circles, in our clubs and coffee houses, there is but one subject upon the lips of men. Who is this man of property? They meet in our dark alleys and ask: Who is this tall, aloof stranger, in short, yourself?'

Rajni Kant laughed uncomfortably, completely out of his depth.

'At long last, after many an intrepid soul had cracked under the strain of curiosity, I undertook to render unto my brethren and fellow-inhabitants of Shilpara Lane all vital information regarding the man of property.' He delivered his words with the stilted oratory of the confirmed rake whose voice is his fortune.

'You are most welcome,' stammered Rajni Kant, unable to resist the man's roguish charm.

'Ah!' breathed Ajit Das-Gupta, pausing before the gramophone and the rack of old lac-disks. 'Some day I must hear these priceless prehistoric pieces of yours. Do you think, if one spun out one of these disks one might perhaps hear the brontosaurus croon?' Then in a hallowed whisper before a large, ugly earthenware vase on the fridge: 'The chamber-pot of the Empress Tsu Hsa Shin, fifth century, terracotta.'

Rajni Kant gave a shrill little titter of laughter. 'That?' he explained. 'I bought it for a few paise at the Chunar railway station some years back. The man was so insistent, he wouldn't take no for an answer. And he looked so terribly poor and wretched.'

Ajit Das-Gupta nodded solemnly. 'And you have placed it here on your fridge as a monument to the unsung artist who offers the fruit of his fingers at the railway station?'

'I . . . I felt sorrier for the vase than for its maker.' Rajni Kant flushed in embarrassment.

'And these delicate pieces of statuary?' Ajit Das-Gupta now stood before the drab little dish of painted earthenware-fruits on the cabinet.

'From Bishnupur in Bengal.' Rajni Kant told him.

'My mistake' said his guest contritely. 'I naturally traced them to Eden. An oven too. And dear me, even a vintage vacuum cleaner.' Ajit Das-Gupta swung round ecstatically and clapped his hands. 'And you have actually carried these . . . these objets d'art to the farthest outposts of civilization with you!'

'Its a lot of junk, I know,' began Rajni Kant timidly, but his guest pooh-poohed him aside.

'And why not?' he glared round indignantly, demolishing an imaginary opposition. 'It's perfectly lawful to own what you so inelegantly call "junk". I've read of "bibliophile" and "scripophile". What law can ban a bit of blameless "junkophile"?'

He planted himself in a chair. 'This,' mused he profoundly, wistfully, '—is what Sankar meant by "Maya". There it all is, swarming round you, crawling about and coming out of your ears, and you can't bear to let the scales fall from your eyes. But when you're elevated enough, ah!—realization descends like a Naxal's bomb—abracadabra and hey presto!—all these wee little mud pies and vacuum cleaners are melted into air, into thin air.'

Rajni Kant began enjoying himself thoroughly. What a strange brother and sister, he thought.

'I shall bear glad tidings. The man of property is an art collector,' concluded Ajit Das-Gupta.

'Scarcely art. Just of . . . of things.' Rajni Kant wrung his hands in a helpless gesture, not finding the right word. And not even a conscious collector at that. For all these things had come to him almost of their own accord, like children, like orphans, stealing up to the master's knee at dusk to be comforted. He felt a paternal tenderness for them in their inertness, their passive self-surrender.

They needed him to realize themselves as indeed he needed them to place himself.

'I do understand' said Ajit Das-Gupta soulfully. 'People cram the inside of their minds with ideas. You, simple man, merely cram your apartment with this charming little mongrelized museum. The schoolboy and his pocket. However,' went on the voluble guest, '—there is one modest suggestion. It will not be amiss to add a useful little household item to your possessions.'

'What?'

'A portable baby incinerator. You know . . . "Instal your own crematorium at home" and all that advertising copy. To answer to your most ultimate need. Elegant, streamlined, exclusive, perfectly soundproof, so the din of the world cannot follow you into the beyond, and eight charming colours to choose from!'

Rajni Kant winced and smiled with effort.

'Guaranteed for five years. So you'd better kick the bucket within five years to ensure perfect performance. But consider it a minor snag when pitted against the manifold advantages you'd enjoy. Hand it down from generation to generation. Oh, I'm sorry, cross that one out. In your case it wouldn't apply.'

Rajni Kant shifted in his chair uncomfortably. The man's macabre humour oddly unsettled him.

'Well, well, well,' wound up Ajit Das-Gupta, bursting into a sinister guffaw. 'I observe, brother, that you are on the verge of touching wood and crossing your fingers. A thousand pardons! And now to business. You will not believe me, dear . . . dear Rajni, shall it be between us two . . . ?' Rajni Kant strove to smile. 'Well, Rajni, it's like this: You must believe me when I inform you that I happen to be a man of rare competence and versatility. I find this the only credible explanation for my numerous seasonal vocations. I have been, to name a few, a singer in a restaurant, a motor mechanic, an assistant teacher, a logician, to wit, a tutor of logic to a boy, and lately an auctioneer's representative from Dalhousie. I come to pledge my troth and ask for your hand in business partnership. You get the idea? For a paltry sum, I shall wave my little magic hammer and all these products of earthly illusion around you shall be whisked away to nought.' He leaned forward in his chair, 'Think it over,' he finished.

A strange dread oppressed Rajni Kant like that of a father bidding farewell to his offspring. He shook his head.

'I cannot consider your kind offer, Mr Das-Gupta,' said he. 'These . . . these objects do not in any way disturb me and I would not part with them for anything in the world.'

'Ah!' breathed Ajit Das-Gupta sadly, shaking his large head from side to side. 'Attachment spreads its malignant tentacles round us all. Well,' he rose to his feet, 'I see that nothing shall sunder you from your junk. Oh, by the way, didn't the boys at school ask you if Rajni Can or Rajni Can't? Can't is my guess, aha!' And with that outrageous sally he was across the floor in a bound and out of the door.

Rajni Kant mopped his brow. What an eccentric! All the same a rising chorus took up a malicious chant within his brain: Rajni Can? No, he Can't. Rajni Kant because He just Can't. Oh, God! thought Rajni Kant, the man's a buffoon but what is this self-doubt he's started in my mind? There was one important way in which Rajni Kant still had not proved himself and the thought did not improve his self-esteem.

A fortnight later, the monsoon broke. Rajni Kant, drenched to the skin, clung to the door of the speeding tram. Shivering, he walked back from the tram depot, wading through pools of muck with his trousers rolled knee-high. With relief he turned into Shilpara lane. The rain fell swiftly, slanting shafts right across his veranda and over the threshold into his rooms. He unlocked the door and the emptiness suddenly filled him with depression. There had been a power-failure and the rooms were bleak and murky. In the still half-light strange objects surfaced. He left his sandals at the door and walked bare-footed across the room, dripping little pools of water wherever he stepped. He seemed to be paddling through an eerie grey fluid element. Behind one of his bookshelves he spied his umbrella, leaning against the wall like an aged bat, fast asleep, its limp, black wings tightly closed in a deep slumber of inertia. He lifted it up, the dust falling away from it like particles of sleep. Sleepily it opened its wide, dark dome above him. Good, he thought, folding it up again, it would do for this season. He must remember to carry it to office tomorrow. His shirt and trousers were spattered with mud. A strange sadness overtook him as he put them away in the corner of the veranda. There they hung, long and shapeless like empty bodies from which the soul has fled. He so much longed to hear a voice, any voice.

Rajni Kant made tea for himself and sat unobtrusively in one corner of his dark room, sipping it. The wind thundered on the window and pushed it open. There was a loud explosion. A vast gusty shriek swept into the room. A tall brass carafe teetered deliriously on its perch, tumbled off and fell, tinkering on the floor. The loud metallic jangle set up a fearsome clamour of echoes; a hundred maniac bells tolled in the centre of the floor, racing wildly away. It was as though all the world suddenly pivoted madly round that single axis of sound on the dark floor.

Rajni Kant's hands shook. The din of the wind had settled in every cavity of his bones. Really, he thought, I'm getting quite neurotic. Trembling, he picked up the carafe. Poor, murdered carafe, felled by the wind, he thought involuntarily. Suddenly he was convinced beyond all doubt that the carafe had just died. Why then did it have that stiff embalmed look when only yesterday it had reclined in gracious curves on his rack? He pulled himself together. Crazed, absolutely crazed!

He returned to his chair and uneasily picked up his second cup of tea. It was then that he suddenly grew conscious of a blinding headache. When it had begun, he could not recall. But the crash of the carafe had swung into all his nerves, starting this pain. Am I, he wondered, now feeling the carafe's ache? Have I picked it up from the air? A fit of shivering seized him.

He simply had to get away. Seizing his umbrella, he fled. A sheet of dark rain flung itself round each house. He crossed the lane and hammered on Ajit Das-Gupta's door.

'Excuse me,' he spoke awkwardly. 'I think I may be running a temperature. Can you lend me a thermometer?'

'What?' roared the loud neighbour in a burst of Bengali Victorian oratory. 'You have everything that the Lord could possibly have created in seven days. How come your Chamber of Horrors does not contain a mere thermometer?' He ushered him in.

Suddenly Rajni Kant felt cheered. The thermometer showed a hundred and two degrees.

Durga Das-Gupta strode into the room, a red and blue pencil in her hand like a jewelled sceptre. Her thick hair was carelessly coiled about her head in what appeared to be, in the candle-light a queenly coronet with a plastic comb stuck, half-forgotten on one side like a peerless diadem.

Her brother studied the thermometer with solemnity. 'What did

I prophesy?' He exploded into rhetoric. 'There you live, cloistered in cowl and habbit. Little wonder that you're feverish just monkeying about in that Tutankhamen's tomb! But wait, we shall summon the tribal medicine man to exorcise this demon . . . .'

He pulled open a cupboard and drew forth a small black case. He pried open Rajni Kant's jaws and neatly dropped the tiny white globules into Rajni Kant's surprised mouth.

'You did not tell me that you are a homoeopath too,' accused Rajni Kant weakly.

'Unhappily, my reputation as homoeopath is somewhat suspect in these parts. You will doubtless appreciate my reticence about this painful subject,' explained Ajit Das-Gupta with detachment.

Durga Das-Gupta returned from the kitchen bearing a large mug of steaming ginger tea. 'Now drink that up fast,' she commanded, ignoring her brother. Rajni Kant complied. The tea scalded his throat. Nectar, thought he blissfully, comes in many tastes and temperatures. He placed the mug on the floor at the foot of his chair. As he straightened up, Ajit Das-Gupta gave vent to a whoop of joy.

'Let there be light,' he hallooed, '—and there is light!' With a creak of tired wings the ceiling fan began whirring above them. The load-shedding hours were over at last. Bright light flooded the room. A tremendous relief washed down on Rajni Kant's soul.

'Thank you, thank you ever so much,' he croaked at the door as he left, his voice musty with gratitude. 'I shall be fine tomorrow.'

He crossed the lane, heart singing. Then he caught sight of his dark, cold apartment and it sent a chill through his thoughts. When he unlocked the door a shock of cold air swept down upon him, issuing from some soulless dimension. He switched on the lights, suddenly alarmed. The room had the still, invisible populousness of a cemetery. Had all these objects died in some former time, he wondered, or had they just never been born? He slumped down on a chair. Every object around him seemed an all-too-conscious creature in some appalling denser world. A nameless fear gripped him that his own body did not belong to him but was an inmate of that dense, malignant kingdom of matter and could rise up against him if he so much as loosened his control. He felt hemmed in. They sat around him, blind and menacing, breathing greedily, poaching on his air. Iron and paint and plastic and brass seemed so much more durable than his tenuous human substance. His single fugitive being crouched in their midst dogged by a sense of inexplicable threat. How blessed would emptiness be, bare clean walls, as white as the moon, long cool floor, large and luminous like a vast lake. Rajni Kant began assiduously philosophizing to quell his terror. These little notches and grooves, lodgements of identity, proofs of possession, proofs of a possessor, weighed down his spirit, he mused. Ajit Das-Gupta was right. He began thinking seriously of getting rid of it all.

He put on a record to aid his thoughts. The music of the sitar rose all around him in tiny trills. One walked the precarious tightrope, note to note. If one's heart slipped and fell, it would plunge into the utmost pit between the very roots of sound. Rajni Kant felt trapped. Was it merely the delirium of fever coming on?—he wondered. The music flared above him in tall arches. He nervously switched on the camel-skin lamp. The kind light welled out, uncontained, uncontainable. Even this, he thought helplessly, is material. Why, I could lift this thin skin of light that rests loosely on the cabinet and stretch it like a shiny gauze between my fingers.

This could not go on, his mind was made up. A clean, uncluttered house it would be. And, his hesitant daydream widened, he would retain only the more useful items like the fridge and the hi-fi and the oven. Women liked such things. Should he consult her as to what she'd like to retain and what dispose of? Here an essential fallacy in his own plan struck him for the first time. How on earth was he going to put the proposal to her? Rajni Kant Swamy fell asleep that night alternating between contrary modes of approach.

And as if in answer to his dream, the first person who rang his doorbell next morning was she! She walked in briskly, carrying a large jugful of steaming ginger tea and a plateful of steamed apples. She was dressed for school in a stiff cotton sari of monastic white, her hair severely knotted and quelled under a stern net. She wore a grim frown. Rajni Kant's heart sank, realizing what he was up against.

'One cup every hour,' was the command. She put down a packet of homoeopathic doses done up in white paper. 'One dose every three hours. Can I trust you to heat this tea up properly?' There was a subtle note of exasperation in her voice which, by a partial observer could be construed as altogether wifely. Conversely it may well have been a habitual mannerism derived from her calling. Rajni Kant Swamy felt more like a tiresome schoolboy than an aspiring suitor. This was scarcely the bedside manner appropriate for a sick visit, reflected he with spouse-like criticism.

'Oh, absolutely,' replied he humbly.

'And these apples?' She looked round the room.

'Please put them in the fridge,' said he.

'Not the fridge by any means!' she barked out. But she turned and examined the fridge with some interest.

'Well, on any of my tables here which pleases you,' he ventured, heroically mustering up courage. 'I . . . I shall retain it when I get rid of the rest, as I plan to.' His heart skipped a beat but she did not seem to notice anything unusual. She unceremoniously placed the dish of apples on the cabinet and suddenly caught sight of the record lying beside it.

'Vilayat Khan!' she exclaimed, her frown vanished. Eagerly she swooped down over the record and read the cover-flap with hungry eyes. 'Raga Piloo is one of my favourites.'

The chink in the armour! He sat up breathlessly.

'My late father,' he began a trifle pompously, 'was a top-notch vocalist. I have about fifty ragas here on my racks. Some vocal renderings and a great many instrumentals. Sarod, sitar, violin, santoor, flute, veena, anything you fancy.' Here he was, baiting her with material things, he thought in silent disgust. What a vicious circle it was!

'Really?' she exclaimed. 'I do so love classical music and I have never missed a single Friday night recital on the radio, but I could never afford to buy a tape-recorder.'

'You're most welcome here,' he said nervously. 'It's all yours if you wish. Consider it all your own.' His voice had risen to a shrill quaver. That's the nearest Rajni Kant Swamy could get to an advance.

'Excellent!' snapped she. 'I shall come when my school examination work is over.' And Rajni Kant blushed all over his face in utter confusion, both discouraged by her obtuseness as well as encouraged by the promise of future occasions to bare his heart.

'No fever today,' she pronounced with her large shapely hand placed masterfully on his forehead. There was an impersonality about her that was totally unnerving. 'All the same you'd better take leave today and rest. And if by tomorrow you're well, I shall send you a pass for our prize distribution and closing function on Thursday. Goodbye.'

He would indeed take leave, Rajni Kant decided. But not to rest. He had a lot of sorting out to do.

But first of all he dragged out an old trunk from beneath his bed and rummaged out a purple silk tie. Would it perhaps be a trifle too garish for a school function? he wondered. Knotting it in front of the mirror, he met himself again, the man with the parchment skin, the pinched nose and the lank hair and eyes so faded that they faltered and shrank from their own reflection. Far from distinguished, thought he sadly.

Rajni Kant began with the camel-skin lamp, a most dispensable item. He studied the lamp; he switched it on. A bowl of light, so brimming, so inadequate, that it let the light overflow, escape over its rim in a thick paste, welling slowly into the room beyond, unevenly coating the surface of his cabinets and clinging round the sides of his tables. The russet leather shade glowed like a fiery cauldron, smelting the light into torrid fluidity. It was a beautiful object and suddenly Siddiqui raised one fine, narrow hand in gracious thanks and repeated a couplet, Siddiqui, friend of many years and dead now. One single memory climbed like a frightened creeper round the tall black post. What a strange, posthumous gift it was, this unavailing loyalty to the dead, thought Rajni Kant, deeply stirred. He was dazed by intense nostalgia. Let that lamp remain, he resolved, moving on to the racks.

But, those racks had held his records for years and if they went where on earth was he going to put them? It was the records she specially liked. So the racks were absolutely indispensable. There was that antediluvian gramophone. But, he had such a splendid collection of old records which it would be a pity to silence forever. There were his cabinets, but where would his books go? And books were not objects, he hastened to assure himself. There remained his old-fashioned tables, and where would the time-piece go and his spectacles and the newspaper and the odd book and the tea-cup and the tired feet, if they went. The bargain would scarcely be worth the wrench, he desperately argued. The wooden peacocks in the carved tables spread their filigreed tails, frozen in mid-dance, heads lifted to the rain. The elephant enamelled on the brass table raised a dusty lotus on his trunk and knelt in perennial homage. Humble, helpless matter in voiceless plea. And I, thought Rajni Kant, moved, almost did not hear this mute beast. Dim evenings by the score he had spent, alone with his tea, absently aware of them. They had left their impressions on his days. How lonely would be life without them, poor and fearful without their solid ramparts, these brass and wooden ramifications of his sureties.

So Rajni Kant went from object to object. The light, from this end of the room, fell in a thin dust, encasing the trunks and tables, curbing their solidities, muting their corners until they appeared the objects of thought alone, insistent spirits that had gathered round him in silent consensus and followed him faithfully from lifetime to lifetime and beyond. What am I, he desperately theorized, apart from these countless histories trapped in their cages of metal or plastic or wood? Where would I look to find myself when these go? For, I call myself by several names but mostly by that of owner of these solid certainties. My name nestles close to these definitions and knows itself proved. Thus, Rajni Kant mused. Ideas impressed his gentle soul, the more ponderous the better. It is impossible to betray, he thought, sitting himself down on a trunk, the distress of the eternally lifeless, the eternally captive. Well, not quite so lifeless, perhaps. Maybe, life itself is a wrong concept because nothing is dead. Just as, perhaps, there is nothing like sleep or death, only degrees of wakefulness. Rajni Kant felt pleased with his little profundity.

But, now he looked around at that multitude of furniture that he had finally resolved not to part with and felt oddly disturbed. He had no love for them and it was a terrible burden to carry these inert creatures he was foster-father to, and could never desert. How much better, he felt, it would have been to have declined to take their responsibility at all. The exaltation of the choice having passed, he felt deflated and somehow cramped. It was a mistake to adopt them and grow one with them. It would be a mistake to adopt anything more, nourish more responsibility, more dependence. Rajni Kant straightened up and caught sight of himself in the mirror on the opposite wall, grotesque in white cotton pyjamas and vest and purple silk tie. He had forgotten the school function. The silk tie curved in a fine, serpentine coil round his neck, knotted firm and tight and relentless. Rajni Kant paused before the mirror and suddenly shuddered.

'Why didn't you come to our school function?' was the peremptory interrogation.

He trembled like a schoolboy caught playing truant. 'Not altogether recovered,' he murmured sulkily.

'I shall drop in for some music but after a week.' She had an odd look in her eyes.

'I ... I shan't be home,' he stammered. 'I have to go out of Calcutta on a tour of North Bengal.' She flushed and he hastened to add: 'I was informed at the last moment. They can pack us, poor confirmed bachelors, off on these dreary tours at very short notice.'

Her eyes froze. Rajni Kant didn't know whether to be relieved or vaguely disappointed.

Rajni Kant Swamy lived in the Shilpara Lane house for three years, an asset to the neighbourhood. And, when the transfer orders came, every article was loaded on to the truck and Rajni Kant got into the front seat beside the driver, casting embarrassed glances round at the full balconies and verandas and drove away. Long afterwards in Shilpara Lane they spoke of him with laughter as that tender, timid man, that meek, mad man of maya. And, the word 'maya' in colloquial Bengali signifies more than mere illusion or the merely measurable. Maya signifies affection, tender compassion, the sort that Rajni Kant Swamy had for his inert family.

PERSONAL FRIEND

My dear Mallika,

You may treat this as a letter from no-one to no-one. You may deny its substance, but I, for my part, challenge anybody to disprove to me the truth of my statements. You may be overcome by moral doubt and insist in that prim little note that we were partners in a pitiable piece of fraud which must end some day. But, to that I say that if we both perpetrated a foolish fraud together, I shall not let a partner in fraud get away that easily. We swim or sink together.

So did you really believe that Mallika is no more? I don't. In case you have lost trace of her in seven years, let me refresh your memory. And my own.

I am forty-five years old now. I was thirty-eight then. I neither wish to know your chronological age nor believe in it. You were thirty then and are thirty-seven now by my private chronology. The magazine which changed our lives was called *Humanity* and the page which we chose to read, by some predetermined accident, was called 'Equations'. The idea was to sponsor what the editor called leisured sharing and disinterested understanding between human beings, friendship having become a defunct concept now. The magazine has long been extinct and I am sorry. Had someone told me that middle-aged pen-friendships could be taken seriously, I would have scoffed at the idea. To think of pot-bellied executives sharing their recipes for gardening or for photography with other balding hypertensive 'pals' across the country or matrons posting poetry or knitting patterns to other matrons across the world—what a perfectly sick idea!

And yet I read that article, condemning but curious, and yet I jotted down a name and address on the last page of my pocket-book: Mallika Mathur, Age—30, College Teacher, 82 Vrindavan Street, Humayun Gardens—a local address. For, I was at a stage of life when anything novel was welcome, however ridiculous. Pornography I had exhausted, and profession and politics.

What really arrested my attention was the observation that friendship is finished. In my father's age, childhood mates remained companions in youth, continued constant in middle age and staunch sharers of one's debilities in old age. Where had those sturdy relationships gone? In my office there were colleagues, in the chartered bus there were fellow passengers, in the colony there were neighbours. But, no friends. I had a wife who was aware of me always, who knew my problems (and often added her mite to them), who understood my appetites but had forgotten my thoughts. Children who asked for objects, never for my opinions. And, the mates of my school and college days? All too often, one of those had risen grandly from a chair in a lavish room and received me with patronage. I was at a stage of life when my mediocre standing hurt. It is these seven years which have fostered a quality of imperturbable control. What arrested me further was your lyrical name, your age and your calling. And, that nebulous hobby you professed—thinking about things! Finally it was the prospect of a friendship of the pen, faceless and free, ideas for ideas, that attracted me most.

These seven years have made me intimately know the rain as it billows across your Humayun Gardens. I can smell the tuberoses growing on your balcony. I have been to the slums behind your colony and known their stench and squalor. I have read the books you read and followed your observations on TV shows and films;

obeyed imperious directions to listen to particular music cassettes, purchasing them from shops of your choice. Alone I have visited restaurants favoured by you. I have received, week after week, general philosophies and confidences. I know, for example, how you dealt with your sister's death and your personal meanings for loneliness and for love. I share your views on what is wrong with us human beings and we are companions in anxiety regarding the future of our country. There is much that we have gone over. How middle age threatens and old age conquers. How best to henna your hair!

In turn I sketched cartoons and sent them across to you, a hobby ever secret with me, I don't know why. I composed silly limericks, cracked jokes and introspections. Often I have sat laughing by myself in the bus or the bank and people have nudged me and asked why I laughed. And, it all came out of a weekly envelope jammed with many sheets of fine blue paper scribbled finely across with green ink, the very handwriting aslant in whimsical flight like so many thoughts air-borne. Why, I can imagine the very fragrance Mallika must wear. 'Pen friend' is too innocuous a name for such intensive haunting.

I asked questions and more questions. I asked for a photograph and received one immediately. I liked what I saw. You were just what I expected you to be, young, poised, withdrawn, chin upon hand, a smile in your eye. I asked for a telephone number and received that too. I dialled and dialled and was told repeatedly: 'This number does not exist. Kindly dial again.' I asked your permission to visit but received no encouragement. And, when I, disregarding, reached 82, Vrindavan Street, Humayun Gardens, why, hell, I found myself before a mammoth Working Women's Hostel with a hundred inmates at least! And nobody knew you there. Mail was collected by claimants from an office downstairs. There were so many letters and none from me.

That was when I began to understand somewhat.

You dreamt yourself up, green ink on blue paper and you were absolutely truthful to yourself there and absolute real to me. I can never hold you guilty. Perhaps, you shall be more disposed to believe me when you hear what I have to admit.

I am not Manager of the Branch of my bank here. I am only Second Assistant. I am not generally considered poetic or thoughtful or even amusing. Nobody ever heard my limericks for the simple reason that I never wrote them before. Cartoons and I do not go together. I am commonplace, unhandsome, poverty-stricken. I have no hair to henna and no humour to spread. Do you know how from plain Rakesh Sinha I became Mrinal Vashishtha? I chose a name to match yours. I selected a picture in a magazine, a man sober, bespectacled, quietly dressed, distinguished, and resolved, henceforth, to be him. Do you know what happened? Except when I stood before my mirror, I quite forgot, for prolonged periods of time, my dumb, desolate self. I visualized myself as that paper man, cut out of a magazine and lying in my drawer. That other man became my chosen station of personality, my mental centre of operation.

Do you realize what we were both doing? Two non existent beings spoke to one another, shared many things, dreamt together, exchanged much across the magnitude and madness of a vast metropolis, never meeting in seven years. Yet, somebody did speak and somebody did respond even if neither existed in the conventional sense. What we did was nothing unusual, if you reflect upon it. Every writer does it and every reader—writing from a deeper place quite at variance with his conventional self; reacting and emoting from an inner ego which is larger than his or her superficial one. So why call it fraud? I accepted your unstated terms that I fall in with your illusions. You entered into a tacit agreement to accord with my self-imaginings and accompany all my fantasies. Together we resonated wonderfully well. I shall never disbelieve your lies, my dear, even now.

The unfortunate event last week may well be another predetermined accident like the one which brought us together. It was all my fault. I had no time to inform you of my transfer and the change of official address.

The lady was thin and nondescript. She entered and stood before my desk.

'Yes, madam,' said I. 'Can I help you, madam?'

'I must rewrite this application, sir,' she spoke quietly. 'The Manager tells me it's incorrectly drafted and if you will be so kind as to help me . . . .'

And she placed upon my desk a sheet of blue notepaper, closely covered with small green words!

I cannot describe the utter confusion of my brain. That handwriting and that paper!

I looked up into her faded face and found it pale, lined, commonplace like my own. Not like that photograph at all.

Mastering my voice, I spoke politely: 'Certainly, madam. Please be seated.'

You know the rest. Deliberately picking up my notepad, I redrafted the letter while she sat, speechless, rooted to her chair, her eyes fixed upon the letters my pen traced upon the sheet.

'What signature, madam?' I asked when I had finished.

'Veena Sahai,' she murmured. 'Mrs Veena Sahai.'

'Address?' persisted I, relentless.

'Stenographer. 82, Vrindavan Street, Humayun Gardens . . . .'

'I know, I know,' said I, ironically.

She looked down, her gaze fixed upon her folded hands and neither of us spoke. Then a light dawned swiftly in her eyes.

'And you?' She glanced at the name and insignia upon my desk. 'Rakesh Sinha, Second Assistant, I presume? Not Mrinal Vashishtha?'

I shook my head.

I was glad when you were gone. To tell you the truth, I could not bear to look upon that woman there. She was the most fake person I ever set eyes upon!

And, here I am once again, at the same table and the same hour, beneath the same lamp, writing to you, Mallika Mathur, invoking not somebody but nobody upon these pages. And I am not Rakesh Sinha any more but the poetic Mrinal Vashishtha, my alter-ego whom I shall eternally miss, if you choose to go now, who is too real to me now and whom I shall forcibly resuscitate, come what may. I am sure you shall understand.

This was the most enduring and the most enriching, the most real and the most unreal relationship of my life. Let nobody write to nobody then. The writing matters, not the writer nor the reader, neither Mrinal nor Mallika.

Yours,
Mrinal Vashishtha

THE FLIGHT

The flight is at two-thirty. Frankly this time I'm nervous. I have not confessed my fear but I know you sense it in me. Why else this forced cheerfulness, this ceaseless prattle and banter? You may possibly be aware of my fear of returning. Twenty years of absence is a long time. Like your own Rip Van Winkle I'm sure to find myself in an unrecognizable world.

We Indians consult the stars and the portents before we travel north or south or east or west. Calcutta is east on a map and west by our flight, so my directions stand negated. But, home and memory may not be measured by cardinal points but by some constant direction in one's being. For me the secret road to home has not changed but it is often no longer there in my mind where it used to be.

Are you aware of my stealthy looks? There you stand, counting the days. And I wonder how you're really feeling, abandoning your home with apparent effortlessness, your vast and glossy America for the sake of this man you have impulsively married. But, you have been an actress, Amantha, and one never knows what to infer.

Not a pang do you appear to feel. 'Shall I take this old Mexican rug or that wild tan thing, Pranob? I could leave it for Martha . . . .'

Your excitement is touching. You forget your questions as soon as they're out. But my heart stops. The way your words formed and fell! Did you know, Amantha, you sounded exactly like my mother did, thirty years ago, perplexedly brooding over her palm-mat baskets when the tongas were starting and the last bundles were being hurled in?

Three weeks of auctioneers, agents, brokers, lawyers. The

mortgage has to be sold; the furniture auctioned; packers contacted; bookings made; good memories sequentially sorted and preserved; bad ones analysed, overcome and demolished, another home, a place in a personal time disbanded.

We're going to live in an old, old house in Serampore, just outside Calcutta, Amantha. It has its thatch, its pond and temple, with the scent of frangipani everywhere in the courtyard. That house has sat blurred in my mind like a corpulent and musty old aunt that one must look up some day and who shall narrate in her cracked voice her smoky tales of father and mother.

Serampore is where I came from but scarcely the ideal home of my deepest dreams. That idyllic status is reserved for a tiny hamlet called Goneshpukur up the slow, slumbrous river, our desh or country-house as we called it. That's where I went with my mother every October. For, to our traditional women, Amantha, home is the father's homestead, seldom the home of the husband's patriarchs. The palm trees leaned low over the family pond and mother looked up at them, wiped her eyes decorously and called on the goddess, and the horse-drawn tongas turned and crawled up the slope.

'Lemme hang on that! Say, that's like the pioneers in their wagons. Like our pilgrim fathers and my pirate grandpop!' You laugh delightedly. 'My grandpop was a sometime pirate, or didn't you know? Proper old sea-dog, the buccaneering type with cutlass and earring! If not him, it must've been my great-grandpop!'

Funny, unsentimental Amantha. That's your way of checking some of my nostalgic wanderings, my beautiful, spurious meditations. For I am constantly narrating my past to myself and to you, investing the images with greater detail and solidity, bent upon an urgent mission to recover and preserve and how tiresome it must get. And what yarns you spin to distract me. Your past is at the beck and call of your random imagination. Your ancestors were once Huguenots from France, and once rustlers, cattle-millionaires, gold-rushers, Texan oil-kings or touchy aristocrats who fought in the Civil War and were killed in Georgia or in Virginia, leaving memorial-pistols to their families. That's what comes of being a practising actress.

'No, honest, great-grandpop found himself in South Carolina and came across the Allegheny Mountains and into Tennessee and then Kentucky in his wagon. He was a pirate-turned-horse-breeder.

That was in the 1830s when Chicago was still Port Dearborn and had only fifty people in it.'

Ah, Kentucky! I love its beautiful bluish grass, that strange blue bloom, the white fences, the great spaces and quietness. And, your rock music. I do not know when this music stole into my life, giving a theme to my restlessness, but I suddenly heard it arguing, appealing, raging and remembering outside the margins of my thought like the distant drumming and sighing of rain. I think that in some ways I'm just as much in love with your America as I was in the Sixties—and not because of the cars and the capital and the consumer goods.

'Oh, gee, you can't kid me,' you chip in. 'You aren't taken in. You never speak all that lustily about how you got your Staten Island apartment through a pert young thing named June or how you came out of the telephone centre with your phone under your arm. Say, you're not impressed. No, not any more.'

Well, I came for different reasons and with different expectations. I came expecting a new sort of integrity and I know I never found it. I came with my head bursting with phrases from a history book. Some abstractions seemed possible here—like equality. And how dumb I was. But, that's because in my part of the world my grandmother sprinkled our threshold with Ganga water every time a pariah cast his shadow across it!

'Bullshit!' I do not miss the affectionate condemnation of your exclamation. Yes, I have been, at best, an academic tourist in America, despite twenty years, IBM and my green-card. I have all this while been taking notes in emotional short-hand, exposing film and developing it all; inscribing it in long-hand in the private contemplation of these long conversations with myself. My first impressions in my memory are still photographic. The streets of New York are still remote canyons to me in a stupendous aerial panorama.

'I thought you didn't like New York any more.' I don't. I don't like restlessness and brash glitter, be it in New Delhi or be it in New York. Brazen lights encrust the skyline and invade all one's darknesses. The surf of sound is like a threat that certain cities seem to mutter to themselves and it makes me catch my breath now to ward off the high-strung nervousness that takes hold of me. You look at me sideways in that special ambiguous way. Spurious they may be but you like these introspective impressions, poetic and eastern they seem to you. You married me for my introspections. I was different from Jim and Willy and Clint.

'Many Americans hate New York,'—is what you say by way of reassurance, as though to smooth away the heresy of not adoring your New York.

I much prefer suburban New England, say Boston or Connecticut, that faint feeling of personal recognition. I love the full palette of California's seasons. I even retain a soft spot for your many madnesses. Like in Dallas I once found the incredible ad—'Dial a Prayer: TE2614—A prayer there twenty-four hours a day'. And, a blinking sign over this commercial salvation centre which proclaimed: 'Jesus Saves'. Only an American could think of turning the Taj Mahal into a bar and restaurant and paint its gracious contours in flashy, prismatic colours! Oh you crazy guys, you Poles, Finns, Italians, Hispanics, Slavs, French-Canadians, you wild talkers, busy-bodies, reformers, tyrants, agitators, muggers, lunatics and bullies!

'Dr Johnson called us a nation of convicts—rascals, robbers and pirates.' You trickle into laughter.

I feel most at home in the Carolinas. The heat is the same as in India, humid, steamy. It calls to mind the Jessore of my old grandmother. I visited it once on an emotional tour. Some stranger must now be living in our old Jessore house.

My mother undertook her annual pilgrimage up-country to remote Goneshpukur and her mother took the same homeward direction east-country to her forfeited Jessore. There is something in us that makes us hanker after the home of our forebears, yes, just to visit it, touch its walls, even when one disdains its discomforts.

Goneshpukur was a green hamlet of thatched homesteads along a single road. On market days this single road turned into a cluster of vendors' carts and low fishmongers' stalls. One circled a giant banyan tree and found flower-hawkers dealing in hibiscus and tuberose, local roses and strings of jasmine, costermongers, grocers, butchers, herb-sellers and old women squatting forlornly behind a square of sacking, displaying a few sad wisps of spinach or tamarinds or half a dozen ducks' eggs. As a child I spent many Huck Finn holidays fishing and chasing chickens in that remote outpost of Bengal. My cousin taught me to fish. And there was Somnath Moitra's fat cow that mischievous village boys drank off, applying their lips to the udders by turns while she stood, calmly swishing her tail this way and that, looking round curiously at us with large somnolent eyes. We broke at least one window a day of the train from Siliguri to Calcutta. And, one awful afternoon Somnath Moitra's shrewish wife chased us up a tree, shouting: 'Burnt face! Spawn of swine!' And ever afterwards we chanted after her in mocking singsong: 'Tell me, my fish, how much water have you in your pond? Up to the ankles or here to the knees, or here right up to the neck, Aunt Fish!'

That was Goneshpukur, pastoral paradise of my rustic childhood. There was another home, one I did not see but heard so much about from the ancient grandmother, who dandled and rocked me and sang to me, that it became a home of the imagination —Chandigram beyond Jessore in faraway east-country Bengal— the home I visited on a sentimental journey years later. She, twelve years old, a nineteenth century bride of a lawyer's son, undertook that long journey across flooded paddy field and marshland and areca nut forest every *sravan* when the rains came. And, for her, she narrated, it was not by train and tonga but by buggy and sedan-chair. Her descriptions were vivid and haunting: 'Each year, child, I had for companion this faithful rain.' Lying beside her on the wattle-mat, fanned by her palm-leaf fan, I could hear the crackle of lightning and see the silver veins tear across the sky and the tall trees thrash and twist in a smoking mesh of rain. Her father was landowner of many acres of prime paddy land, master of many menials. They received her with the blowing of conchs and chafed her with many indulgent quips. How thin she is, the little Krishnakali. Maybe, her mother-in-law beats her for leaving pebbles in the rice and scales on the fish. I never, insisted the child-bride emphatically, set foot in the cook-house! They sat round the lanterns before their banana leaves and dined on fried spinach, ladies' fingers, aubergines, rice and drumsticks, fish cooked in curd, fish simmered in mustard, fish wrapped in banana leaf and baked in cauldrons of slow-cooking rice. After dinner, all the servants came splashing across the flooded fields to greet the child-bride, bringing strange, humble gifts. 'Each time I visited my home the rain followed me,' repeated she wistfully.

She continued going year after year, switching from sedan-chair to cycle-rickshaw, from buggy and tonga to bus and train, even when riots broke out, even when famine came, even after her father, her mother and her brothers were all dead and gone and from child-bride she became an amorphous grandaunt. In her nephews and grand-nephews she sometimes detected a curling lip like her brother's or a pair of thick lashes like her mother's or a wild temper like her father's and that was her reason for homecoming and her personal continuity. She made history come alive those steamy afternoons on the wattle-mat, the palm fan slow-fluttering above us both. The hero of the narrations was always her father, the despotic monarch who made the sons line up outside the lavatory or the bath-house and recite Shakespeare's speeches while he hollered out corrections from within. He loved his violin, he loved his verses—Bengali, English, Urdu, Persian—and he loved his paddy fields and his sumptuous meals. She recited one of his favourite poems to me in a peculiar stretched and swerving language that she told me was English, confessing that she knew no English herself except for that single poem. But, one phrase clutched fast at my memory—a reference to 'the rain-loud night of June'. Twenty years later—or was it twenty-five?—I found that phrase in a volume of Tagore's poems. But of course! A little poem called 'Krishnakali' and the lines in question; 'I call her my Krishna flower . . . I remember a cloud-laden day and a glance from her eyes . . . . She is the surprise of cloud in the burning heart of May. A tender shadow in the forest in the stillness of sunset hour. A mystery of dumb delight in the rain-loud night of June. . . .' Then I remembered that her father had named her Krishnakali! And to think that I found this poem here in the library of a friend, incredibly, in the middle of a Canadian winter, snow-bound in his Montreal apartment, the temperature well below zero. Suddenly I smelt the rain in the dust, heard the chirp of the crickets, saw the glow-worms on the queen-of-the-night bushes of my Serampore garden; a single strong image laid waste all my adjustments and reconciliations and filled my mind with a troubled and uncompromising insistence.

After 1947 she went home no more and Chandigram was lost to her. She was there when the carnage broke out, it being August and the peak of the monsoon. The old matriarch wept for her pots and pans and pestles, wept as only a Bengali woman can, and for things which could not be carried—the well in the yard, the old cow sheds, the pools and the shyuli tree which rained flowers in the courtyard all October through. Taking up handfuls of soot and rice, thrice she cast it upon the desolate house, blighting its future claimants forever.

That was the dreadful exodus from Chandigram to Serampore. The old matriarch yearned for her well and her homestead until she died, Chandigram gone forever.

'Now how about me telling you my own little story.' You interrupt quietly. 'My maternal grandmom spoke only Yiddish.' You reveal most astonishingly. 'She was Jewish, you know, and so was my Mom.' I am silent and I know this isn't just another amusing act. 'She was a pole evacuated from Warsaw and learnt English too late to speak it, at all, comfortably. I guess there isn't much about a pogrom that my mother's family doesn't know. And, this is the story, yeah, a bedtime tale like yours that she read to Martha and me. It happened while David was hiding in the Cave of Adullum and was being pursued by Saul. One night David had a great yearning to see his old home, Bethlehem, which was in the hands of the Philistines. He longed for the well where often he had watered his sheep. 'Ah, that someone could bring me a drink of that well in Bethlehem which is in the hands of mine enemies!' sighed he. Then Adino, Eleazer and Shammah the bravest of his generals, swore that their king should have it and one night, quietly, they slipped away from camp and made their way to the well in Bethlehem, fighting all the way. They drew a flask of water and fought their way back again. And, when they brought the water to David, so moved was he that he poured it out unto the Lord of Israel for 'be it far from me that I should drink this elixir which only the Lord is worthy of receiving'. But, you know, Pranob, I was always angry with David for doing that, for being such a punk and the Lord for being such a kill-joy . . . !

That's you, Amantha and why you're special. Out of a confusion of contrary inheritances you produce for me, repeatedly, a corresponding experience, a moving resonance. Yes, even when you're only acting.

You have been an actress, though you insist an unsuccessful one. Have I ever narrated my only experience of acting?

It was a real-life performance and it helped to kill a woman, whether mercy-kill or unmercifully-kill I'm not even sure. It was absolutely unrehearsed, without script or stage, the scenario my old Serampore veranda, my co-performers a benign old gentleman of the neighbourhood, my leading lady a broken old wisp of a woman. The offer had been sprung on me the previous day and quite without warning. It sounded, at first hearing, too weird to take seriously. 'Pranob,' ventured the old gentleman, a friend of the family, 'I have an old mother, a fretful old creature of ninety-two whose poor wits are all addled and whose body is now confused in all its functions. Of her ninety-two years but one or two decades are clear in her memory; the rest, time has wiped out beyond all hope of recovery. Her teeth are gone and her poor bowels and bladder beyond her conscious will. And, yet, the Lord God has granted her life—breaths without end. And, there is this burning demand in her infant heart—"Take me to Sabzi-bagh, my Patna home. Take me back to Father. Once, just once . . . ." In the last five days the weeping has not stopped. What am I do, Pranob? That Patna house is now not even standing. There is nobody alive who belongs to that time. I am at my wits' end, my son. Yesterday my wife had an idea. And I wonder, I mean to say, her father was tall and thin and wore glasses and had a beaked nose. And, so have you. I shall show you a photograph. Her old home was a thatched bungalow and so is this one,. And if we were to bring her here, Pranob, and if you could . . . . Her wits aren't such that she would know any difference. And it would be an act of great kindness to us, to her . . . .' His eyes waited, anxious. I sat up slowly, too astonished but also quite fascinated.

No stage-fright can be worse than mine on that extraordinary day as I waited, costumed in gold-banded dhoti and silk shawl, upon my veranda. He brought her in, a tiny, shrivelled creature in a wheel chair, limp as a flabby, crumpled object. He pointed out my veranda and told her: 'Look, Mother, you're in Patna now and that's Pushpa Bhavan, your Sabzi-bagh home.' Then he pointed me out, seated stiffly upon my tall-backed chair, and said: 'Look, Mother, that's our granddad, Badri Narayan Ghosh, and your esteemed father.'

A panic seized me. Too much was at stake. I wondered what to do. How would an elderly Bengali father behave towards a favourite, married daughter? Would he display authoritarian inflexibility of expression? Would he lavish melodramatic emotion? Then I grew emotionally conscious of that ninety-two-year-old child, seeking the vanished home of her childhood. She stared up at me from her wheel chair, her feeble mind hungrily assenting to my play acting. Recognition awoke the lines of her face. Her ragged eyes filled. Words formed in her mouth and would not attain speech. A quaver sounded somewhere down the deep pit of her throat and a single tear sprang down the dry waste and hung upon her trembling jaw. I became aware that she was trembling convulsively. I threw aside all resistance then, all insistence on being my own emphatic self, well-located in time. I discovered, most startlingly, that I was her father, that it wasn't difficult being anything I chose. I could live any relationship, find a home in any supposed self and make it tenable, ally myself to any country and any identity, so rich was my sudden flight from myself in that momentary self-denial. I stooped over her, ran a hand over her bald pate, lifted the other withered claw with my other hand and held it fast. She wept and wept in her wheel chair, leaning her birdlike head against me, the sobs of a child eking themselves out in the cracked voice of an old woman. She turned my hand this way and that, looking vaguely perhaps for a familiar ring or a mark. Curiously she sniffed at my shawl. Was it that something failed to convince? She, who was incapable of thought, could still detect a fallacy. All of a sudden she shied away from me like a frightened and reproachful child. She sat very still and looked me straight and piercing in the eye. Then she leaned back and sobbed in long, broken gasps. I never knew for certain if she smelt any falsehood. That was all. There was no dialogue in this skit and its duration was about ten minutes. Then her son stepped in and wheedled her thoughts away from me.

She was brought only for that fake assurance but for me the experience was anything but fake. Do you know, Amantha, she died a fortnight later. And, I was told that in that last spell she never once asked for her home again. I shall never know if I helped restore her home to her or confused and denied it to her for all time. More, I have never been able to decide if I ever succeeded in becoming another person by the force of my will for a while or remained myself inescapably. Actually it is vain of me to imagine that my petty performance could claim such a large consequence. But, I proved to myself that I could, if I chose, take at least a brief flight from myself and that was truly enriching. So, that's how I can love another country with a personal emotion. I love this nation of refugees and adventurers. I love its abstractions. I even love the native names of your rivers, the Talahatchie, the Yazoo, the Kaskasia, the Arkansas, those roaring, hell-bent allies of your Old Man River. Their names taste so sharp and tangy, so fresh and pungent, they burn their way down one's throat. I love your Washington where history seems so curiously contemporary.

But there it is—I am leaving. Once when I was six, my aunt, Purobi, offered me a choice between two coins that lay on her palm. One was a large, ugly eight-anna. The other was an exquisitely sculpted, curly edged little two-anna bit with a young queen on it. I chose the smaller of the two. 'Ach, Nityanondo,' rasped the old lady. 'You have taught the boy nothing. He can't even distinguish less from more!' Then, turning to me, she demanded: 'And why, boy, did you choose the small one?'

'Because it is so pretty,' faltered I in confusion.

That explains why I'm going back. I can't articulate it entirely to my satisfaction but I know that I don't want to drive at a regulated sixty miles an hour on a thoroughfare. But, each time you put away an old rug or armchair or juicer, some disturbing association returns to me. I lost my home before and I am losing it again. And changing homes is confusing, like stepping from one dream into another adjoining dream or walking from one thought into an overlapping thought. And we Hindus believe that there is only one way to come home to ourselves if we are tortured by homelessness and that is to fall asleep.

And, then this dreaded last round of the yard, this awful locking up. You almost drop the key in your bag before you remember, laugh nervously and hand it over to Max, smiling brightly. A riot of images runs loose in my brain. My old grandmother wouldn't even let them have an easy entry. I can still visualize her vigorously putting up the bar: 'Let them sweat to get in!' she spat with venom before she turned to pray for the last time before the tulsi in the yard. You shall miss your flowering cherry tree. In life, as in a journey, it doesn't do to carry too much luggage. But I am hastily scooping up these last sights and scenes to remember. 'Do you remember, the cherry tree was flowering in the yard, Amantha,'—I shall ask. And you shall laughingly dismiss the thought—'Why, no, Pranob, it wasn't that way.'

It wasn't that way. Memory plays tricks. The mind furnishes its own fulfilling fictions as my poor enactment perhaps requited an old woman's longings. All that remains roughly reliable is feeling recollected. And, I can recall just one constant feeling—I was restless in Serampore and restless in America. Like my East-Bengali parents I have remained a refugee everywhere, dreaming of the rivers of Babylon.

You smile bravely at me over the rim of the cup the stewardess has just handed you. 'We could be birds migrating, Pranob. Let's be some place else for a while.' You might as well exercise your actress's choice and declare—let's be someone else for a while. There's nothing I'd like better than to take the flight away from myself if that was really as feasible as a change of homes. But, I suspect that there is really only one ancient home for us and only one poor self that one must take the flight back to, like it or not, for it is as irreversible, as irreplaceable as a parent of the past.

So, I turn my back to America and wish this Pan Am flight would last forever. This is the most decided region, this place of the upper air, where there is no country, no constant time, just movement, migration, and the blessed poise of a stone as it hurtles through the air.

The man who died on the pavement that day was Vasant Thakur. I knew him years ago. For six months of my life I underwent, in his company, the most intense infatuation and the most fitful despair. He was stepping across the pavement in Connaught Place when a bomb went off nearby. That was the most futureless interlude in my life and it remains intriguing in a way. Still, purposeful is a word I should hesitate to use for a man like that—purpose was outside his script. I have never experienced so threatening a state of impermanence and wasted effort as I did when I was trying to reform him.

When last I ran into him it was in a restaurant. He still had enormous style. In dress-suit and tie, arty fingers twiddling a pen and notebook, whispering quiet words, you'd imagine he was stepping about on a rarefied plane of contemplation and composition, the eternal wayfarer poet. But no, here he was head-waiter and still a class by himself and, I may add, extremely attractive in his way with such a depth of puzzled tragedy on his face. I kept my eyes fixed on the menu card as he jotted down our order. I'm quite sure he did not recognize me.

Vasant Thakur died when he least expected to. That's what scares me about life—the absolute uncertainty, the ignorance we labour under and our own futurelessness. Yes, even he who made no plans, stepped across that pavement under an assumption of continuity. But, conversely, for argument's sake, one may well observe that the end allotted to him was of a piece with the bent of his being—even in the rash and the accidental one may detect a general consistency of design.

I was twenty-one when I first got to know him. Everyone

warned me that I was inviting trouble. But, he walked in through the glass-panelled door into the lobby, a faded brown blazer slung across his shoulders and a terribly wretched look on his grecian face. He walked right up to the counter where I sat.

'So you see, madam,'—he spread his hands in a fine, expressive gesture '—you simply must lend me the money.'

I had never seen him before. He expressed surprise. He explained that he shared a room with a Mr S.M. Talwar who occupied Room No. 39 on our third floor. I checked up in our register and found it correct. Mr Talwar was his friend and mentor, he said, and was paying for his stay. He had left the evening before on a lightning visit to Delhi, leaving behind some money. And he, Vasant Thakur, had most unfortunately 'spent' the money and now had none with which to pay a certain bill.

How did he spend it?

He looked vague, irritated, as though it was a senseless question.

'Oh, here and there. At a bookstall. In a music shop. In a folk handicrafts emporium. On taxi fare driving up and down the city, and picking up, in a curio shop, most remarkably, an antique jade paperweight.'

'Why did you ask me, of all the people here, for the money?'

If I expected to hear about my kindly face, I was in for a bitter disappointment.

'You were the first person I caught sight of.'

Was he even aware that I was a woman? That I was young and comely, as hotel receptionists invariably are?

'Mr Talwar pays for your stay but don't you have any money of your own?'

His face was supercilious. 'I don't believe in owning money,' was the crushing reply.

'But you just asked me for some.' My amusement must have shown.

'This is an exceptional situation,'—he bristled impatiently, raising intense eyes into my face.

I am not usually described as naïve by my friends but for some reason I gave him the money. That otherworldly disdain of his, those looks, that shrugging despair, that shabby aristocracy that was his. Everything provoked curiosity and made this an exceptional situation. He thanked me with a graceful bow, out of place in the lobby of a hotel but somehow absolutely appropriate, with its suggestion of courtly, romantic acknowledgement upon his lanky frame. One would have thought that I had applauded a couplet rather than lent a hundred rupees, so fine and gracious was that slight nod of the head, that weary, warm, thoughtful smile.

'And,' I added, quite disarmed, 'please don't hesitate to come to me if you ever need anything here'. Was it pure hotel punctilio? I suspected my own motives.

He turned the suggestion over in his mind, then his distraught face lit up.

'I was wondering about dinner,' he said like a child.

'Right,' I said before I knew what I was about. 'I get off duty at six. At eight we meet for dinner. The Camellia is on our eighth floor.'

'Excellent!' said he enthusiastically. 'May I have the honour, then, of claiming madam's company at dinner à la carte?'

'Thank you!' I could not help laughing at the absurdity of the situation. 'The honour is granted, sir!' I knew that the dinner was on me and yet, true to courtly gallantry and grace, it was he who was taking me out. That's the way he made people feel. That wretched superior air of his—they loaded him with favours and thanked him for accepting them. It was something of an honour to be seen with so distinguished a being. And I, a young girl then who dreamt of meeting the rare and right man in irregular, fantastic circumstances! I don't know whether to despise myself or dismiss myself for my youth and silliness. I am not a silly woman but I have done some silly things in my time.

'You resigned from your job in Cuttack? Why?'

I wore my favourite turquoise silk that suited me well. That silk itself should have made me suspect myself. His face seemed cast out of grey shadow, I told myself in the vocabulary of the romances, and lovely descriptions multiplied in my head. Some of the ancient furnace still lay locked miles within, I reflected. He looked down, frowning at the table linen. Some intense story of rejection, some lofty, idealistic revolt . . . .

'There was a girl in Cuttack,' he suddenly disclosed, blighting my hopes. Of course, thought I, with an air like that there was bound to be a girl somewhere. The icy white curtains of the Camellia frosted the world out of sight. A crimson light ripened on the walls. The narrow vase on our table caught a slim, burnished world on its copper skin, slender and finite. There are images of the past one retains forever. They were playing a strange, forlorn music tonight. A note split in two like a broken twig or a very very tired voice. The violinist raised his bow in a high shivering passion on the summit of an octave.

'You resigned from your job just because of a girl?' But I was not surprised. 'And before that you abandoned your master's course at the university because your mother died? That's no reason.'

'Because several times in life I wanted to make an abrupt end to a certain personality. I didn't want to carry any meagre leftovers of one self-projection into another. It was some . . . some inner necessity.'

It didn't make much sense but it certainly sounded impressive to me. I had read too many romantic books and their vocabulary was my usual emotional currency. So I fluently perceived that when he spoke he seemed to forge each word anew, fluidly melting speech into its first shapes. Each thought seemed to occur like a pang, never before uttered. The notes of the violin leapt over, fleeing their own rapture. 'Why had I come?' I questioned myself as the heroines of fiction do at some point of the tryst.

My curiosity got the better of me. This was no ordinary Casanova, I had already deduced. This was a lost soul, a sojourner on an alien and inhospitable planet, a troubled, storm-tossed castaway upon a violent and lethal ocean.

'And why did you leave the other one, the one who was in college?'

He made a helpless gesture. 'I'd try talking to her sometimes and she didn't know what in tarnation I was talking about.'

'So you just broke the engagement and rushed off because she couldn't understand your profound utterances.'

'I didn't break the engagement,' he protested. 'I just rushed off.'

'That certainly does lend a different complexion to the matter, does it?'

The waiter brought our order.

'D' you know,' he said. 'I'm not used to this rich food. And I make a frightful ass of myself with all these fancy spoons and knives and forks. I've lived for weeks on just buns and tea picked up from roadside stalls.'

'When?'

'The time when my father wanted to force me to return and pursue my law studies and I left home and lived with a friend.'

A friend like Talwar who footed your bills for you while you emptied his purse on antique paperweights?—I wanted to ask.

'Why did you buy that jade paperweight?'

'That? It just caught my fancy.' He looked evasive, perplexed. 'How?'

'It's like this—when you dream you don't see images in the visual sense. A dream is a feeling which includes the properties of vision and sound and what have you.' He drew fitfully upon the table with the fork. 'You don't dream in terms of black or white or technicolour or even in terms of shape and size and dimension. Your dream contains the essence of colour without the property of colour. There are some shades which seem to exist only in essence—like . . . like the soul of a colour without its body. That's what I fancied about the colour of that paperweight. It seemed to be beyond shape itself, above colour and outside touch. To feel its texture was to find the smoothness of water in the disguise of stone, as though it were deliberately pretending. It looked like a green lake carved by some superior craftsman along the natural outlines of water—which, you know, has no outlines, save what you give it. Yes, that's it! It had a shape that seemed somehow a transitional shape, ready to overflow into a further shape that you could somehow foresee but not prove because it wasn't there yet. That paperweight had a nebulous present but a somehow predictable future shape.'

Suddenly, this impassioned orator grew self-conscious. His eyes grew tense. 'Sorry,' he said. 'You wanted to know why I bought it and paid through my nose for it.'

For a fantastic price. And you have neither desk nor paper to put it on, I thought. But never mind that: I was already floored by the unexpected overflow of self-expression upon the unlikely subject of a paperweight! To a girl like me, Vasant Thakur stood forever vindicated, all his irregularities explicable and natural.

He rested his thin elbows on the table and spoke and spoke. In his urgency to express, he moved his hands in the empty air. Behind us a fluting note tripped over another, recovered itself, went shining down a steep staircase of scales. The erratic music came to an end and the raucous silence which followed stung the ear. I seemed to be hearing his voice for the very first time—that's how the books describe it. Needless to relate, Vasant Thakur, his words, his mannerisms had all earned tremendous respect in my eyes. Youth is like that—that is also what the books sagely pronounced.

'And what of the one in Simla?' More than the speculations and the intuitions, I was keen to learn about the women. But he did not seem to find my curiosity strange.

'She was an IAS officer and she gave me everything,' he said candidly. 'She gave me everything a woman can give—herself, presents, comfort, money, complete security. She gave so much that it began to feel like a cushy multinational job and that wasn't what I wanted out of life.'

What innocence and what remorselessness.

'What do you want?'

'I don't know,' he said. 'I know what I don't want.'

'But if one considers anything deeply enough one comes to feel that one really doesn't want it. Still we go on.'

'No,' he insisted. 'As soon as I don't want anything I just drop it.'

This, I told myself, was integrity, the guts to face the void, the power of action and choice, the uncompromising standard of the implacable individualist. Other than soft emotional pieces I also read serious books very seriously.

'But one's got to climb down, alter one's choices. That's what continuing to live is all about.' Wisdom was a stance I had successfully cultivated. Besides those were the days when I actually paraded a neatly formulated philosophy of life and I was given to speaking often of the business of living and the meaning of life.

'Not for me,' he said emphatically. 'I don't prune and pare and trim myself. I terminate the entire circumstance.'

I particularly liked people who spoke in instant metaphor. It conferred a pleasing intensity to their speech.

'Did you ever think that you might be causing suffering?'

'Never,' replied he outrageously. 'I've been through tremendous suffering myself in order never to settle for the slightest disappointment.'

'Perhaps,' I reflected sentimentally, 'you are a special being, unlike all others and seeking in our inadequate situations for something that no situation can compass. You are looking in the drab, shabby substance of life for something which it cannot contain.'

'You're one of these crazy artists?' I laughed.

'Yes, but an artist who created nothing, only destroyed.'

'Pardon the presumption, but may I make bold as to offer this?' I placed the cigarette pack on the table, also an envelope containing a fraction of my meagre savings.

He raised an enquiring eyebrow.

'It is an occasional delight to serve the Devil in distress, let alone the damsels'. I explained, laughing.

He helped himself to the money and smiled. 'When pain and anguish wring the brow, a ministering angel thou?'

'And that,' I quipped, '—is another instance of the Devil citing scripture for his purpose!'

We both laughed but a strange misery stirred in my heart, as the books put it.

Is it that at that time most emotions came to me clothed in the idiom of certain phrases and that experience was my unconscious attempt at their exorcism?

He brought out a small volume of Japanese poetry and offered it to me. My acquaintance with poetry was an old one but I had not had the pleasure of having it introduced to me through the medium of such a poetic personage. I told him so.

'Wonderful!' exclaimed he. 'I seize the pleasure, then, of doing the honours between poetry and you.'

His voice opened large visual landscapes. A mesh of white streamlets twinkled into laughter. A thin young tree awoke and stretched its arms, warming its fingertips in a simmering bowl of sun. The sky was an up-turned rice bowl. A thin garment of mist spilt round the throat of the mountain. Birds bloomed on white cherry-blossoms and a young man grew meditative and old and the essence of a lifetime found speech in a stanza. A tilt of tone and strange half-shades appeared in his voice. A supple descent of breath and a nameless distress stole over my mind. And yet, it came to me suddenly, that something was amiss.

He looked up in surprise.

'What do they know of anything!' I almost sobbed bitterly. 'It's only a fools' paradise, all this describing and expressing! It's only a . . . a refugee camp!'

That was when I looked at myself in surprise. I may not have grasped the truth of it all, I may have given vent to a rash dismissiveness, but I had felt something that I had never read anywhere before, that was violent and personal, inartistic and unorthodox, uncultured and incorrect and absolutely authentic to me.

'And how will you explain me?' My voice was harsh with pent-up hysteria. When someone asks you—And why did you leave the fifth one, the one who was a hotel receptionist in Calcutta?—what will you say this time? That you were killed with kindness? Or that you learnt too late that your ardours are all for yourself? Or that she did not understand things? Or maybe that she understood everything too well? My voice rose shrill, out of control.

'Do relax.'

'How can I? Can you relax in the middle of something so brief? Something that you're sure will end?'

He sat up and spoke eloquently, sensitively in his best voice. I found him hateful.

'Is there anything you're sure will never end? The fact that life has an end does not prevent you from living it? There is something like creative forgetfulness. Euripides or was it Empedocles?— claimed . . . .'

'Do you know that you can be loathsome?'

There were two kinds of ways in which words could be used— real meanings and fake meanings, I deduced in another unexpected burst of understanding. I think that my present middle-aged belief that a good author must be a good man springs from that insight. There is such a thing as spurious depth. I added another conclusion to my staircase of conclusions.

But we met again as usual.

'I spoke to Talwar. When his work in the National Library ends I shall stay back in Calcutta.'

'You don't intend throwing up this new assignment at the archives that Talwar has wangled? All because of me?'

'Why not?'

'What will you do with yourself? An unemployed, self-professed wandering philosopher on the streets of Calcutta?'

'I shall study the underworld. I've always wanted to. I shall step out of the ivory tower of academic orthodoxy and taste a few humble professions. I shall write a book.'

'Poetry?' My scorn left not a dent on him. He blew a couple of smoke rings in the air and chuckled. This world shall yet see me as a law-abiding and stolid householder. Can you picture me as a pompous paterfamilias, dandling a gaggle of brats with my rationcard in my elegant breast-pocket where a carnation should be?'

'I tremble to think,' I quipped. 'Besides, I'll warn you not to speak to me of the foul institution of marriage. I may end up demanding a colossal alimony and then where would you be, my Percy Bysshe Solzhenitzyn? Better buy up a few more paperweights to pawn.'

'Have you no sense of sanctity, woman?'
'Have you?'

Talwar, before he left, invited us for lunch. He was a large man whose voice was straight and sturdy, striding evenly forwards on a few hard, sculpted syllables. 'So Vasant has found yet another protectress on the premises,' he said ironically. 'May it do him good. Do sit down.'

Talwar was annoyed. 'I've had the misfortune of being Vasant's knight-errant ever since he stepped out of his swaddling bands—if he ever did so, that is.'

'I hope,' he continued after an uneasy pause,' that you, young lady, realize the implications of this new decision of Vasant's. It means another long spell of unemployment. It was with some difficulty that I secured this archives assignment for him. But I observe that it's another of those chapters in his chequered career. The number of times Vasant has renounced our poor market place world of work and common sense, would put a Buddha to shame.'

'Common sense is much too common for a man of my mettle,' declared Vasant and quoted a French proverb—*Le matin je fais des projets, et le soir je fais des sottises*—In the morning I make resolutions, in the evening I commit follies,' he translated with a sidelong glance at me, laughing provocatively. Talwar snorted.

The waiter brought Talwar's cigarettes and change for the hundred rupees that he had handed him.

Suddenly, Vasant was on his feet, gathering the loose ten rupee notes. 'Back in a minute.' He vanished through the revolving door.

'The trouble with Vasant,' said Talwar, is that he knows what displeases him but rarely what pleases him.'

'Neti, neti?' I wanted Vasant's mentor to think well of me.

'A perilous philosophy,' he observed. 'Just suppose you cut away all the real, solid things and find nothing?'

'But Vasant believes that experience is like a globe—if you remove the crusts of hindering rock, you strike the fire beneath.'

Talwar shot me a sharp look. 'Is that what he's been telling you?' he asked, his lips twitching suspiciously. 'You can match wisdom for wisdom by talking of the proverbial onion— you remove sheath upon sheath and find nothing beneath.'

The door swung open presently and Vasant sprang jauntily in, a large, glossy, volume under one arm. 'Sorry, just popped off to the arcade. I saw this book on astral travel in the window yesterday.' He put the single tenner on the table. 'I've always,' he declared, sinking contentedly into his chair, 'believed that events may be reduced naturally to psychic vibrations just as a melody is reduced to minute scratches on a disc. Talwar, old man, let me illuminate you on the subject.'

Talwar pocketed the single tenner with supreme insouciance, then his eyes stopped on mine and there was in them a look of infinite pity. My cheeks burned. Vasant expounded.

Talwar left for Delhi that evening. I could not understand why he had supported Vasant, why he went on supporting him. They were very old friends, Vasant explained. Here, I suddenly thought, was something real and no narrations or speculations were needed to render its reality.

During the next two months Vasant changed his lodgings thrice. We took to dining in a tiny south-Indian eating-house nearby, for my money was running short.

'I want,' I said one day as I paid at the grimy counter, '—to fling all my money away on something trivial, something meaningless and pretty and easily breakable, something utterly, utterly useless that I can place upon my desk and laugh at!'

'Aha! One more convert to the creed of the paperweights.'

'It would celebrate the fact that you and I aren't going to last much longer.'

'How dreadful you sound!'

Calcutta that summer was terrible. The little eating-house with its asbestos roof was like a furnace. He sat opposite me, unshaven, sallow-faced, smoking bidi after bidi, eyes tangled with the distance. Each time we met I clung to the hope that somehow our complicated relationship would be sorted out. I knew the inevitable.

'I want to overhaul myself,' said he ominously one day. ' To renovate myself completely. Inside my brain there is only a musty, faintly sour consciousness. I want to clear my mind of its obscure, tiring rhythms. I'm sour with the taste of my own being. Maybe I'm falling into that old sin of self-analysis and you will be another person to condemn me . . . .' He looked up, haggard with poetic weariness.

'No,' I replied. 'I don't even know what I sense in you. Maybe I shall find some reason to justify you to myself. Or maybe,' I added bitterly,. 'I'm only using you to teach myself something important but I wish I knew what it was.' I was ill with nervousness and anxiety.

'I've noticed,' he remarked petulantly. 'That you're just waiting for me to pack up and go, the sooner the better.'

'Please,' I begged, 'let's not go into all that again. Why do you live in small things so intensely and dismiss all the larger ones so casually?'

A strange look curdled in his eyes. 'That's exactly what the one in Simla used to say. I am haunted by a sense of the provisional— that is my answer today although another day I may find a different answer to give you.'

The bell-boy handed me a sealed envelope. A Delhi postmark.

'Dear Miss Choudhury,' Talwar wrote.

> It is my unpleasant duty to inform you that Vasant returned to Delhi yesterday. I apologize on his behalf for the serious breach of propriety that he has made himself guilty of in not intimating you of his departure.

> With regards, S. M. Talwar.

Vasant always made fun of Talwar's old-fashioned expressions. I found them strange but in no way comic.

Reading that stiff little note I knew that I was relieved, I had learnt what I had set out to learn. And I lost the vocabulary of my girlhood naturally in a few months.

I always considered that period as a wasted one in my life, until I met Talwar again in Delhi and married him. After all, hadn't we both supported, liked and despised the same man? I shall hazard one more general statement about life—a practice I strictly discourage in myself ever since—between the happiness one seeks and the happiness one eventually achieves there is a vast area of the unpredictable. There are many more things in the world, other than the ones we consciously look for, capable of affording us far greater fulfilment. Disappointment is a blessing if one learns its lessons intelligently. I am not the best authority on myself now. But

I suspect that in the perfect design of things, I was to put up certain illusions on trial, test whether they survived or fell before I was allowed to proceed with my life.

Vasant Thakur was on his way to an interview, a real job at last. And that was outside the scope of his personality. He believed in terminating unwanted situations abruptly with that special artistic intolerance of his. Is it at all amazing that he died on the way, as though by some intervention? In this fools' paradise there do seem to be some erratic regulations.

A MAKER OF MIRAGES

Some Calcutta buses have low ceilings. If you are unfortunate enough to be a weary, standing passenger, peeping into your neighbour's pockets, your neighbour's cleavage or your neighbour's conscience may afford you some scant comfort. The neighbour's comfort is quite another matter.

He was standing just behind me in the bus and craning his neck to peer over my shoulder and at first I didn't even notice.

'Bad composition, dada,' he remarked, peering interestedly into the bunch of photographs I held. 'Yours?'

I nodded coldly, edging away to look at the next. I was new to this city of garrulous strangers.

'Overexposed,' declared he, unabashed. I turned and gave him a nasty stare.

'Here your camera shook ever so little, *moshai*. Always use a tripod for such shots, my friend.'

'Here,' I said, turning and thrusting the entire bunch into his swarthy hands. 'This is for you to deliver your unsolicited criticism in greater comfort.'

'With pleasure, *moshai*, with pleasure!' beamed the obnoxious stranger, reached out and took the proffered bunch of photographs eagerly. And when my partner got off at the next stop, he instantly took his seat beside me, his face burning with enthusiasm.

'I am Manager in the Behala Branch of the State Bank,' he smiled broadly.

'You may be the madam of a bawdy house for all I care!' I cursed silently.

'Which camera are you using?' An urgent whisper.

67

I told him, too astonished to think up an adequately stinging reply.

'Why do you like photography?' Another urgent, breathless question as though his life depended upon my answer. The Calcuttan makes you give yourself away, draws you into conversation even against your disposition.

I found myself talking. The mobile world, the dynamic image. The exhilaration of taking aim. Like a hunter felling down a fugitive vision . . .

'Wrong, wrong. That's not the idea at all!' exclaimed he. 'An image must stay alive. A dead bird in the hand is a violation of nature, my friend. The idea is not to encroach like a hunter, to wait and watch and ensnare but to invoke or rather to invite a fresh fluttering image, like a sentient creature, still wet with God's paint, to rest upon one's palm. Good pictures aren't the result of accident or luck. They need the right attitude, reverent devotion, patience, a sense of psychological moment. One clicks not to overcome the image but rather at the precise instant when one is wholly overcome by the images . . .'

In Bengal one can find all-purpose mystics and here was a photographer mystic! I groaned inwardly.

It is a mystery to me but I actually accepted his invitation. A solitary man in a large, untidy apartment down Rai Bahadur Road. His name was Sulochan Mullick.

'You live alone?'

'Sad to say, yes. I lost Shobha, my wife, five years back and we married off our daughter, Ruchira, a year before Shobha went. My son, Udai, lives separately so that leaves just myself. Let me show you my albums.'

'This is the first serious photograph I took. 1950 or thereabouts. A faulty picture as you'll notice. Ill-composed, under exposed. This was about the time when I met my guru, Keshab Chandra Roy. A remarkable man who made black black, and white white, and gave all the shades of grey an individual, fierce identity. But his camera made no compromises, no forgiving interpretations. Women who wished to look like memsahibs ended up looking like wistful tribals in his pictures. Naturally he was a failure. The customers complained: "But you have made me so dark, Keshab-da!" He died in poverty which was a pity for he was a very talented man. Now look at this one!'

A girl asleep over a book, flushed cheek, long inky lashes and uncoiled knot of hair.

'What a pretty girl!'

'My daughter Ruchira.'

'Your daughter liked books?'

'Come to think of it, I really don't know. Now in this study the impact is due to the tremendous contrast between the face and the background; the strong human interest element and its Raphaelite suggestions.'

Two despairing faces of a woman, shadowy and forlorn.

'Shobha was a perfect model.'

'A beautiful woman, yes.'

'Very camera-worthy. This photograph was created from two negatives. Observe the elongated construction. The shape provides easy travel for the eye. The triangle or pyramid was a favourite compositional form of the old masters. Here it was important to keep the interest centred within the triangle formed by the eyes and the lips. The hands on which she rests her chin have been darkened during printing to stress the triangle effect. The two negatives were taken within a month of each other. Shobha was very ill in between, I returned from Delhi where I'd gone to attend the Annual Photographers' Meet and found her pale and wispy and her face had turned almost abstract. Excellent, in fact, for the alter image.'

'What was she suffering from?'

'I'm not sure. High blood pressure, anxiety and some sort of cardiac complaint perhaps. Now here's another interesting study.'

An armada of swans cruising on a dark sheet of water.

'Yes, I remember. Long ago it was, and Ruchi was only three. A lovely day and the light was perfect. The wind splashed the water and the swans cried aloud and the two sounds met with a clash in one's heart, and everywhere a strange disturbance of delight.'

'Your wife looks quite ill here.'

'Yes, she was quite over-worked, poor thing.'

'No servants to help her?'

'I can't say. I have an abominable memory for facts outside my pictures. Besides I spent most of my time that vacation doing nature photography. There's a striking one of a Bengal tiger. Wait till you see my Kodacolor slides . . .'

'This is the late Ronnie, our dog. This is Ruchi and Udai in Gulmarg. Udai on his fifteenth birthday. Myself on my motorbike. My mother at prayer. This is a spot near my village that always affects me very strongly. Just a bare clearing between these thin, frowning trees. Some intense memory lurks here, somebody's emotion, a satanic anger and despair. The silence seems choked. Even time seems to slope backward in regret. These trees, here to the right, seem to fling agonized hands to the sky. I always think of martyrs tied to the stake or frail, bony witches damned to hell fire. Notice the misty effect. No colour used is a complete statement but seems more in the process of discovering itself. The angle of shooting is higher than eye level. This has helped to create the required perspective and has helped in covering more area. The area towards the right is underexposed as compared to the area to the left. I used a 100 ASA film with aperture 4 and shutter speed 1/30 seconds . . . And this is Ruchi at her wedding, crying in her mother's arms just before leaving'.

'She seems to be crying rather badly.'

'You know how it is when a daughter leaves you. This is Ruchi's baby. Notice the balance of light. No light, no picture, that's one of the simplest rules in photography. But in colour photography, however, the colour of the light is also important. D'you know that light has many colours which must not be recklessly mixed? The depth of field must be considered in focusing. For extreme close ups like this one, the depth is very shallow. And this is Udai's son. Udai lives in Laketown.'

'Why not with you?'

'I hardly know why. Udai and I never got along. When Shobha died he accused me of criminal neglect towards her and all of them. We seldom meet. But, on the birth of his son I was invited, so I went with my camera.'

'This is Shobha just before we carried her away. We dressed her in bridal red and I took a few colour photographs.'

'And here your camera shook.' I observed with a viciousness incomprehensible even to myself. I almost quoted him to himself on the use of the tripod.

'Yes, the composition too isn't all it should be,' he answered with a strange rueful smile'. And, this is one of the night sky. I took it when I was all alone with Shobha gone forever. D'you know that the stars are as colourful as land objects? Probably not, because dark adapted eyes have low sensitivity to colour. The constellation Cassiopeia contains two blue, one white, one golden and one green star. A good camera that can make time exposures, a rigid tripod and fast film are all one needs to capture the colour of the stars.'

GODDESS OF CLAY

Whenever old Manik Das shuffled down to Robi Mullick's grocery store in the village for a trifling loan or a bagful of fluffed rice and sugar or a pinch of snuff on credit, great was the laughter.

'What, god-maker?' jested the village wags. 'Can't conjure up a handful of sugar with a mantra? Of what use are all those gods and goddesses in your yard?'

Or Robi Mullick, our grocer-financier, pronounced heartily: 'Ish! The number of loans you've taken this month can only be counted on Ma Durga's fifty fingers, Manik da, certainly not on mine.'

The wags crowed. 'Ma Durga's given up warfare, no? Counting loans, is she now, ho god-maker?'

'Silence!' roared Robi. 'This is Kali-yuga, my young sparks, so what better use for the ten hands of the holy than counting loans, investments, assets, taxes, interests. These things have their spiritual counterparts in heaven, yes, even taxes, even soap and tea for free, so look sharp, my lads.'

And they hooted and slapped Robi's back and begged him for a bidi apiece to celebrate his wit. Those wags were our village chess players, good-for-nothing layabouts who carried on their intent game, come rain, storm or riot in Robi's corridor.

Old Manik Das smiled mildly. He was a lanky old-timer, vague in the eyes, uncertain in his movements, gone stupid over the years. It was common for all young men of superior intelligence in the village to smile after the old one and tap the forehead to denote complete senility, and they did so now as he tucked the packet carefully into the greasy bag and left.

But he it was that made those clay idols for our village Durga puja, our Lakshmi puja, our Kali puja, even our Vishwakarma and

Saraswati pujas. For, you know, between the monsoon months and
the next year's summer our goddesses must be feted. He had his
ancient shack down a bylane and lived in a ramshackle room
behind it with two of his sons and a spitfire of a daughter. Forty
years he had fashioned the goddesses for our village. And his
hands worked miracles. Nobody could give our Saraswati's face
that tender thoughtfulness or Kali's that dark rage. He was even
better than his father, Nimai Chandra Das and his grandfather,
Abani Shankar Das. Great pains he took procuring his material.
River clay and paddy husk, the firmest, most supple of bamboo
shafts, old paper, shreds of cloth. He did not like these modern
moulds that made the goddess look like a simpering starlet or an
overblown matron. He patted out each separate face, rendering it
lyrically with his leathery hands. He lingered long over each
arching brow or slope of cheek or bridge of nose or curl of lip.

And he did not like being watched. The children used to gather
outside his shack. The old one was too mild to chase them away,
but his creaking song ceased abruptly, his fingers faltered and his
face grew tense and ashamed. A little later he abandoned his work,
lit a chillum, slunk into the room and waited for them to leave.

Naturally, his work was slow. He took weeks to finish each
Durga idol. 'Hurry, hurry, baba,' urged his sons. For in the time
that old Manik Das took to complete a single idol, other clay
modellers would have finished six. But the old man was roused to
one of his mad fits of rage.

'Ho!' he fumed wrathfully. 'Does one stand before a blest
woman before the nine months are done and shout, "Hurry, hurry,
deliver before thy time?"' And his sons knew there was no arguing
with him.

The old man would stand, lost in introspection, drape his fingers
lightly over a clay wrist or ankle, think deeply, hum a verse from
the 'Song of the Goddess', add a dimple, soften an angle, bend a
little finger and that was that. He never seemed to realize how little
he earned. For with Manik Das it was the verse no less than his
hands which wrought the perfection of the fiery woman, the lady
of the lion. Shail-putri, daughter of the mountain, he mumbled.
Brahmacharini, chaste one. Kal-ratri, night of the aeons, protectress
of the ten directions. Each attribute, each utterance, surely left its
impact upon the clay. The beauty of her names! Chhatreshwari, he
whispered, giver of shadowhood to the shadow; bearer of the

virtues of ego, mind, intellect, bearer of the thunderbolt of the five breaths; adorner of well-being; Yoginidevi, of all essence, form, fragrance, word, touch; Narayani, to the three gunas; protectress of dharma; Swar-rupa, she whose very shape composes the subtle stuff of sound!

He stood back to survey the work of his hands.

And does one stand before a blest woman and say! "Hurry, hurry, die before thy time?" '

Manik Das's hands shook.

'What's the matter, Ma?' Of all his six daughters, this one, Uma, was the worst.

'Matter? Ash in your eyes if you still can't see!' she leaned against the wall in bitter melodrama and addressed the clay idol with scorn: 'He lets me grow into a dry old crone, dry, dry, dry as the sugarcane stick when all the juice has been crushed out! Then he looks at me as tho' butter will not melt in his mouth, no, neither butter no jaggery, and he asks—"What is the matter?" Huh! How long will I go on stirring his rice, ha?'

Manik Das shook inwardly. What was the vixen's problem? True, she was an abandoned woman and her husband's folk had cast her out, but she didn't want for anything. He had brought her back and willingly. And here she sat and accused him day after day. He was the usual victim of her tantrums and her perversity knew no limits.

'Ha!' she scoffed, delighted with his shock and dismay. 'See the way he lovingly carves those full arms and buttocks. And he has the nerve to ask me—"What is the matter?" '

Manik Das trembled. 'For shame, daughter, have you lost your mind?'

With a wild sob she rushed out. A daily scene this, reflected Manik Das helplessly. He could not work with a mind so troubled. He lit a chillum.

The village wags knew what the matter was. So did our women, beating their clothes at the community pond. Between them, our wags and our virtuous women could render accurate accounts of the contents of your coffers and your conscience both. A woman on heat, and not even worth your lechery, held the young sophists at Robi's store. Dark as night, a belly like a rice pot and a skin like a toad's, a shrewish tongue and no morals to boot. The women at the pond did not blame her husband for throwing her out. After all, Somesh Chandra of the next kasba belonged to a proud family, had a large patch of land of his own. The women of his household had skins white as milk or turmeric pale. Heavy gold bangles they wore. Why he should have married that spitfire, no one knew. For Uma, it was relentless war.

'I heard what you just said, Aunt. And why should I put vermilion in my hair and why should I wear a shell bangle? He threw me out, didn't he, the swine? He's dead for me, that son of wanton birth!'

Mark how she flings her pitcher into the water, muttered the good women at the ghat. At least maintain a decorous silence about your situation, my great lady, held those moralists. At least maintain that your husband has now got a job in Calcutta or Ranaghat or Burdwan and that's why you're here. If you don't please him, my queen, he has the right to give a kick on the buttock! Brazen hussy! Dirty slut!

'Go, sit in a balcony with flowers in your hair if you're that desperate,' teased the wags. 'But do, do let us know when you're taking to the anklet bells and we shan't fail you, madam, for old times' sake.' And no less than a dozen brave men made their claims and narrated the incident and all the ladies, listening behind the scenes, shook their heads and affirmed that they'd always known that she was a bad lot. Each day Uma raced away from the pond in a whirlwind of hysterical confusion, mouthing venomous imprecations, sobbing, like one possessed.

Old Manik Das still sang as he modelled the clay. She is the victorious one behind, the victorious one before, unvanquished to the left, unvanquished to the right. Udyotini, her crown illumined, her forehead bears a garland, the renowned one where her brows are, the three-eyed one, she, the breath of whose nostrils gives birth to time, conch shaped between the eyes, inhabiter of the doors of the ears, Kalika, of the cheeks; fragrance at the nostrils, speech at the upper lip, immortal nectar at the lower lip, Mahamaya, at the palms, Bhadrakali, at the throat, bow-bearer at the spine, bearer of the thunderbolt at the arms, Mahadevi, at the breasts, grief queller for the mind, Kamini, for the navel, granter of all desires, Mahabaladevi, at the thighs, Vindhyavasini, at the knees, oh, she, possessor of the lion force at the ankles, lance-bearer of the heart, rider of the buffalo . . .

Uma's lip curled in scorn. Sullenly she turned her back to him and strode into the inner room.

Uma stared at her reflection in the cracked mirror. Kalika, of the cheeks, she muttered bitterly; fragrance at the nostrils, immortal nectar at the lower lip, Bhadrakali, at the throat, Mahabaladevi, at the thighs! She looked at the mirror and her own ungainly form in rage. If I flung this pitcher into that wall, the crash might stop his crazy chanting.

She lowered the pitcher down beside the earthen hearth and thought—'I shall carry this ugly face like an evil karma till I die.'

'Hurry, Baba, hurry,' urged the sons. 'The third day of the goddess's advent and still a lot of the paint remains to be applied, and what if it rains? You waste time singing and dreaming. If, for instance, you let me apply the paint on this order, Shubodh can attend to that Kartika there while you rest in the afternoon.'

But the old one would have none of it. He was possessive about his creations. Each year they noticed the madness that claimed him as the ten-day advent advanced. His absent-minded concentration and his irritability grew, so did his senile murmuring. He helped drape the folds round her form, arranged in her ten hands the conch and the discus and the club and the hatchet, the lance, the massive bow, the trident.

'He who wears the armour of your name,' he whispered softly to himself, 'in the three worlds shall he be blest. Desires fulfilled, all victory his, disease, all ghouls of the sky, sea travelling powers, female spirits, movers in space, destroyer forces, all, all cast away. For him your ultimate sanctuary, Mother, for him shelter in your form beyond which no form exists.'

On the fifth day they came with their carts and took away the idols, shouting, clashing cymbals, blowing conchs, beating drums and dancing. The sons stormed and haggled themselves hoarse.

'Thieves!' roared Proshanto. 'You'd cheat your very mothers of their last drop of Ganga water! Not Brahmins but Shudras in soul are you!'

'Next year take an advance!' shouted Shubodh and followed it up with a string of profanities. Manik Das watched her borne away in silence, not seeming to mind anything, not the broken assurances of full payment, nor the lying and the ribald abusing in her sacred presence.

Early on the sixth day he stood outside the festive tent, watching from afar. The lamps swung on their chains, dense fragrance rose from the censers and the dizzy drums thundered. Armed with her weapons, she towered astride the writhing demon, no longer clay, and her scorching eyes raged with an intense cosmic wrong. Every year Manik Das witnessed the miracle, a mood that was not of his making emanating from her face and a different expression each day.

Armed with the celestial weapons, mounted upon a lion, Durga emitted a blood-curdling cry. The seas trembled. The earth shook. The mountains rocked. Mahishasura's heart skipped a beat. 'I have come to fulfil Brahma's boon,' she said. 'You wished to die at the hands of a woman? So be it'. And as she breathed, thousands of soldiers came into being and fought at her side . . .

'Kanto!' cried Uma, catching up with him, gushing winsomely over the handlebar. 'Fancy seeing you here! Father and I were speaking of you just the other day. Why do you neglect us so, you forgetful thing? With these eyes I saw you cycle past our door and not a thought you gave us.'

Head inclined coyly upon the shoulder, Uma's voice is teasing music. 'Too learned for a tailor boy, yes? Too big your friends? Fine new clothes too. My!'

Suddenly she reached out and gripped his arm. 'Come!' she laughed gaily. 'Today is Shoshti day. Won't you come to sweeten your mouth and touch Baba's feet? Won't you measure me for that new choli you promised me?' She winked naughtily. 'I simply won't let you off.'

Kanto recoiled, filled with revulsion and panic. He shook her importunate arm off, a deep frown of disgust upon his swarthy face. It may have happened twice before, he scarcely knew how, but never, never again. He shuddered at the memory.

'Listen,' he spoke hurriedly. 'D'you know who saw me at the shop recently? Your brother in law, Ashit. "Look after your health, tailor"—that's what he said. Everyone is afraid of Somesh, your man. You know what he did to Milon Bose when he gave you money? I wish you would not come after me and insist on this thing going on. There was a to-do at home too. I don't want any trouble for the family . . .'

She could have slapped him hard. The screaming words exploded shrill and hot upon her lips. 'After what happened in the boat and the riverside reeds, you're on Somesh's side too? You hang together, you men? Burnt face! Field mouse! Stinking mole!' She was aware of herself racing away in that old primeval flight away from all people and things. She was aware of the tempestuous thoughts. 'And to think I almost bore this gutter-snipe's child! This worm's! Oh, thank the goddess my womb burbled forth its refusal today!' Only another woman could soothe and in this hellish village all the women hated her, the bitches! Except one. It is only in the festive tent of the goddess that she can find something for herself. So she stood in the corner and seethed with rage.

And the goddess told her what she had to do.

It was with grim decision that she sought him out.

'One minute,' she stepped in his way. 'There is something I would have you know, dear Kanto,' she said sweetly. 'There's something you must tell them all from me—it has festered too long inside me! "Everybody's afraid of Somesh, your man,"' she mimicked in bitter mockery. 'Not everybody, my little snivelling prick! And never call Somesh, my man, ever again. There was a man who wasn't afraid of Somesh and his filthy clan and I bore him a son! Yes, do not think that I am alone, tailor boy. His hands hacked off the heads of goats—phut, like that, and snapped the chickens' necks in two, so look sharp, tailor.'

Kant gazed at her in horrified suspicion. 'Waseem Khan, the cobbler?' he whispered. He'd heard it before. A caste woman too.

Her eyes glittered in malice. 'Yes,' she announced recklessly. 'That was a man made of beaten gold like Kartika, with sinews like Durga's lion. And a face as compassionate as the goddess's and as thoughtful as Saraswati's. He fed me the nameless meats of his poor hearth when, bruised and broken, I crept to his door. Do you know the bride price Somesh ever gave me—beatings and beatings, red weals and blue-black bruises, hunger, insults and filth. Not he alone but also his vile father and, his foul-mouthed mother. Barren, they called me, barren and ugly and poor. Waseem Khan never called me ugly or barren. He applied turmeric on my bruises and told me the story of the Prophet and the man who was beating his slave. Do you know what the Prophet said to the man, tailorboy? "You should know, Abu Masood, that God has more power over you than you have over this slave." He sent me back to Somesh with another story out of his big Book. The Prophet said to Abu Jandal: "O Abu Jandal, have patience for God will soon show you and your kind a way out of your suffering." "Go," said

Waseem Khan, "and weep not. If man only foresaw the hopefulness of tomorrow, he would never despair over the defeats of today." '

She frowns into the distance and suddenly, in her abrupt, vicious way, bursts out laughing. 'To remember all that rejoicing in Somesh's household when my womb filled. Somesh, gloating oaf, so proud of his virility! And as my belly grew, they fed me milk and fish, nuts and festive sweets, I, their starveling! I stole away each day to see him in his shoe maker's hut and he gave me new mangoes for the palate and meats of many kinds for strength, talismans against spirits and sacred stories from his Book. "Do not spend so much on me, cobbler. You're a poor man yourself, you know," I said to him. But he had a pious answer for everything, that man. "What should I do with my earnings, girl? Hoard them up! No, by God, for the sake of tomorrow, I will not disobey God today." The Prophet said that God told him: "Mankind, spend and you will be spent on." To think that I betrayed a man like that for a snivelling like you, may I be punished for that, slut that I am, may I be punished for a hundred lifetimes!'

'Why didn't you go to the fellow for good?' Kanto's outraged honour smarted under the lash of her tongue.

'I did, many a time,' she replied and there was now no sting in her voice, only a boundless nostalgia. 'I took the child for him to see even before the forty days were done. I took him flowers and coconuts and sweets from my goddess. And I bent and touched his feet, for my gratitude knew no end.'

'And Somesh let you go?' Kanto's sneer was lost on her. She herself was lost to the world and enclosed in her own story.

'He did not know. I lied to him. I'm a cunning one—doesn't the entire village know of my cunning and my shamelessness, eh, tailor boy?'

Curiosity had long overcome all of Kanto's fears. He drew closer, goaded her on with searching questions. A pretty story for the village this would be. Nothing like this had ever happened.

'I touched his feet,' she recalled in a dream. 'And he chided me and said: "Don't do this. This is *kufra* and it may not be done. Man must not bend his head before man." '

'And then?' prompted Kanto.

'Then I burst out laughing and said: "But I am a woman, dear cobbler, and a woman must bend before man, must she not? Keep telling me nice stories out of your Book. I like them but keep your way for yourself and leave mine for me and please do not preach. I have brought you some prasad." And he laughed and took the coconuts and I said: "May my goddess bless and protect you from all harm, good cobbler. I shall ask her for it every day of my life for you have done me a great favour."'

'Oho,' taunted Kanto, insidious. 'Why didn't you go wed him, then? He'd have put you in a black burqa and pyjamas and done you the same favour year after year and you could've peopled the village with your brats. Everyone knows how they breed.'

'I wish I could, I swear before all!' cried Uma fiercely. 'But Somesh would have cut my throat with the kitchen *bonti*, yes, beaten me to pulp with the iron pestle. I have many marks and bruises on my body and they aren't the marks of love, be sure. So I left him and returned until … until they finally threw me out some weeks later.' She closed her eyes and was silent. Then she opened them and they fell on Kanto's surly face and a passion of fury swept over her. 'Go, worm and to hell with you!' she screamed. 'Go, tell them all. Be my talebearer—that's all I ask of you. Tell them that the god maker's daughter has gone to find her son and her paramour and may all of you rot with my curses!' She gave him a little push. 'Go!' she hissed.

In the pandal a deathly conflict was in progress. Enraged Mahisha leapt upon the lion and rushed at her but Durga soared over him and pinned him down. Mahisha struggled to free himself. As half of him emerged from the mouth of the buffalo, Durga raised her sword.

That was the first and finest woman and only she could be of help against the wretches who took away her son, her trunk of sarees, her gold jewellery, her good name. Uma cast a shamefaced look at her faded saree, her bare arms. She looked around. Today was a day for Murshidabad silks, gold-ridged combs, Dhaka-crisp cottons, tinsel tasselled braids. It is the eighth day of the goddess's cycle and the third day of mine!

And when Manik Das, lifting the rice to his lips that night, queried: 'Ma, what ails you?'—she said nothing, just sat, head in her hands beside the extinguished hearth.

If, she thought, I take the Tentul-tola bus, I'll have to pay a rupee. If I take the boat ferry, boatman Dulal will recognize me and open his big mouth in the village. So Uma resolved to walk all the way. Carefully rolled in a bath-cloth, she carried her only presentable tussore silk and knotted up in a kerchief a tiny pair of earrings. Not as a pauper but as a conquering lady would she appear at her worthless husband's doorstep. Give me back my trunk of sarees, she would demand. Give me back the gold mango collar and the thick bangles I wore at my wedding. Give me back my little son for he is mine, not yours and the time has come for the truth to be told at last. Her rage was weapon enough to quell an army of demons. By the oath of Goddess Kali, this Oshtumi day was the last one in my life that I went to the puja pandal clad in rags.

With a blow of her sword she felled Mahishasura. Victory, victory unto you, goddess! Bearer of all the energies! From Shiva you received your mouth, from Yama the tresses on your head, from Vishnu your arms, from the moon your twin breasts, from Indra your *katibhag*, from Varuna your thighs and calves, from Brahma your feet, from the sun your toes. From Agni came your eyes, from Sandhya your brows. From Shiva you got your trident, from Vishnu the discus, from Vayu the giant bow, from Indra the thunderbolt, from Yama the celestial staff. The sun fed you with his flames. Mighty Kal gave you the sword and the shield, Himalaya your lion, the Ocean your garlands, your lotus and your gems. Victory unto you, Shakti, Upholder of Dharma, Mahavidya, Mahamedha, Mahamaya, Mahasmriti, Mahamoha, Mahadevi, Maheshwari . . . !

Today was her tenth day of conquest. No longer did Manik Das discern clenched rage in her painted face. Today there was soft regret, a speechless transfiguration of leave-taking. Her eyes shone limpid, unusually bright. Thus did a woman leave her father's hearth for her spouse's, reflected the old man, quite carried away. Today she must go. And Uma, after her mysterious absence, was back again.

Today the battle was over and won. But Uma stood alone, her lower lip cut and swollen, her hair disarrayed and her eyes smoking. What a victory there was, she addressed the goddess in the strangest of personal prayers. Your worshippers desert your tent for their own celebration. Only I, forbidden menstruating woman, dare enter and defile your tent with my impure body. But of course you do not bleed unholy blood and you do not shed human tears, Great Cosmic Woman!

Quickly she pulled the fringe of her saree over her cheek and bent her head lest the mark of shame become visible—Somesh Chandra's five flat fingers, still stinging upon her cheek.

And Waseem Khan, that man of honour, that icon, that god among men with the face of a lyrical sage and the words of the valiant defender sat busy in his shop when she came in.

'I have come to you again,' she said simply. 'Please help me.' He looked up at her and a shocked, suspicious alarm appeared in his face. 'Why have you come?' he asked.

He threw a hasty look towards the interior of the shop and spoke aloud: 'A pair of slippers for mending, sister?'

Ah, she thought, how very fitting. A dangerous sweetness stole into her voice.

'Why, no, dear cobbler. Don't you remember, I never, never wore slippers when I came to your house. They made too much noise in the night so I left them behind.'

The panic in his expression changed to desperate sternness. 'Be quiet,' he rasped and resumed in his normal voice: 'A pair of shoes for your little one, sister?'

But Uma was not to be outwitted by a mere man today. 'Our little one, you mean?' she asked loudly. She sat down cross-legged upon the floor and put her bundle beside her. 'And how is he now, cobbler? Surely you see him in the village often? I am going to bring him here soon, this very day, in fact . . .'

Alas for Waseem Khan, that lion among men. His terror before his holy Islamic wife, his shame before his four legitimate brats, was a sight to remember if only it were not so demeaning. 'This is an insane woman, begum,' he pleaded. 'Believe me, O Farida Khanum, truth and falsehood are one to her; can this creature be the landowner Somesh Chandra's wife, tell me? And what would I, a cobbler, be doing with a pious Hindu woman?' And more to the same effect . . .

'Who is this funny woman, Mother?' asked a little boy of a young lady outside Somesh Chandra's homestead.

'Hush, the woods here have a rakshasi, a demoness who comes to take away children,' answered the lady.

Manik Das had never missed a single immersion. He tramped the seven miles to the river's edge, ahead of the crowd and the bullock carts, and waited by the promontory above the mango orchards. His emotions were mixed. An immersion put an end to what was begun and wrought with love, a death rite against the

setting sun with the river as witness. What a din and
clamour, blowing of conchs, shouting and beating of drums.
Dancing, clapping, burning incense, they carried her and her
attendant gods far downstream before they let her go and the
boats returned.

Above the Tentul-tola bridge, Uma spoke incoherent words into
the air. 'See what they do. They're careful to remove all your silks
and your gold and your weapons, your sword and your lance and
everything else, before they cast you away. Another goddess shall
get them, come next year, a younger goddess. Stretch out your ten
naked arms to the sky, Goddess Durga, before the dark waters
receive you, for such is the forgetfulness of man . . .' There was
much else she uttered. A crazy woman often makes speeches to the
gods or to the empty air.

And Durga's billowing tresses spread out on the water. On the
Tentul-tola bridge, a passing carter thought he heard a splash.

THE OLD FOLKS AT HOME

You will say I talk too often of old age. How can I help it? Twenty years of my life I lived among old people, old parents, old aunts, old uncles, old family friends, a solitary, moody child. I lived old age as many times over with as many variations as there were aunts and uncles, elderly cousins, old servants. All old, all waiting.

My old uncle Debashish was our writer, a peppery old man who periodically went misty-eyed and talked at great length about the current play or the current poem (short stories he frowned upon). A pigeon sailed in to settle on the sooty blades of the ceiling fan and Debashish mama spotted a symbol. A platter grew musty with age and Debashish mama made a speech. A tree toppled down in the yard and Debashish mama cited scripture.

Debashish mama took me to task often. 'Now,' he said, firmly bandaging my grubby paw. 'Let us look at the recent events. You lit four crackers and they all turned out to be damp squibs. Nay, you said, I shall persist. You lit a fifth and lo! it exploded in your hand.' (Debashish mama's diction, nurtured on a staple diet of Ruskin and Carlyle, was inclined to turn a trifle flowery.) 'It is a symbol, boy. Miss not its significance.'

'What is a symbol, uncle?' Debashish mama scratched his head and looked chagrined.

'A symbol is something which means something else,' he replied helplessly. He quailed beneath my frank stare.

'Yesterday you said the bird was a symbol and the flour dish was a symbol.'

'True,' Debashish mama did not seem to be too comfortable with his literary conscience.

'What something else do they all mean?'

84

'Leave me, boy,' said Debashish mama wearily. 'You're enough to corrupt all the elders of Athens!'

Debashish-mama wrote a little, published nothing. After his retirement he dug out stacks of dusty files and tumbled them on the old ornamented four-poster bed to the great dismay of my Aunt Basanti. Now that the fifty-eighth birth anniversary had come and gone and the farewell gift clock adorned the wall beside the well loved framed Kali, now that he had rendered unto Caesar the things that were Caesar's, now Debashish mama set himself to the task of rendering unto the Muse the things that were hers. The Muse was decidedly stirring. 'You will kindly put a cup of tea outside my door every hour, Basanti,' he said crisply. 'And keep that infernal boy out.'

It was to be a *magnum opus*, a monumental work. Debashish mama had a lifetime's notes in readiness.

'Well, Rabindranath,' chafed my mother when Debashish mama sat himself down cross-legged in the kitchen before the platter of rice and bowl of fish. 'And has the zamindar whipped the hero and kidnapped the wife yet?'

'Twenty-five cups of tea should have inspired him to greater flights of crime, Mira di,' quipped Aunt Basanti.

'Debashish has turned to crime, no? Rabindranath, *chi chi chi*. What of your heritage, what of your obligations to society, what of our moral values?' said my father mildly. Debashish mama was the youngest among the men, a stripling of fifty-eight, and, therefore, exposed to a lot of chaff.

Debashish mama ignored the banter. 'Dada,' he said reflectively between mouthfuls of rice. 'At twenty-five I outlined a theme. I won't go into details. I went through the files today. What do you expect of a lad of twenty-five? There was nationalism, you know, those days. There was romanticism. There was lyricism. Complex, subtle, never-resolved relationships, fine distinctions, unchallengeable finalities, overdoses of sensibility, intense abstractions. In a word, nonsense,' he said, with sweeping modesty. He swallowed, raised another handful of fish curry and rice to his lips and thought deeply.

'At thirty-five I found cleaner lines but honest confusions. Also, a certain crudeness. But, inevitably, more nonsense.'

Father nodded, the old great aunts nodded.

'At fifty I made a startling discovery. That I had not changed at all. Just a shift of idiom, a different angle of the same theme, a slight check on the same emotions. The same nonsense.' He paused for effect.

'I wrote today and I may tell you, Dada, I wrote very well. But there is this nagging suspicion: am I still writing the same sort of modified nonsense? Old age has its share of follies . . .'

Our Big Kakima, our ancient great-aunt, chortled. To hear that young Debashish call himself old! Let him, she seemed to feel, let him if it pleased him.

Debashish-mama stopped writing after a fortnight's labour. 'All aesthetics are relative, Dada.' My father nodded. He made a principle of nodding when Debashish mama spoke. 'All literary maturity is relative,' continued Debashish mama. 'What I haven't learnt is literary conviction. What I haven't learnt is literary finality. I'm not blind enough.' My father nodded.

Debashish mama went around again, sermonizing, spotting symbols, nursing a beautiful, flowing beard. Long afterwards, when he was past seventy-five, it is said that he took up his pen again. He was ailing then but he claimed to have won some final insight. He was forbidden to exert himself but he wouldn't listen. He wrote and wrote and without the cups of tea. It was a race against time. And he never made it. He had a couple of strokes and that was that. Nobody discovered what he was writing about, for all the chapters grew garbled and obscure and petered into references and notes, more notes.

I have never understood by what destiny Debashish mama was forever denied utterance.

A large photograph of him in a graduation gown and bearing the scrolled degree hangs, garlanded, in the east veranda. 'This was our uncle, Debashish Chattopadyaya.' We have fallen into the habit of saying. 'He was a writer.' If anybody ventures to ask what he wrote we still look baffled. Does it matter what he wrote or did not write? So many books stand, gathering dust upon the shelves.

My parents too were old, quite old. I was the product of a late marriage and to all intents and purposes a happy one, save for a certain streak of competition in my mother's nature. All her life Mother competed with Father. She may not have been conscious of it but it was there for all to see. 'If you claim to work hard, I work much harder. If you are tired, I'm worse.' She even competed in sickness. If Father complained of an attack of his colitis, Mother promptly spoke of her angina. 'Woman, don't harass me with petty problems at my age when my days are numbered!' exploded Father. Mother bristled. 'Mine are numbered too,' she said defiantly. Father groaned, 'I shall go before you.' 'Wait and see,' said Mother menacingly. 'We'll see,' he said grimly. 'We'll see who goes first, you or I.' 'You'll be the one to see, not I!' she fumed. Suddenly her mood changed. 'Let me not live to see it!' she shouted, her eyes bright with angry tears.

Both lived to be eighty.

My Aunt Suparna was yet another intriguing being. At sixty she loved writing letters to God, her formless Brahmo Samaj God. The habit had begun at the age of ten and had lasted fifty years. Her letters to God were a standing joke. Those who claimed to have taken a peep into the blue-bound diary said they were full of strange complaints, childlike, innocent, scarcely different from the ones written in childhood. Her husband, my uncle Manik, was twenty years her senior and could scarcely walk. He had to be helped to rise and to eat and to go to the bathhouse. Then she sat him down carefully on the mat before the prayer niche and for more than an hour he arranged the little gold eyed gods, dusted the holy books, polished the bronze offering dish, the oil lamp, the little worship bell. But he never prayed. All he did, morning and evening, was dust and arrange the prayer niche with thin, trembling hands. She scoffed at his dry, doctrinaire faith.

Strangely in their relationship there was a coyness, a freshness of love and anger and wooing. They quarrelled. He got annoyed. She made up to him seductively. Perhaps it was because she was his second wife and younger to him by twenty years.

'Ish!' she exclaimed sadly to Aunt Basanti at the water tap. 'Would you believe it but "he" says he dreamt of a woman, alas.'

Aunt Basanti, prim and proper, laughed uneasily. 'How slowly the bucket fills,' she said.

'And what is worse, Basanti di, the woman wasn't I. It was a nameless young woman in a century old costume. It made me sad that it wasn't I. I told him I was surprised. He said he was surprised too.'

'The bucket is overflowing, Suparna,' said Aunt Basanti severely.

Aunt Protima at forty thought herself very old indeed. She returned from her school (she was a teacher), shrill and querulous, and sat down to her embroidery. She was working on a large ornate bedspread, large as a carpet, bridal rich, with a hunting scene. She had designed it all herself—fawns, trees, slip of water, dashes of green grass. She did not seem to have any regrets, this lady of Shalott. If anybody complimented her or spoke of a marriage proposal, Aunt Protima grew extremely angry. She liked to play at being old, just as I liked to parade about in my father's shoes.

Only about half the bedcover was done. The rest lay empty, white. 'In another thirty years I'll have filled all that up,' she said happily threading the needle.

They doted on me, the single child in the household. Astounding powers of intellect and imagination were ascribed to me. Lozenges, toys, woolies, they lavished all possible gifts on me. A bright future was assured for me. A leading place in the world of arts and letters. No, a place in the ICS itself! I did not grow up to be great in any way. With difficulty I landed myself a petty clerical job in a jute firm. My wife too was very ordinary like me. What was amazing was that none of the old people were disappointed with me. Their delight in me continued. So did their gifts. A misshapen jersey knitted by Aunt Basanti's stiff fingers, or a pre-war blouse, all brocade and lace, part of somebody's trousseau, for my wife.

I manage a trip to the old homestead every other year or so. Aunt Protima no longer embroiders. I've never dared to ask her about the fate of the massive bedspread. She hates being old, is seldom well and is full of complaints. She sends me a jar of pickle once in a while. She looks after the property and lives alone in her corner room. The rest of the rooms are empty.

A DIAGNOSIS OF DESTINY

And talking of homoeopaths brings me to the most unusual case in my career as a homoeopath. A strange man he was. You say you knew him slightly? Well, listen to this:

He came to my clinic on Morrison Road in the August of 1982. That day I had few patients so I kept each one in for an entire half hour, talking. For apart from my practice and my hobby of writing passionate letters to the editor championing the cause of homoeopathy, I delight in the role of family counsellor and moral scourge to the erring, the unmarried, the unemployed and the insolent.

He entered my cabin, a not-too-tall but undeniably impressive man, a man of pleasant aspect, good education and evidently of ample means for he was quiet and dapper and neat as a new pin.

'Alarming things have happened to me in the last three months, Doctor Babu,' he began and his voice was shrill and troubled. 'Friends directed me to you. I don't know how to explain my case but I have begun to fear for my life!'

Ah, thought I, recognizing a familiar type.

'Well, my good man,' I beamed, 'and what do you claim to be dying of?'

'Will you be amused if I tell you that I'm dying of . . . of destiny?'

This tickled me so much that I made a note of it.

'We all are, we all are,' I agreed generously. 'But I regret that I have no antidotes against destiny, my friend. Now just when did you begin dying?'

I took up my pen and got down to business.

'Symptoms?' I confess that I derived a quixotic pleasure in these types. One felt so blessedly sane, so securely real in contrast.

He shook his head nervously and with a supreme effort of will, began. His mind had turned feeble, dull, incredibly forgetful. Its reliability no longer convinced him. The shine and suppleness were gone. Everything was strange, a nightmare. Irresoluteness marked his character. He was low spirited, disheartened. He feared he was pursued. He feared everything and everybody. He was full of anxiety. There was no peace. He was separated from the whole world and in despair. Unsocial. Feared some dreadful thing would happen . . .

Here I interrupted with a routine query customary in such cases. 'Are any of these complaints reduced by eating?'

He looked stung. 'There was no relation whatever,' he replied curtly.

Did his skin burn? Had there ever been any kind of eruption, I pursued.

He sat up abruptly. 'Let me tell you, Doctor Babu, that in the last three months I have consulted three renowned allopaths and one eminent psychiatrist. I have no use for analysts of my first five years or for nerve-soothing treatments. I seek real solutions, not palliatives. It is said that homoeopathy treats the individual rather than the disease and I am given to believe that you are a homoeopath who is free of medical dogma and allopathic superstition, hence this visit.'

He stopped and scowled at me. 'My case cannot be separated from its strange antecedent circumstances.'

'Please go on,' said I, getting a word in edgeways.

'I worked as a music critic with the *Forum*,' commenced he. 'Until a year ago I hadn't a care in the world. I earned well, both in money and in reputation. I was happily married, promising, living well and fully, and well content with my lot. I remember the exact moment when my troubles began. It was at a party hosted by *Forum* for some delegates from the *New York Times*. Somebody congratulated me for my insightful interpretation of a composition by a German maestro. I smiled and made the expected graceful, self-effacing reply: "My insights I owe to the oversights of better men." There was a ripple of appreciative laughter, then someone uttered a loud exclamation: "I've heard Mrinal Dutt say that once."

'I was annoyed for my *bon mots* are my prized, original surprises, hand-picked from the random introspections of many years and carefully crafted to suit every cultural occasion.

'Who is Mrinal Dutt?' I asked, piqued. But the gentlemen had by now moved away.

'It happened again. "The secret of public appeal is a certain commonplace imaginative accessibility but shot through with a certain distinction." I intoned sententiously for the benefit of the young lady journalist at a musical evening.

'"Yes, sir," said the young lad accompanying her. "Mr Dutt once told me the very same thing in the very same words."

'"Who?" asked I, incredulous.

'"Mrinal Dutt, our Associate Professor at the Institute," he explained.

'"Oh," said I shortly, conscious of a strange unease.

'When it happened yet again I was utterly nonplussed. "Truth can never be a discovery for the world. It is always a rediscovery, or more aptly, a recovery." I pronounced with a flourish at the Annual Music Conference.

'"Why, that reminds me of Mrinal!" exclaimed the elderly lady usher. She turned to her companion. "For that matter, he resembles Mrinal too, doesn't he? See his profile, his physique, his style of intoning words."

'I was at the end of my tether. "Who is Mrinal Dutt? Where does he hide himself?" cried I.

'"Don't you know him? But you must meet him. You simply must," said the old lady. "When I first set eyes on you, I took you for a brother of Mrinal's."

'"I haven't the foggiest who he is."

'"Well, I must bring the two of you together in that case. Why don't you both drop in for a meal and some music at my place? Wait. I shall scribble an invitation to Mrinal and you can carry it to him yourself on my behalf."

'I was sceptical and, I confess, a little apprehensive. "Where was I supposed to take the invitation," I queried.

'"The first lane to the right just off Patel Avenue," she said.'

'At the fourth ring the door opened slightly and a head peered cautiously out.

'"Thank God!" it uttered an explosive exclamation. "Thank God you aren't one of my friends!"

'I was staggered by this uncivil opening.

' "At any rate, not so far," said I, covering my pique with a grand show of merriment.

' "Then you're welcome," said this changeable man. "It's my friends who aren't. God protect me from my friends; I shall take care of my enemies myself." He emerged into the light, loudly quoting Voltaire and ushered me in. And what amazed me was that that quote, too, was one of my favourite utterances.

'No, Doctor-Babu, this is not a melodrama of long-lost brothers. We were not related. We were absolute strangers to one another. Yet those who discerned a stunning resemblance between us had a point. I was myself taken aback. He was a little taller than I, perhaps. His face was thinner, more tired, and he was grey at the temples where I was still black. But it was like getting a glimpse of myself as I would be some years later in time.

'And as I stepped into his room I had a strange sense of returning, of the familiar, a feeling of belonging naturally to the space. It had the same musty light, the same dull, indefinable aroma as my own room possessed. I felt as though every article of furniture, every stray book and scattered paper, every ashtray and picture recognized me immediately and unmistakably.

'I produced the invitation I had brought along. That was how we got acquainted. Like me, he proved to be an institution of satire and mimicry and predictably proceeded to ridicule the silly old lady who had invited us, garnishing his observations with the most literary of darts and the most comic of caricatures. He had her speech, her eager air, her manner of earnestly seeking the listener's approval on every point down to perfection. He had a quiet, innocuous innocence of expression when the most vicious barbs were forming in his conversation. And when he spoke of women, be they old or young, every statement was a marvel of multiple *entendre* and pitying mockery. He could gaze speculatively into the distance, uttering philosophic insights of rare originality and suddenly surprise the audience with a glaringly erotic metaphor. He could be crude and so very cultured, effortlessly throwing himself from Queen's English into polished French, to literary Bengali or Urdu and just as suddenly into native four-letter words expressing the same general ideas. I held my sides and laughed, we were so much attuned, our humour of a piece, our understanding equal.

'We met frequently after that occasion. In every word he spoke, every astonishing phrase or theory, I met myself. Even our voices were almost identical. My mannerisms, my habits, my way of holding a book or a cigarette, turning the pages of a paper, crossing my legs were the same as his. I was fascinated by him. And as time passed I conceived a violent dislike for him as well. He was diabolically clever and original but he could be a humbug and a bore. He had horrible intellectual affectations. At all times, though, he thought himself painfully sincere. I realized with horror how I must appear to other people, a shoddy patchwork of intrinsic qualities and shabby pretences, pleasant but more often contemptible. And yet to meet him again was such a relief. I found myself sinking restfully into the field, as it were, of my own self, into my own idiom of expression and experience, without any discomfort or conflict or need of explanation. Knowing Mrinal Dutt I entered into a new relationship with myself.

'And by this time we had become what is commonly termed very close friends. For Dutt too was amazed at the uncanny similarity between us. Many evenings were spent speculating over this singular identity of natures and circumstances. Dutt spoke of the curious case of Manet who was accused of imitating the pictures of Goya even though he had not set eyes on them. He read out to me with great excitement a passage out of Baudelaire's letters in which Baudelaire impetuously asked: "You don't believe what I'm telling you? You're sceptical about the possibilities of such mathematical parallelism in nature? Well, don't they accuse me of imitating Edgar Allan Poe? And do you know why, with such infinite patience I translated Poe? It was because he was like me! The first time I ever opened a book by him I discovered, with rapture and awe, not only subjects which I had dreamt, but whole phrases which I'd conceived written by him twenty years before. I found, believe it or not, poems and stories which I'd already conceived but only in a vague and formless manner, which Poe had planned and brought to perfection." For my part I excitedly discovered the extraordinary case of Darwin and the botanist Russel, both of whom hit upon the same theories at almost the same time and independent of one another! Dutt and I enjoyed making a philosophic or scientific enquiry into our own singular case. As an enlargement of our own phenomenon we felt wondering whether in every century there were beings exactly like us, who thought our thoughts, who dreamt our dreams, who bore our faces and who knew our sadnesses. And the natural question arose for us. How far could these several persons, if such there were, be construed actually several and not, as we daringly deduced, one and the same person in a field beyond historic time!

'And not only were our personalities and thoughts and words similar but our lives too had followed the same pattern. He told me that he'd been educated at Sherwood College, Nainital, and that he had two older sisters and had lost his father early in his teenage years.

'"Remarkable!" I exclaimed. "I had my schooling at St Augustine's, Kalimpong. And I have two older sisters. And I lost my father when I was fourteen."

'He told me of his interest in mountaineering and of that fall in 1966 when he had broken a shin and been laid up for six months. That was strange, I said; and I proceeded to tell him of my interest in mountaineering and of that toss I had way back in 1970 and of my smashed ankle.

'"Well, well!" he chuckled. "This lends a further dimension to the case history. Let's go into this systematically. Did you get ploughed in mathematics in your high school examination?"

'"I did," I laughed.

'"Did you aspire to be a military dictator?"

'"I aspired to be a top notch vocalist but became a second rate music critic instead."

'"Come, come, that's enough of self-deprecation and it doesn't deceive me. And did you ever lose a fortune at cards like I did in 1974."

'"I did lose a tidy sum at the casino at Kathmandu but that was in 1978. But you're four years older so we were both the same age at the time of the event."

'"And," said he, "did you marry outside your religion?"

'I was dumbfounded. "I did. Rashmi is a Catholic." And added in a rush: "But I always believed you to be a widower."

' "Which in a sense I am," he said slowly,"—considering the fact that as far as I am concerned she is dead for me." There was fury in his voice, the pent up, smouldering anger of the wronged husband which the years had never muted. "She left me four years back for an Air Force man. We had no children."

'And neither did I!—I realized with a pang of alarm.

'"I'm sorry," was all that I could trust myself to say in that complicated moment.

'Did he take the denied man's pleasure in upsetting me. He spoke deliberately: "She was steadily unfaithful to me from the day we were married and I never knew for years."

'From that day on, my own married life was on the rocks. I took to badgering my wife with suspicious enquiries each time she returned late from the company where she works as a Public Relations Officer. I took to telephoning her at odd hours to make sure of her activities. I subjected her women colleagues to searching interrogations. I tormented her with burning accusations each time she was seen with a delegate at a hotel or the airport. She was bewildered and angry. "What's the matter with you?" she tearfully demanded. "It's my job and I have been doing it for years." "Exactly," said I ironically. "I want you to know that I am aware of what you have been doing for years." Matters came to a climax when one day she nervously told me that she was pregnant.

'My rage was fearful to behold! I shouted, I sprang on her and demanded the name of the father, since precedent had already established in my mind that I was to remain childless and the example of another's life had unshakeably decided my own. My mind was possessed by a demon. I threw her out, the slut, Doctor-Babu. What man wouldn't in my place? Only one thought made me uncomfortable. I did not know if Mrinal Dutt's ex-wife ever had a child with her Air Force lover. I asked him. He said he did not know and did not care. Was that reason enough to call my wife back, her guilt disproved. I resolved that it was and I went to her parents' house to fetch her back with apologies and entreaties. But my wife is a proud and independent woman. She refused to return. So there I was a divorcee or soon to be one. Fate had taken a little liberty with the design, introduced a small variation in the theme but the style ended up the same.

'Do you understand, Doctor-Babu? This is not a case for symptomatic analysis. Consider the correspondence between Dutt's life and my own. Consider your patient and his situation. Mrinal Dutt's life and mine were following duplicate destinies—or almost duplicate ones. And we weren't even born under the same stars. It was at this point that I became afraid. I had already wrecked my marriage through my obsession with this situation. I now unaccountably began fearing for my life. That was because Mrinal Dutt was suddenly preoccupied with thoughts of death. And inescapably his thoughts had a way of infecting mine. What was this evil fascination? Does destiny have a few recurring motifs, a few recurring designs by which human fates are fashioned? There are lookalikes in physical form and I was sure there were lookalikes in fate as well. I continually asked myself the tormenting question: do we mould our fates to fit our selves or does some determinism of the genes, not only parental, but you may say, Platonic and archetypal, ordain the motif of our personalities? And was this philosophy or madness? Fatalism or folly?

'I am keeping you long, Doctor Babu. I see that there is another patient now in the ante-room. I shall wind up my story. At about this time Dutt and I were both extremely depressed. Dutt did occasionally display manic-depressive tendencies. There were losses and failures he spoke of vaguely, disenchantments, old griefs, a belated hatred of all, a noxious self loathing.

'Then on the morning of 7 May this year somebody telephoned at the *Forum* offices and informed me that Dutt had died the previous night under suspicious circumstances! The two sisters had been wired. The body had lain for nine hours undiscovered, and was in a bad state. The police declared a case of suicide, but other causes could not entirely be ruled out ...

That case is still pending. And what of me, Doctor-Babu? I am like a madman now. I am divided against myself into victim and killer. When I awake every morning it takes me some time to recognize and place myself. Then a diffused sensation of doom overtakes me, becomes palpable in my consciousness. And the far flung items of my being draw unwillingly together, summoned by some blind dictate into unity. Suddenly I spot myself, solitary, shaken, confronting another terrifying day. I wish it were possible to reverse time, to run headlong back into the refuge of the previous night, refusing to concede my being. I am continually defending myself against everybody, especially myself. I am constantly examining my will to live for any sign of possible dissent ...'

As his doctor I can furnish the end. I gave him my patent *Anacardium Orientale* and it must have had its effect for the man never came again. It is one of the greatest triumphs that homoeopathy has every demonstrated. I unhesitatingly wrote yet another letter-to-the-editor, citing the case as one of chronic paranoia that undoubtedly responded to treatment. It is quite possible that my patient responded to the month's course I gave him and is now a stable, well adjusted and happy man, that his wife has returned and his life is salvaged from certain ruin. Yes, that's a valid point you have raised—I was coming to that myself. As you say, its also possible that he has carried paranoia to its logical, or rather its illogical conclusion. But, my dear sir, the possible is often not the probable, nor the proven. You have reasons to believe that my patient killed himself, distractedly seizing the choice that destiny willed for him from the example of his demented friend? Rubbish. This is not a Russian novel, sir. He died in an accident, collided with a speeding truck in sheer distraction? You have the wife's version of it at fourth hand? Frankly, if you don't mind, I find it hard to believe that you have the facts straight. And in this case words like destiny lie outside the scope of scientific concession, and I am a man of science. Did I make enquiries at the *Forum* office? My good man, I have too many patients and time is scare; and why ever should I wish to be publicly connected with a case which may well be of an unsavoury nature? No, I merely content myself with narrating this sinister case to a stray patient or two whenever my clinic is a little less crowded.

HONOURABLE MENTION

Do you see that man there, hunched upon that microscope? His name is Abhijit Das.

You have heard of success stories. I shall tell you a failure story. That is my teacher and my friend. He taught me all I know. Of course, I superseded him. I do not know whether what I feel for him amounts to detestation or devotion but I can't get him out of my system.

There isn't a bus he hasn't missed, an opportunity he hasn't lost or a promotion he hasn't been denied. And, what enrages me most is his endless justification, his declaration that every failure was of invaluable profit to him. I have never known a man who so emphatically defended loss. 'This supersession is, in the ultimate analysis, very good for me, Ramendram, it will stop me exerting myself so much and I shall have time for my photography. This setback is just what I needed, Ramendram, it has prevented my blood pressure from shooting up—success can be so tyrannical, so demanding, you know. This rejection is a blessing in disguise; who knows, maybe it has saved me from becoming a crashing bore. I can see my own limitations better and hope for excellence next time. This lost promotion is, in the ultimate sense, a great asset—at last I have come to terms with injustice, a formative growth, you'll agree. And, most absurd of all—this heart attack has actually proved so good for me, Ramendram, it's shown me the worth of life in its broadest perspective, revealed to me the time wasted, given a new focus to my vision, Ramendram.' 'In the ultimate analysis', 'the broadest perspective', 'when all things are taken into consideration': those were Abhijit Das's favourite phrases. Everything was *sub species aeternitatis*, we mocked. I never saw such an organized and resourceful philosophy of escape.

I was his junior research assistant for seven years and I am now his senior, I, Ramendram of the swarthy face and the lantern jaw, penniless rationalist from Madras, who admired Abhijit Das passionately, baited him with a ferocious joy that was keenly akin to scorn, young, ironical, hostilely defensive about my ardent disbeliefs. I was by his side when Abhijit Das, fifty, class two and desperately unfulfilled, threw in his last stake. Those were the most meaningful years of my life. I remember that day of discovery, the only scientific miracle I was ever privileged to share. Wet Calcutta, August 1978, it was.

He must have missed at least half a dozen buses and stood shivering in the rain at the bus terminus that morning. I can see him even today, soaked wisps of grey hair, a battered briefcase under his arm, myopic eyes straining searchingly through damp spectacles and the fine spun rain to discern the numbers on the buses. Do you know Calcutta in the monsoon? The streets are roaring ravines; the buses squelch past, crazily tilted, cruising round the corners, gorged with clammy humanity, men sealed tight in steamy interiors, clinging to window bars, balanced upon mudguards, spilling out of the doors. Flogged and spiritless, the chilled palms dangle ragged fronds, drip slow, slimy drops. A sky choked and tense with rain. Umbrellas an oily black retinue toiling up the avenues. Drenched trams rattle past, jammed with men, reeking, humid flesh and shivering skins, one arm clutching the bar, galley slaves chained to the oars upon a wearisome voyage. Waiting for the bus, Abhijit Das could so easily be elbowed aside by the first flashing-teethed, mahogany-faced youth. 'Sorry, Dada!' The lad would have waved a mirthful hand as the bus growled off. Did he smart at the effrontery of the young or lapse into the thousand natural self-pities that late middle-age is heir to? I honestly do not know. Somebody gave him a lift, I guess, some acquaintance from better days. I can just see Abhijit Das sink timorously back upon the cushioned seat in relief, saying: 'How lucky to miss that bus, after all! I can now reach the institute much earlier in your car.'

I have no patience with negative philosophies. But here was a man who doggedly translated every negative experience into positive deductions and congratulated himself constantly. I thought Abhijit Das did protest too much and I told him so.

And what an exasperating fool he could be sometimes. Absolute strangers were detained and compelled to listen to his eager babbles. I can visualize him in the car, wagging his large head, eyes shining, gesticulating in passionate self absorption, talking, talking, while his unfortunate benefactor with an expressionless face, steered through the raging traffic.

'Do you realize what that implies? Can you guess at the tremendous possibilities? It can only point at some sort of botanical individuality, even within plants of the same species. Not determinism but botanical decision. Individuality with all its attendant implications. We have experimented on FS with as many as 150 different species. A hibiscus, for instance, has been proved to register higher FS than, say, a carnation. One may suspect that some connection exists between higher pollen productivity and higher FS but we have no conclusive evidence yet. Nature is not singleminded, I frequently reflect. Everything does not revolve round fertilization. There is room for the lawless, the erratic. You have heard of Heisenberg's "uncertainty principle" perhaps in the domain of physics? Ah, no, I recollect that you were not a science student in the old days. Well, to return to the subject in hand, we have stumbled upon an unfamiliar dimension, sir. The electrograph has some very interesting data to offer. Exciting, to say the least . . .'

And his audience so frequently responded with a polite, well intentioned query like: 'What is your basic salary at the institute?' or 'What upward mobility can you expect in your particular line?'

And Abhijit Das's voice would suddenly die away.

On his pedestal the Marquis of Hastings sat drenched aloft his prancing stallion, one hand strained upon the reins, the other shading carved, empty eyes which sought something indiscernible behind the troubled rain.

What a despicable babbling old romantic!

The Institute of Botanical Studies loomed vast, Georgian beige, large ornamental gateway with brass eagles and victorious crossed bugles, the triumph of science over superstition. The paved drive was washed clean by the shower and the hedges so sharply green that they shocked the eye. Round the corner went he, past the old moss-blackened fountain, into the porch and up the stairs. The lab was on the second floor on the southern face. He opened the white door and stepped silently in. That morning the windows were shuttered against the slanting shower and the eucalyptus turned and tore forlornly against the shut panes. We had all the lights on.

'You're early today, sir.'

'Yes, I got a lift. Do I see you entering yesterday's readings?'

'It's that *Discus Allegoria* we did yesterday.'

'Let's hear it again.'

'30 and 16. PLT 12 in the first round. 45, and this is amazing, sir, actually an FS as low as 4. Then a fairly stable return graph. Last month when we were doing those projections the same thing happened. The electrograph kept swaying round to the most absurd counts and all my calculations were upset.'

'Can petals wince under sound frequencies, sir?'

He would take that sort of dubious sally with such grotesque gravity.

'You wretched pundit, you botanical buffoon!' I took such liberties with him, so long as I did it in Queen's English. I object to all these poetic vapourings! Wake up, you shabby slob! What are you trying to construct? A philosophy of Botany, here in a third-rate government institute, here in our jaded lab?

A quarter of this I spoke aloud, sirring him between breaths; three quarters my voice implied. He only laughed meekly.

'Ramendram, spare me your onslaughts. Mridula, we shall have to go over those reactions again.'

And yes, there was that girl whom Abhijit Das endlessly watched with strange, mellow eyes, to our secret merriment. An ugly girl, some would have said, with her still, abstracted eyes behind thick school marmish glasses and her hair gathered into a severe braid. She could not have been more than twenty-seven or thereabouts but she always dressed in those stiff whites and greys and browns, a woman one could never picture in scandalous pink or an explosion of orange. I guess that was a gesture of defiance or despair. An unattractive girl who had pledged to leave beauty alone. And I guess Abhijit Das, doddering old knight errant, fancied failure above mere beauty. But her hands as she wrote were startlingly exquisite, calm and impersonal and complete. She was Abhijit Das's Girl Friday at the Institute. She was also our Ashok Mohapatro's fiancée.

Abhijit Das never drank so that a single beer had him dithering. Oh, help, now the confessions come pouring out in true Augustinian self laceration, with me for Father Confessor! Who wants to listen to your sordid fantasies, you slime?

'Sometimes, Ramendram, I wish I was born twenty years later.'

'You mean, circa the year two thousand?'

'No, no,'—he wagged his head vaguely. 'I mean twenty years after I was born. I have missed a woman by about twenty years.' Mercifully for her, thought I. No names but I grasped all.

But A. Das had more to reveal: 'When I was fifteen, Ramendram, I desperately wished I was about thirty. Maya was about twenty-five then, a cousin, and I was a callow school-going lout. Strange, isn't it?'

'Very. And your wife? Have you aired these hopes in her presence?'

'Hopes?'

'Twenty years younger or twenty years older . . . ?'

He sighed. 'I wish I had. Anyway, I wasn't the one she was supposed to marry. She was engaged to my elder brother. And what were the recordings on those *seboria eltonias*?' From mawkishly personal, he could turn briskly professional.

'When I switched on the Gama screen the graph appeared very uneven. Sylvan high sap pressure.' I essayed to laugh.

'And by the way, Surendranath plans to attend that Seattle conference in February. He told me to get on with my FS paper. He intends to read it at the conference. Oh, I knew you'd rear like a cobra, Ramendram.'

'Like hell he will! I shall find myself sabotaging all our apparatus if that old skunk is planning to steal the show.'

A. Das held up a warning hand. *'Noblesse oblige.* After all he is Director. So we stay in a couple of hours extra and work, full speed ahead. In any case you're leaving in October.'

'I'm not.' Scowled I. 'I flunked the exam.'

'What a pity.'

'Missed by three marks.'

Something in my dead pan voice made Abhijit Das melancholy. 'I must now be infecting all those who come in touch with me,' ruminated he. 'There's a pattern in these things. I don't know if I pursue the pattern or the pattern pursues me but I have come to recognize the symptoms all right.'

The last thing I wanted was philosophic consolation. But A. Das grew reminiscent. 'Three attempts at the Pre-medical Test, all missed by a hair's breadth. For eight years I missed everything I tried my hand at by the narrowest margin possible. Earlier in school, sometimes the Headmaster's son had to be given a promotion in my stead or a bout of flu on the day of the exam. A careless examiner or an irritable interviewer or a theory unknown to the expert himself. The proudest and saddest moment of my life was when I bagged the second position by a single mark, mind you, in my B.Sc. . .'

I listened patiently, my thoughts busy elsewhere. There was nothing I wouldn't do for this empty old anti-hero, even kick him up the ladder if I could. Overtime we would work, we fifteen research assistants, and that paper would not go to the Seattle conference first, I suddenly resolved.

She was a bird of passage in his uneventful life or some such horrendous piece of shabby poetry. Ashok Mohapatro was our brilliant engineer.

'You're very painstaking, Mridula.' The silence was getting oppressive. In my own corner of the lab I bent over my ledger, my face expressionless.

'Ashok is leaving for Connecticut in November, isn't he?'

'Yes,' said she tonelessly.

A. Das, I saw out of the corner of my eye, concentrated tensely upon the page before him.

'I do hope the project is complete by then. We don't want to lose both you and Ashok before that. Where would the team be without you?'

'If the unit needs me, sir, I can't think of leaving.'

When Abhijit Das spoke it was in a hearty rush. A bogus paternalism, a phoney note of disinterested patronage, sounded false and unconvincing, in his reedy voice.

'Come, come. Cut out all that dedication stuff. When was it decided?'

Her voice was low. 'Very recently,' said she evasively.

'Listen,' spoke he and there was now nothing phoney in his headlong appeal. 'Don't be indecisive about important things. Learn to arrange your priorities wisely. Don't keep things waiting. I know our work here matters to you but I don't want you to go the way of Ramendram or Bhupen or, for that matter, myself . . .'

Oh, I could have thumped him on the back, this Hamlet turned Polonius, for his crisp delivery, his precise prescriptions. His performance couldn't have taken in a child, let alone an intuitive woman. And, when he tried to be jocular he was positively outrageous. 'I give you these flowers of middle-aged wisdom, etcetera, etcetera, etcetera.' 'Congratulations, A. Das!'—was what I was tempted to shout across. 'What a succinct, clear-sighted philosophy you have just enunciated!' Flowers of middle-aged wisdom!—I almost choked. 'Go,' said he to her. 'Or you'll miss your bus tonight.' And she left.

September and our endrometer whirred incessantly. The tapes raced, wheels turned, the dial turned green, the magnetic needle slid on and off the rotating drum. The silence in the lab was intense. On the table Bhupen spread out the graph sheets while Mridula worked upon the slides and I recorded the shock-pulses for the month-old *Arboria rexus.*

'What I fail to understand,' mused A. Das,'—is why the counts are so unbalanced between the synclinal swings and the anticlinal stops . . . '

Change the plates. With a dim rear the E.G. started again, clicking rhythmically. The lights in the lab switched off, the dial turned a slow, burning green.

'Stop!' cried A. Das. 'The readings again.'

'A-52, lapse 200, A-40, lapse 196,

A-42, lapse 203,' read Bhupen.

'If the speed of the drum is lowered, sir . . .' suggested Mohapatro.

'We must pursue the speed of a phenomenon we cannot yet define,' ruminated A. Das. 'Speed. What a questionable word in this context. Lower the speed to record frequencies of what? I am often suspicious of all my primary hypotheses.'

An obscure process shaped itself under our very noses, and, try as we did, we failed to keep pace with it. Our artefacts told us some things which our recordings affirmed; on the glowing dial the needle swung, clicked, hesitated, swung to higher figures and then, unaccountably, dropped. The magnetic needle jumped once, twice and then the dial went dead. The lapses between the anticlinal and synclinal readings barely averaged a hundred. I thought A. Das would explode in frustration.

It was a bleak, windy October morning. We had worked all

night. Mridula cleared away the mugs of tea and I lifted my heavy head from the table, sleepily protesting, when A. Das, who had continued working while we snatched a catnap, suggested that we resume. Then I noticed that strange, taut spring in his voice.

'Look . . .' said he, and in the middle of a pin-drop silence we saw the dial turn dim green like the eye of a jungle deity. The two arms circled slowly and swung to a stop. 52 and 52. 52 and 52. 52 and 52.

'As I always suspected,' was all that Abhijit Das could trust himself to utter. 'Ashok, the dimensions of the magnet had to be altered. That's all really . . .'

Nobody spoke. Then suddenly the shell of silence cracked. Bhupen gave vent to a loud whoop and Mridula drew in her breath sharply. As for me, my first impulse was to hoist A. Das upon my shoulder, footballer that I was, and hurrah him down Roy Choudhury Avenue! 'You blithering priest of science! You've done it!—somebody was roaring incessantly in my ear and I rather believe it was I. But, A. Das, I recall, only pulled out a chair and sank, exhausted into it. Then he remembered. 'Now to formulate the findings in a paper for the Seattle conference,' said he wryly. 'Surendranath is worried, you know.'

Formulate the findings in a paper we did, all fifteen of us, and much good A. Das's dutiful dedication to the Director did him. He never suspected a thing. If Surendranath received his copy in early November, ours was despatched a good three weeks earlier. It was I who sealed the envelope, Bhupen who drafted and typed out the covering letter and it was our Mridula of the bird-like hands who forged, yes, marvellously duplicated Abhijit Das's meandering signature! And when we stood outside the GPO, the operation complete, we felt we were the self-appointed arbiters of fate, titanic agents of a superior destiny, who had craftily outwitted our teacher's objectionable habit of surrender.

So when Abhijit Das received that large blue envelope a month later and perplexedly fussed over it, turning it this way and that, now studying those American stamps, now re-reading that type written address as the truth slowly dawned upon him, all work ceased in the lab and one by one we stole around his swivel chair, triumphantly awaiting the belated decision of fate.

The long sheet fell out.

My dear Dr Das, we are happy to receive your paper entitled etcetera etcetera. We invite correspondence on the subject, so on and so forth . . .

And then, unspeakably, damnably, the words which fifteen pairs of eyes devoured with a growing sense of the impossible.

Of course it must be made known to you that your interesting theory has almost wholly been anticipated by Doctors Klein and Humboldt of the University of Berlin only this July. Your findings happily coincide with theirs . . . The Klein-Humboldt formulae have recently been applied and found valid in all our institutes . . . We are despatching our quarterly journal containing the Klein-Humboldt paper printed this September . . . etcetera, etcetera.

Yours sincerely,
damnand blast!

It was then that Mridula, who was late that morning, appeared upon the threshold. Her face lit up at the sight of the envelope and with a bound she was by A. Das's side, eyes sparkling, voice asnap with excitement.

'Washington! Oh, what does it say, sir?'

'Thank you all,' said Abhijit Das very slowly. 'It says in short that our work deserves an honourable mention.' He handed her the sheet and turning, passed a hand over his forehead and looked away, shading his eyes, out of the lab window, past the Marquis of Hastings and the distant grey warehouses, at the murky, unmoving river.

So we walked by apparent accident alongside him that evening, tense and speechless, and a little awed, yes, even I, noisy Ramendram. We queued up for the Thakur Pukur bus, and, as always, when the milling crowds jostled and fought for a foothold or a hand-hold, A. Das just made no effort, and stood listlessly by, and we, who could push and shove as well as the next man, for some unspoken reason, chose to stand unresisting by and miss the bus with him. If A. Das understood, his face registered no response but inevitably the situation oppressed him into inane talk.

'Look,' said he, 'are all of you coming home with me? Don't. Mira is away and what with the load shedding and the mosquitoes, my house isn't exactly a picnic in the evenings.

'Besides,' he continued, 'we must separate at the Taratalla Crossing. I go straight down Diamond Harbour Road, you know, but all of you go different ways. No point walking me home and then walking back. You'll only waste time and it'll be dark by the time you get home.'

Nobody agreed or disagreed. This was a collective experience and nobody knew quite how to explain or understand it.

I still don't know what to make of that day, whether some science simpler and superior to our own, intervened to tutor us in fate's complexities or whether the complexity was speedily taken out of our taxed wits with a curious, brilliant and brutal twist of resolution. Life is full of such constant allegories. For, half an hour later, as we approached Taratalla Bridge a ghastly spectacle met our eyes. I have never forgotten that scene, police whistles shrilling, the bottleneck that had developed on the flyover, the surging crowds, the noise, the shaken, eyewitness narrations, and above it all the wailing siren of an ambulance and cries of pain, death in the air, the confused buzz of voices and vehicles wreaking silence upon our shocked senses.

It was A. Das who spoke first. 'Bhupen, look! It's that Thakur Pukur bus we just missed. Number 69, I distinctly remember. Ah, poor souls!' And his hand went involuntarily to his head in an old fashioned, instinctive gesture of respect for the dead, the dying and those who would die.

Not that we were superstitious but the day's developments were too concentratedly significant for our threadbare control to endure. We did not actually shake but some sense that was already disarrayed, revolted within us, totally dashed in the face of an ironic enormity.

'It could have been us,' was A. Das's inane afterthought. 'Had we not missed the bus, Ramendram. Oh, God!' He mopped his brow, smiled wearily at us, a smile of pity and terror, of relief and thanksgiving, above all, of a curious new release from complaint or secret inner argument.

Abhijit Das had found a reason, made order out of chaos, I slowly guessed, made his own version of sense of the pattern, made peace with it and accepted its reckless terms.

'Go home now,' said he to us. 'Be grateful you missed that bus today.'

THE SECOND ATTACK

If you haven't actually watched cancer devour somebody close to you, you know nothing about it. Believe me, it isn't a pretty experience. I know. I watched a mother die of it. And she a woman with such a keen sense of fun.

Carcinoma of the left breast. Something in her body betrayed her, treacherously gave her unknowing consent, and the large sluggish cells began multiplying in their millions. When diagnosed it was already too late. The breast was removed. The wound healed well. There were many visits to the hospital for radiation and chemotherapy. But with awesome inevitability the strings of wicked reddish nodules reappeared like beads upon an evil rosary of death. Don't they say once it's there in your system, nothing, no, nothing can get it out? Metastasis, they call it in medical parlance, or relentless migration, relentless recurrence. This and a second heart attack.

It was then that I saw her performing those many ceremonies of self-immortalizing. She used up all her prized perfumes. (The terrible association of the thought—for later when the stench of her sores grew intolerable we burnt incense round her bed for twelve terrible days! Can you picture it? Funeral, sweetish incense round the bed of a living person?) She wore out all those seldom used silk sarees, sent for the gold ornaments in the locker, dressing up for those radiation therapy sessions at the hospital as one normally would for a festival. She had the backyard cleared and fruit trees planted—guavas and Chinese oranges, lemons, even an apricot and an almond. And when those first awful bunches of hair came off upon the comb, the inescapable side effect of her chemotherapy, she rushed to the photographer and posed for three glamorous portraits, decked out in her best, a fixed, studied smile of cool graciousness upon her face. It was a prolonged gesture of denial and defiance. And it could not last long. Her hair went in exactly four days—all of it.

Then came those terrible black days when she lay in a dirty house-coat, quite bald and absolutely shrill and fretful, disbelieving our cheerful assurances, our wretched baby-talk. Everyone had come to be with her, her brothers, her many children, their spouses and their children. The house was packed to capacity, some of us even spreading our bedrolls on the floor. It might have been a marriage or a thread-ceremony or a child's head-shaving feast! There was even room for quips and cracks and solemn games of chess and long speculative political discussions late into the night, for everybody was meeting after a long time. The last wedding was six years back.

Alone in her corner room, attended by two or three people by turns, Mother became a different person. She was no more the good-natured woman we had always known her to be. She uttered bitter, spiteful words. She told her two daughters-in-law how much she detested them. She told me and my brother how casually we had always taken her. And as for my father, she had no words in which to express her abhorrence. Her earlier anxiety lest she should utter damaging words upon the operation-table under anaesthesia now changed to imperious contempt. 'Oh, go and wear your hearing aid, Mr Bose!' she dismissed him with a wave of her hand. 'You can neither hear nor understand me. Not that you ever did, of course . . .' She found us all a set of selfish brutes and had so many things to denounce us for, so many accusations to make. The tantrums began at daybreak and continued all day with a brief respite after lunch when, mercifully, she slept. We were at the end of our tether. We had no idea she hated us so much.

It was the same with visitors. Friends and local relatives came to see her and she lashed out at them, raking up old quarrels, pouring scorn over everybody. She seemed to derive a peculiar joy in being perverse. We stood around, our faces crimson, and didn't know what to do. When the visitors left her sick room, Father apologized, saying that Mother was now no longer herself. Why did she do this to us? It seemed that now that she was more or less certain that the end was near, she felt released from all social discretions, all worldly bargains, equations and observances. She was tasting a new sort of freedom in her self-expression and liking it. It seems to me that our terrible emotions are valuable props and there are circumstances when hate and bitterness serve one's vitality. It now seems to me that she derived a certain strength from them and used them to nourish her will to continue.

One particular day continues to trouble my memory, a month before she went.

She had woken up in a peevish mood, refusing to eat, being difficult and tearful and sarcastic by turns. Several visitors came to call and she excelled herself in general rudeness. With old uncle Pitamber Nath Ghoshal she brought up that twenty-five-year-old matter of the loan of two thousand rupees that he had refused to advance her when her younger sister, our Aunt Mohua, was to be married. With Aunt Shefali she had bitterly recollected the details of the time when the latter had done her little bit in getting my earlier engagement broken. To our neighbours, old Mr Shantanu Dutta and his wife, Mother narrated all the nasty things about her that they had regularly told our common servant. She made it clear that she neither forgave nor forgot. The morning wasn't exactly a social success.

Naturally, therefore, when the doorbell rang yet again late in the afternoon we looked at one another, agitated. Who was it now?

It was my father's friend, Bijon 'Jethu' or elder uncle as we say in Bengali, and Aunt Juthi, his wife. Bijon 'Jethu' and his wife used to be frequent visitors at our house when we were kids. We feared the worst. Especially as there had always been an unexpressed dislike between Mother and Aunt Juthi.

To make matters worse, Aunt Juthi had remained youthful and sweet-tempered after all these years, still slender and attractive, tastefully dressed and her hair still raven black while Mother lay there bloated in her dirty house-coat, bald as a husked coconut. No wonder we were subdued as we led them in. I escaped into the kitchen where my wife was making tea.

When I returned I was surprised to see how smilingly Mother spoke, how she laughed, how she talked of the old days and the fun they'd had at so-and-so's wedding and on such-and-such a puja. Her sharp eyes took in Aunt Juthi's elegant clothes, the bangles on her wrists, her neat, sleek hair, her unwrinkled face and her gentle good-natured responses. Aunt Juthi had brought a box of sondesh for Mother, which, of course, she could not eat. But she laughed and lied: 'Of course I can have them. There's nothing much the matter with me. There's this physical disorder but it has nothing to do with me. I am not ill.'

I laughed uncomfortably. 'We daren't call her ill, Jethu,' said I. 'She isn't ill. Only her body is.' That's the way we put it in colloquial Bengali—'my body is bad'. Not I.'

To Uncle Bijon she said not a word. After they left Mother became very silent and very sad.

The next day she called me and said: 'Son, will you do something for me?'

'Of course,' said I.

She hesitated. 'Will you . . . please tell your Bijon Jethu that I'd like him to come and see me again soon.' She looked afraid. 'Don't even tell Maya,' she added. (Maya is my wife.)

I said I'd get in touch with him.

That evening Bijon Jethu came, as reserved and subdued as before. I had an impression that the visit was unpleasant to him, an unavoidable evil.

'You asked me to come?'

'Yes,' said she. 'Yesterday I could not talk to you.'

And then she began talking feverishly. She talked and talked. She talked without logic or continuity. She narrated how her mother-in-law had taken away her gold mango chain. She spoke of her terror of losing me as a child. She related her thwarted hopes of getting a teachers' training certificate. She spoke of acute headaches. She spoke of the time Father retired and we lost the bungalow and the servants, and the vintage car was sold. She described the second heart attack. She seemed to be rendering a comprehensive account of the years, compressing all the backlog of suffering into that feverish trivia.

But Bijon Uncle uttered not a word. And, when I pushed open the door, helping my wife with the tea-tray, he had just put his first cold question:

'Why did you ask me to come?'

I retreated discreetly behind a screen.

'I must return something to you,' replied Mother in a small voice, chided by his coldness.

He looked at her questioningly.

'A book in manuscript. Yours. Do you remember that one you wrote? *A Boat Across The Hoogly*?'

Suddenly he gripped the arm of his chair, consternation in his face.

'I do not understand,' he muttered.

'How can you understand?' she mocked indulgently. 'It was the most intelligent deception of my life! Don't you remember? You persuaded the *Tollygunge Sanskritic Patrika* to serialize it. You never heard from them, did you? I intercepted their acceptance letter. Yes.'

She was smiling in triumphant glee now. 'I went to our little post office and even intercepted the manuscript when you sent it. And that pleading little epistle you wrote them a little later. Postmaster Choudhury's daughter was my friend and I often carried his lunch for him and waited in the office whilst he went to wash his hands and gargle at the tubewell in the yard. That's how. You waited, alas, poor Bijon, so pathetic, ah, the failed disappointed poet, ah, the unrecognized genius, upon your terrace. Weeks and months and no reply! Ha, your lovely Bengali calligraphy, poor Bijon! As I waited behind my barred window across the lane . . .'

The light fell upon her face and I saw an expression of unbelievable pathos and rage in her wasted eyes.

'Maybe,' she said insinuatingly, oh, ever so malicious, 'maybe you could have become famous, a writer, a well-known writer like our Sarat Babu or our Bimol Mittro, instead of a petty accountant in an insignificant tea firm, eh Bijon?'

What sophisticated revenge shone in her eyes. Truly, hell hath no fury . . . and this was, Oh God, my old mother!

Then suddenly her face set in a waxen mask and her eyes grew limp, imploring.

'Do you remember those little Calcutta papers, Bijon? And the things we used to scribble and send? You wrote very well, you know. You had what it takes. Do you recollect how you corrected my little verses on champak blossoms and joba-flowers? Do you remember that Puja play in which you were Maharaja Harishchandra and I could not read Taramati's lines well enough? Ah, Bijon, do you remember that flock of herons in the paddy field in New Jalpaigudi? And the way the blue mist boiled up from the valley in Darjeeling that summer our theatre group went there? 1949 it was—just after the war. Do you remember the pink plume of cloud upon Kanchenjunga's crest . . . ?'

But Bijon could endure no more of it. Eyes glazed, he sprang to his feet.

'Wait,' she called after him. 'The manuscript. *A Boat Across The Hoogly*. It's lying in my old chest of drawers. You don't want it back?' Her voice shook, a little shameful.

'No,' hissed he in a low snarl and made for the door.

After he left Mother lay down very quietly, her face to the wall, and took no notice of us. Only Father looked upset and angry and said: 'Why did you let her babble so much and tire herself out? You should have barged in and told him to leave and let her rest.'

I chose to say nothing to that.

That was my mother and the confusion she wrought in my filial picture of her.

I refuse to call hers a failed life despite the excruciatingly painful death God gave her, despite the great unsuspected disappointment of her life. If success is a positive feeling about things, I always looked on her as one of life's anonymous successes. What else can be said of a woman who admitted to physical breakdown but denied that she herself was ill? And, what better can be said of a woman who even when she lacked money, never called herself poor. In all my life I never knew her to read a line of poetry, real or fake. She loved her little morsel of malice. And, I don't think she ever had a profound thought in her life save the saws of inherited folk wisdom. Her photographs are now upon the wall. And, the fruit trees in the yard are all abloom. What is there to do but nurse her in my mind and the memory of that strange evening? What is there to do now save put her behind me and go on, striving to make sense of what remains of life?

I have now integrated her two big defeats in my understanding in a dim conjecture of what appears to be one of God's many formulae. I step into her garden and intuit its perennial laws. To make a plant grow well you must feed it and sun it and water it. You must encourage it but you must also disappoint it regularly, cutting down its shoots mercilessly after all its laborious growth, denying it judiciously, slashing out the leaves and the hoary old stems so that the energy that sustained them be renewed for other, younger ones of its kind. There are those which are cut down by the wise gardener; there are those which drop off naturally on their own; and there are those which are irreparably ravaged by disease and suffering as they decay. And, new leaves everywhere. Metastasis and metempsychosis—the truth of the garden.

I could make a second rate poem of it to send to a little Calcutta paper as my mother did in her youth. Now I never will.

THE PASSING OF PERCIVAL

Once a headmaster always a headmaster. When Arthur Peregrine Clements, M.A., L.T., Ph.D., D.Litt. (Glasgow), retired headmaster of St Christopher's Academy, opened the door of his dilapidated Muirabad apartment, I found him little changed in thirty years. The chins had multiplied but the steel grey eyes were just as peevish and censorious as before.

'Come on, come on, Sinha. For a man on a mission of mercy you are exceedingly tardy about your business.'

Dr Clements's opening address was enough to reassure me that my erstwhile headmaster had changed in form not in content.

I apologized. At the veterinary hospital there were always things cropping up to delay appointments.

A seedy little room it was, a veranda really, enclosed by green-painted bamboo screens and set about with old, creaking cane chairs, ancient revolving book-cases.

'Martha!' shouted the peppery old man. 'Come out and meet this physician of the furred and the feathered!'

'Coming, Arthur,' trilled a fluting voice from the interior.

On Mrs Clements, time had left its mark. A tiny grey lady in faded print dress and rubber slippers. She had nothing in common with the elegant first lady of the campus I remembered. Gracious she had been, soft spoken and correct in smartly tailored suits and white parasol. It had been kid gloves and net veil on Prize Distribution Day. She had bowed slightly and extended her hand to us like a queen, an arch, languid smile playing about her lips.

'See this fine young man, Martha? I had once the singular pleasure of giving him five of the best. What was it for, Sinha? My history is, I'm afraid, ah, somewhat shaky. Bursting a cracker in class, was it?'

'Smoking a bidi, sir.'

'Ah, yes. It all comes back.' He chuckled. 'You even had the honour of having your Byronic locks shorn by my inartistic fingers—hey?'

'Not me, sir.'

'Not "I".'

'Not I, sir. That was Suresh Verma.'

'Verma? Yes. You remember Verma, Martha? Fellow with a Roman nose. We made him Caesar in the Shakespeare festival in 1964. Couldn't act to save his soul. And, what is Verma up to now?'

'Teaching Business Administration out in the States,' I informed.

'Still hear from him?'

'No, we're rather out of touch. An annual New Year Card. . .' My voice trailed away in embarrassed confusion. But my old headmaster continued smoothly: 'And, talking of cards, thank you very much indeed for the ones you sent in the initial years.'

'Tell us about yourself.' Mrs Clements filled up the uncomfortable pause. 'Are you married? How many children?'

I found the surroundings uncongenial. I did not like the shabby little flat, the worn out rug, the chipped paint on the chairs. There was something depressing in the demure little lace doilies, the cabinet of china. I looked from the Jesus on the wall to the scrolled text which proclaimed "The Lord Is My Shepherd". There was something uncharacteristic about the drab, soft-spoken old lady in her rubber slippers and that massive deposed monarch in his chair. It seemed like a reversion of a law of nature. Arthur Peregrine Clements, Headmaster of St Christopher's was fashioned by the powers above to stride about a quad in tropical suit and sola hat, puffing at a cigar, his Malacca cane atwirl, sharing satiric observations with his handsome Dobermann, Archibald, who lolled his tongue and flattened his ears and fawned up in adoring agreement. Lear and the Fool.

'And how,' demanded he, '—did you stray into this—this Franciscan line of yours. Do the dumb beasts tell you their secrets? Do little singing birds perch upon your shoulder and twitter in your ear?'

'I had to settle for it. Couldn't get into General Medicine.'

'It's all the fault of that good-for-nothing Ron Carson. Should've given him the sack right in the beginning,' muttered Dr Clements. 'Calling himself a teacher of Biology!'

'How are your sons?' I asked.

'Both fine, thank you. One in Bombay, the other in New Zealand. They wrote sometimes. Mike and Ashley visited us last year,' said Mrs Clements. 'This terrible cubby hole of a flat can't hold us all together. We were packed together like sardines last Christmas. So now it's been decided that Mike and Alice and the kids will come down for Christmas, and Brenda and Ashley for Easter. I guess none of them quite likes this.' She stressed the "this". I looked away in discomfort.

Where, I presently asked, was the patient?

'Our Percy is in a bad way,' said Mrs Clements. 'You remember Archie? Well, this Percy is his grandson. Arthur named him Percival.' She dimpled. 'If ever we have a dog again I'm positive Arthur'll name him Lancelot.'

'There won't be another dog, Martha,' said Dr Clements in a flat voice.

Mrs Clements was right. Percy was in bad shape. He lay stretched out on his mat. He gave me a dour, sidelong look.

'Just can't walk,' whispered the old lady. 'He could limp around till about three days back. Yesterday he began falling about.'

I bent over the dog.

'His blood pressure is fine,' whispered Dr Clements. 'I've been checking it. So is his heart rate. I specially procured a stethoscope . . .'

'Poor Percy has been very cooperative,' said she.

'I've been trying to keep a temperature chart,' explained Dr Clements. 'There's this stick-on thermometer that Ashley sent from Australia.' He gave an embarrassed laugh. 'Well, not being familiar with your coarse veterinary methods, I've been doing the best I can with my clumsy common sense.'

I worked the dog's rusted limbs up and down.

'For some time I've suspected rheumatoid arthritis,' went on Dr Clements. 'We're old men, Percy and I. I managed to lay my hands on a handful of medical journals on the subject. What I haven't read up about arthritis isn't worth knowing.'

'What haven't we tried?' put in Mrs Clements. 'Cod liver oil, lard massages, liniments, herbal fomentations, walks, baths in warm, salted water.'

'Of late I've begun suspecting progressive paralysis. I am in mortal dread of paralysis myself, I may tell you. It runs in Percy's family. Archie had it too.'

'There certainly does seem to be a total loss of sensation on one side. How old did you say he was?' inquired I.

'He was eleven last February, poor chap.'

Lumbar paralysis perhaps. Percy was dying of old age, nothing more and nothing less. So, I wrote the name of a strong sedative, obscure enough to mislead even the knowledgeable Dr Clements. Mrs Clements put it carefully away on the old fashioned chest of drawers.

'You'll have to go down to the chemist, Arthur. Mind you take a rickshaw. With that gout of yours, you're as bad as Percy himself. Oh, I do wish it does him good. I couldn't bear to see the poor fellow limping round and round the room, nosing into dark corners and behind the furniture. With a sort of craving, you know, as though he was blindly looking for something, looking for something, and quite, quite crazed. All day he went, round and round.'

I stood up. 'Don't worry, ma'am. Percy'll be fine.'

'It's good to hear that. Percy means a lot to us, old folks,' she said. 'Come and sit in the parlour while I make you some tea. I could give Percy some too, with a spoonful of glucose, perhaps.'

There was only one thing to talk about. The old days, the old days . . .

How was old Reginald Barth, the Principal? How was Miss Sarah Sewell? How was His Excellency, the Bishop, the Reverend Walter Pereira?

'His Excellency, the Bishop, died recently,' was Dr Clements's disparaging reply. He, who was committed to disapprove of everything the Reverend Pereira did, could not let this bit of irresponsibility pass easily. Then he brightened up. On his puffy face there appeared a fleeting expression of grim satisfaction. That he had worsted the irascible Pereira in this last bout could not have failed to have afforded him a blameless pleasure.

'Went suddenly,' he muttered. 'Awoke in the morning unable to use his arm and within a couple of hours lost his speech too. What was it that Dr Johnson wrote on the morning of his stroke, Sinha?'

I shook my head, at a loss.

'"It has pleased God this morning to deprive me of the power of speech". That's Boswell's version. The Reverend Pereira could scarce be expected to exhibit the same graceful surrender.'

He fell silent. The Reverend Walter Pereira, big and beefy, in flowing satin robe and skull cap, expansively held forth from the pulpit each first day of term. 'By midday he was gone. Never spoke again.' Dr Clements spoke with sinister meaning in his voice.

'I didn't know of this. Did the papers carry the obituary?'

Dr Clements looked piqued. 'Lies, damn lies and statistics, was it? Well, now we can add a fourth class—journalists,' he grunted. 'I went through all the dailies specially to see what they were saying about him.'

'Well, he was a man with a controversial reputation,' I ventured.

Dr Clements brooded. Then animation flooded his face. He rose and hobbled into the inner room.

'I have here some cuttings.' He placed a large, battered folder on the table. The table was soon littered with snippets. If I expected accounts of school functions or pictures of a youthful Dr Clements cutting the red ribbon with a rosette upon his lapel, and trim accounts of speeches delivered, I was in for a minor shock. For spread out before me was a rich assortment of obituaries! He seemed as pleased with his scrap book as a little chap with his treasured stamp collection!

'Here's one,' exclaimed he, picking up a ribbon of newsprint.

'Our dear and beloved Reverend Walter Pereira, Bishop of St Christopher's and the Uttarpara diocese, left for his heavenly abode on the evening of Saturday, 6 March. He passed away following an acute attack of cerebral thrombosis. He was sixty-four. He leaves behind a host of grateful students, seminarians, friends and a grieving fraternity. Awaiting the Second Coming of Our Lord Jesus Christ . . .' Here Dr Clements held the snippet distastefully away from his nose.

'Humbug!' he scowled. 'Poor composition, uncertain grammar, and a mawkish lack of artistic restraint.' He tapped the paper speculatively. 'There are,' he said austerely, '—several little errors in this—this document that I take strong exception to.'

And, I recognized the thin, exact voice of Arthur P. Clements, M.A., L.T., Ph.D., D.Litt., standing authoritatively over his desk, arms folded commandingly over his chest and face intense in its merciless exploration of the niceties of English as she is spoke.

'Not errors in the strict sense,' he made a grudging concession. 'Let's call them inelegances. (a) I disapprove of the use of "dear" and "beloved" in succession. There is nothing so shabby as excess and tautology. The entire thrust of the primary adjective is lost by the needless interference of the second. To say nothing . . .' His beetling brows shrank. His mouth tightened ascetically. 'To say nothing, of course, of the maudlin sentimentality of repetition. Slobber, dribble, nerves. Not the cool control of sublimated emotion. An obituary, being as it is the last pronouncement upon a man, must be composed of sharply chiselled syllables.' He turned lyrical. 'Syllables as white and pure as the lilies on the tomb. Cool as a marble tombstone, nobly symmetrical as the Cross.' He fell silent, evidently overcome.

'Further,' he continued, tapping the paper. 'I detest this heavenly abode business. Quite apart, of course, from the fact that I very much doubt whether the worthy Pereira would have gained admission into the Kingdom of Heaven as easily as the one to the ecclesiastical chair.' His eyes twinkled roguishly.

'I feel it brings in an obnoxious medievalism into our attitude. A smelly hangover of popery. Nor do I like the phrase "passed away". I much prefer the phrase "passed on". Now there we have an interesting suggestion of spiritual continuity'.

'Then,' he moved on, '—there is this chronic mixing of tenses that we in this age of linguistic chaos are heir to. "Left for his heavenly abode" is followed by "He leaves behind a host of grateful students" etc etc! Lacking in classical uniformity. I know, I know your objection. Might it not be, you will ask, that the earlier past indefinite tense is linked to the finality of death and the latter present continuous tense suggests the continuity of the living. That is only a matter of grammatical allowance.' He dismissed it with a deprecating wave of the hand.

He selected another snippet from his collection.

'This,' said he profoundly, '—is yet another type. Captioned "In Memoriam", if you please!' He paused to snort and stare balefully at me over his spectacles. ' "In memory of our dearest sister, Ethel Bray, who left us this day, four years ago, in Bangalore." And then the half-witted piece of poesy—

> *I lost this flower I cherished*
> *This lily chaste and pale.*
> *Behold, the Lord said unto me,*
> *She blossometh in my vale.*

Ach!' swore Dr Clements with feeling. 'Shrill. Shrill and idiotic. Biblical, Wordsworthian, country churchyard mush! If you knew poor Ethel Bray you would hoot at the mockery of the second line. Whatever made Brian and Linda take to composing disastrous elegies at their age, I can't fathom.'

I sat in deferential silence. This was perhaps one of the rare occasions that now came by Dr Clements's way to renew touch with his former vocation.

Mrs Clements, appearing with the tea tray, cut short the literary criticism.

'Oh, Arthur!' squealed the little old lady reproachfully. 'Not again!' Then she turned to me, apologetic and concerned. 'He hasn't been showing off his little album, has he? Arthur has this macabre hobby and nothing that I say or do can discourage him from sharing it with all our friends. I often say: Arthur, other people collect snap-shots of living people and look at you—all you collect is obituaries of dead folk. Now Arthur.' She said primly, placing his tea before him. 'No more of this. Don't bore the lad.'

Arthur Clements protested. 'Just one more, Martha,' said he appealingly. 'Here, Sinha, is one obituary which I composed for my brother, the late Randolph Clements. It appeared in the *Statesman*.' He placed the prized snippet carefully before me and beamed with honest pride. 'Read it out,' he commanded happily.

' "My brother, Randolph Wright Clements, passed on this morning, 4 November 1965, at 6 a.m. at the Elizabeth Barden Memorial Hospital following a severe cardiac arrest. The burial service was held at St Patrick's Church the same evening. Unto him may the Lord grant peace in his onward progress and unto those who hold him dear fortitude in our loss." '

'There you see!' Dr Clements triumphantly thumped the table. 'Neat and aphoristic. Stoical reserve and including an . . . an intimation of immortality.'

Mrs Clements burst out laughing, shaking her head. 'Oh, dear,' she trilled, very red in the face. 'Oh, dear.'

'Hush!' glared Dr Clements. 'We are forgetting Percy, now mercifully asleep. Well, Sinha, dare I hope that you shall keep me company down the lane to the chemist's store yonder?'

'Tomorrow, eleven a.m., sir,' promised I when we parted.

And, when I rang the bell next morning, one glance at Mrs Clements's puffed face was enough to disclose the inevitable truth.

Percy was no more and Dr Clements, in faded dressing gown and slippers, sat in woeful reflection upon the aged working chair, head philosophically sunk upon his chest.

He shrugged feebly in mock despair. 'Well, Sinha, there lieth Percival Clements, meaner than the dust he trod upon, and all his days and ways as airy nothings now.'

'It was in that half hour that I slipped off to sleep,' sobbed the lady. 'Between two and two-thirty, Mr Sinha, oh, the Lord forgive me to abandon him in his last half hour!'

'More likely he upped and left when the coast was clear and no tears being rained down the back of his neck,' ventured Dr Clements, gruff and facetious but with a sinister quaver in his thick voice.

'And now?' asked the lady as I stood uncertainly in the doorway.

'Ah, now,' declaimed Dr Clements. 'We do unto that muddy vesture of decay what needs be done, alas for us, Martha. Ring out the knell, lay him under the yews, assure him of the resurrection and the Lord, cover the poor blighter up and leave him to rot, poor beast.'

'Oh, Arthur!' whimpered the lady in appeal and even I, uneasy in the midst of this Act Five resolution of the tragedy could sense, in the farcical play acting, a terrible mockery of his own mourning, an appalling terror and accusation, and I could not meet his eyes.

'I can always,' he continued, '—distract myself with composing an obituary but the dumb beasts die outside history. It little matters, Martha, that he was my friend, faithful and just to me . . .'

'Arthur, please,' begged the lady. 'Mr Sinha,' she turned to me. 'We have no orderlies now. Where does one give a dog a proper Christian burial?'

'Comfort thyself, dear heart,' recited Lear in his chair. 'We shall erect a mausoleum to his memory here, lady, 'neath this waving ashoka tree outside your window. A modest barrow, three by three, on which the turf shall wave and I compose my autumnal elegies!'

'Oh, you are impossible!' Mrs Clements burst into pent up, exasperated tears.

'Madam,' I tried my best. 'I'll have it all fixed in half an hour, don't worry.'

'And, we shall plant dog flower upon the hallowed mound,' whispered Dr Clements quixotically. 'And, recite: "Not fare well, but fare forwards, O Percival, son of Adam." ' And the tears at last shone in his old eyes. He bent over his spectacles, intent upon cleaning up the tell-tale mist. 'I'll have to sound Sircar, my landlord, upon the subject,' said he, rising abruptly.

But, Earnest Prabhudhan Sircar, Dr Clements' pious Bengali landlord, was a particularly difficult specimen of Christian orthodoxy and Christian practicality, and his objections to the proposal were both pragmatic and theological.

'A dog cannot claim redemption or salvation, so why the cross, sir?' The old Bengali knew his Scriptures well and trilled off excited passage after passage, citing chapter and verse.

'Besides,' he went on shrewdly, 'a grave right in front of the front door shall be most inappropriate, ah, shall I say unappealing, to the next tenant, whenever he comes.'

Dr Clements took long to comprehend.

'Next tenant? What do you mean, man? We have no plans to move, Martha and I. Make no mistake, man, we stay here.'

The old Bengali had the grace to look shamefaced. 'You are an old man, sir, and so is your wife . . .'

Thunder shook Dr Clements' brow and his torrid eyes bore into the man's embarrassed face as they did in the old Malacca-cane-sola-topee academy days. For one moment his fleshy, apoplectic face flamed a furious red. Then, suddenly, before my eyes, he shrank and seemed to lose all confidence and a silence fell.

'Well, so long, Sircar!' intoned he and we came down the stairs, uneasy in a reciprocal and reluctant realization of the forbidden.

'Why not float him down the Ganges the Hindu way?' suggested I. 'After all, Percy is an Indian dog . . .'

'Ach, yes,' sighed Dr Clements. 'A dog at least is above dogma.'

I brought the jeep from the Veterinary Hospital. Shrouded in saffron, garlanded with jasmines, Percival was driven to the ghat by me and Dr Clements who insisted upon coming. We paid a boatman to row Percy downstream and lay him in the stream.

And, as the tiny vessel diminished in the distance, Dr Clements was seized by another suspicious paroxysm of poesy.

'Do you remember "Morte D'Arthur", Sinha?' he barked, expressionless.

I nodded.

' "Hearest thou," muttered he, "—this great voice that shakes the world . . . O Bedivere, for on my heart hath fall'n confusion, till I know not what I am, Nor whence I am, nor whether I be king. Behold, I seem but king among the dead . . ." '

He turned to me in quickening emotional excitement.

'Ah, Sinha, those lines, I forget their order—"I am so deeply smitten thro' the helm . . . Ah! My Lord Arthur, whither shall I go? Where shall I hide my forehead and my eyes? . . . the days darken round me, and the years, Among new men, strange faces, other minds."'

I now remembered that elocution contest and I, a snotty, knock-kneed stammerer. 'It also says, sir, that God fulfils Himself in many ways and that there is, in some unintelligible sense, a place where one may heal oneself of the grievous wound.'

Dr Clements' face creased into multiple folds, his chin shook, his eyes grew brilliant and he turned upon me in keen gratitude.

'Thank you, my lad. If you, a vet, remember those lines at this moment and can supply them for me when I need them, I have not been entirely unsuccessful in my vocation.'

Then the mask was back, Senecan, expansive. 'That, Sinha, is the ultimate utility of literature. The stock poetry comes back to you when you are shaken and vacant of words and relieves you of the responsibility of articulation—eh? Those masters had every feeling defined and every mood explored and recorded for our reference. It is now that Shakespeare and Tennyson come back to me, fluent friends returned . . .'

'Martha!' cried he, stepping in and waking his drowsing lady in her armchair. 'That's farewell to Percival now, God rest his soul, dear beast. It was a burial by water, I'm afraid, rather like those ceremonies on ship, you know. You remember Tennyson's— "Down that long water opening on the deep, somewhere far off, pass on and on and on, from less to less and vanish into light?"'

She did not speak. She looked strangely at her voluble husband and went on looking.

I took my leave.

'And so, goodbye, Bedivere,' was Dr Clements' parting address. 'See us sometimes.'

Some years later I chanced upon a back number of our St Christopher's journal. There, located finally in the syntax of life and death, sat a stern-eyed Dr Clements in cravat and horn-rimmed glasses, many-chinned, a grammar unto himself.

Dr Arthur P. Clements. Born 1912. Died 1990.

Those were the days when a single breadwinner supported a horde of children, a wife or two, some odd brothers and sisters and frequently half a dozen cousins and mates of the village, all on a salary of forty or fifty rupees a month. All were welcome and all were accommodated, for did not milk then sell at a paisa a *seer* (and that included a crust of cream, one finger thick), and silk at a rupee a yard, and a pair of the finest Flex shoes at five rupees a pair? Did I say 'welcome'? Forgive me, in our house there were some that were not. For when Bade Chacha Imam Bux came to stay, quite without notice and for months at a stretch, it was only we children who rejoiced.

An ancient musician was he, stooped, wiry, tapping his stick down the wet alley, shooing away the chickens and the curs. I can still see the discoloured, quilted jacket, out at the elbows, and the gathered trousers, grey with dirt.

My sister, Afeera, nudged me. Together we peeped through the trellis on our mouldy terrace. Afeera's eyes shone. An evening of fun! But I was doubtful, for whatever would our Ammi say?

Ammi had a lot to say. Her eyes snapped dangerously, her two dozen bangles jingled furiously on her wrists as she rolled out the dough and slapped the muslin-fine bread onto the skillet.

'Now do be silent, mother of Ilyas!' shouted my father, 'He'll be here any minute.'

And no sooner were the words out of his mouth than Bade Chacha seized the heavy door-chain and hammered upon the door. 'Abdul Hamid!' he roared, 'Open up! This fakir is here again!'

Ammi bristled, bent over her woodfire. Fakir, foresooth! She was ready to bet her seven tola anklets that his crafty eyes never missed a comely wench! 'Afeera!' she hissed, commandingly, 'Stay inside. You're a big girl now.'

But my brother, Ilyas, and I crept into the courtyard where Bade Chacha Imam Bux had made himself comfortable on the divan, drawing up his dirty feet on Ammi's precious coverlet and reclining sideways upon her embroidered bolster. He pinched my cheeks: 'Aha, little two anna bit!' cried he, addressing me by his special name, 'And how many teeth have you lost, old timer? Abdul Hamid, Allah grant you of his bounty, and will it please you pass me that handsome hookah there. Also that beauteous spittoon and give your Ammi my salaams, and will she send for a clutch of betel leaves?'

He poked Ilyas in the ribs. 'And what has your Ammi made for dinner?' he asked cheerfully. Then he motioned to my agitated father to be seated and, taking off his muslin lace cap, ran a grimy hand through his shoulder-length hair. He took a long pull at the hookah, a man content.

'What does huzoor fancy?' muttered my mother spitefully. 'Lion-meat roasted in saffron or a peacock in almond gravy? Hish!' she sneered, venomously tossing her yard of tinselled veil over her shoulder. 'Lived all his life on a flake of garlic and a bunch of dry loaves like a yokel and comes here demanding a white-sheet feast!' But she sent me for the betel leaves all the same and I ran down the wet lane, clutching the coin in my haste not to miss out on Bade Chacha Imam Bux's oratory.

For Bade Chacha Imam Bux, ne'er-do-well, up-to-no-good, ancient rolling stone, call him what you will, was a prince among storytellers. The pigeons came crooning down under the dark cornices, the sky grew dim, a flimsy rag of shadow lapped and fluttered about the lantern base, and behind a pillar even Ammi flopped down on the last step of the staircase and listened, suppressing a laugh or announcing her scepticism with a snort.

Many were the tales we remembered. There was the eerie adventure, with its numerous artistic variations, upon the dark road that ran from Faizabad to Lucknow and along a cemetery notorious for its vengeful denizens. There was the chilling demon-drama that occurred in the lane mansion of Ashraf Ali—'the same Ashraf Ali who went to madrasaa with your esteemed father, Abdul Hamid'—in which the intimate proximity of the Evil One and his cohorts made us hold our breaths and steal closer round the lantern. All night long, through the hours of peril, curtains caught fire; filth descended on the courtyard; chandeliers exploded; gilt mirrors fell off their nails and terror reigned until dawn, at the hour of the first tremulous minaret call that went searching the tall sky in quest of God, the holy words scattered the evil spell. The Devil was very close to us these days and Bade Chacha's profound understanding of the dreaded one's ways filled us with deep respect. And so it happened in every tale. Sceptics came, dissenters, heretics, and questioned the Evil One and the Evil One responded with resounding smacks, with clods of excrement and the women fainted. Only the renowned Pir of Rehanabad, he that spent his leisure hours, atwirling and atwirling in incommunicable ecstasy, did the Evil One hold in some respect, and thus did the holy man arrive, with many tangled incantations, and amulets and exorcisms and seven nails were driven into the musty walls and joss sticks lit to sweeten the soul and the Evil One questioned, gently at first, then with ringing authority, upon the nature of his grievances.

But this evening Bade Chacha seemed to have lost his flair both for the sensational and the supernatural.

'Oh, to have fallen on evil days, Abdul Hamid,' he sighed in uncharacteristic melancholy, thoughtfully seized a leg of chicken and tore at it with his scanty teeth, meditating on the trials of fate. A trickle of gravy crept down his chin and he mopped it with his sleeve.

'My father was Quanungo. From Patwari to Quanungo, from Quanungo to Naib Tehsildar, fate took him, so sweet was his flattery and so winsome his wit. And his father?' He looked down gravely at my brother, Ilyas, who hung upon his words. 'His father was dewan to the Emperor Aurangzeb.'

I heard my mother mutter something behind her pillar and Afeera tittered, but we? We believed all, my brother and I, so willing was the suspension of our disbelief; we'd have believed him had he told us that his great-great-great grandfather had been dewan to Allah himself!

'I, misguided wretch, sought to be a musician,' said Bade Chacha. 'Fourteen years I offered up, practising those tangle-throated tricks. The tremolo that is like an echo revolving in a brass bell. The cadence that is like a note swooning down a veena string. And the regurgitating cascade that is like water emptying out of a broad-mouthed earthen pitcher. Ragas of the morning, ragas of the evening and of the deepest night. The difference between the "re" of Marwah and the "re" of Poorvi. I was, I do not blush to say, Abdul Hamid, a local celebrity, a prodigy of unparalleled versatility. Thumri, ghazal, dhrupad, khayal, all were my province! And truly, my teacher's teacher, the illustrious Barkat Ali Sanvaliya, was descended from a long line of maestros, yes, from the durbar of the ill-fated Muhammad Shah Rangila himself. Now when the invader Nadir Shah sacked Delhi and withdrew, our sad king, the colourful, music-loving one, our Muhammad Shah, grew disenchanted. Wherefore this music, asked he, wherefore this art? Never more shall the strings sound and the drums beat in these portals. And, he sent away all the songstresses, the fluteplayers and the fiddlers. Then it was that the two old masters, Mian Jani and the shining Ghulam Rasool, sought refuge at the court of Asaf-ud-Daula of Lucknow. Well, we soft-souled ones, we musicians, you know how tender is our temperament and how quick our ire. Ghulam Rasool left Asaf-ud-Daula's court, slighted, I never learnt why. To cut a long story short, his pupil, my master's master, Barkat Ali Sanvaliya, became durbar musician to Nawab Hashmat Jung, the 'Baawan-hazari', the fifty-two thousand one, and the Farrukhabad gharana was born. And what a patron he had, Abdul Hamid! One of his servants, a Maghru Khan, sang Raga Des as only Allah's minstrels can.

'My own master, Barkat Ali Sanvaliya, was presented with a baby elephant and a golden shawl by the nawab. Alas for him, a grey beard will not teach one anything. One cold night, returning from the nawab's court and beholding the famous *tawaif*, Munna Jaan, warming her hands over a wood fire, our master gallantly offered her the shawl. Words passed, I know not what , and the shameless hussy angrily cast the precious shawl into the fire, crying— "There, that much for your fine words!" That was the year when the first railway line from Farrukhabad to Kanpur was opened.

'Another one of my teachers, Nabi Bux, received five thousand dhrupads as his holy wife's dower, secret notations of sound and style, family formulae preserved for nigh three centuries and more precious than all the gold in Hindostan to the music-loving one's eye. Twenty children the couple begot, each one a musical prodigy. Then, true to the law laid down in the Book, *Nikaah* was read out—and the old couple united in matrimony anew, and lo!—two more children followed, twins, then the good lady died and Nabi Bux composed the most memorable mausoleum in sound to her memory, which did perish with him for no son of his approved of it on grounds of classic purity though all who heard it felt it clutch the heart in the simplicity of final woe; yet the maestroes reluctantly agreed that certain combinations in it were just not permissible, and a debate did divide the sons for two decades and more.

'I was born during the great famine, they say. That year Mallika Victoria died and a song went round our lanes— "Ah, the Mallika is gone, alas for us, our shops are closed."

'I was born with doom writ in these palms, you see. Music, Abdul Hamid, has proved my undoing. It took me to seek my fortune at the durbar of the nawab of Santoor. Truly a man of feeble wit. Fourteenth scion of a noble line, titular head of a tiny state, a one-cannon, four-elephant state, a kerchief-breadth of barren land. A man who saw phantoms everywhere, tossed and puffed upon his brocade bed all night, wrestling with direful anxieties even as Yaakoob in the Holy Book wrestled with the Unknown Stranger. But the begum was a veritable queen; she revealed her proud blue Persian blood in every measured utterance and every chiselled movement.

'The nawab affected to like music. He preferred the coquetry, the teasing flirtation, the sweet, strong passion of thumries. Songs of the rain, songs of the swing, songs for the wearing of bangles, yearning love-songs, wedding ditties, songs of complaint and accusation. The begum, alone in her villa, listened to pure, speechless music, long, melancholy meanderings of mood, subdued and reflective. One evening as I let my voice loose in a cascading welter of trills she interrupted me. "Maestro," said she through her veil "—give me something quieter." I bowed my head. I thought a while. Then I began a smoky Aheer-bhairava.

'Ah, the ultimate loneliness of Aheer-bhairava, Abdul Hamid. The notes lit up slowly like lamps in the dark. Each note flickered like a flame blown upon. Then it moved away, lone, silver-chill, into stellar dimness. She sat very still. I knew everything, or so I thought, about the misty terrain of this raga, how to shade a note, inflect it and hold it steady; mute it, and, placing it effortlessly upon the air, argue beyond it, impelled by its own classic logic, how to set each note with infinite perfection, symmetry and finish.

'Thus I ended, extinguishing each exquisite phrase slowly.

Never had I sung thus. "Now you, sir," said she, turning to my old master.

'Now old Sajjad Ali's voice was long past its prime. He opened wide his jaws. He made monstrous faces. He emitted raucous, cackling trills. He slapped his thigh. He flung one trembling hand into the air, drawing it this way and that as though 'twer a kite at the end of a string. He clapped the other hand to his ear.

'My face went red. What shame! What was wrong with the old man? He was trying so hard to outdo me. I never realized he was so bad. And he had taught me all I knew. I sat embarrassed. The ladies covered their mouths with their *dupattas*, yawning genteelly. But the begum sat listening intensely with her deep, grieving eyes. I could not understand her concentration. What was the old man uttering and what did she understand? It has taken me thirty years to grasp that, Abdul Hamid. She presented Sajjad Ali with a ring. She gave me nothing, not a word of praise. I burned in indignation.

'She must be dead. A very strange woman. She detested her husband though once, it was rumoured, she had poisoned one of his courtesans. She cared not a whit but when he came she bowed low and touched her fingertips to her brow and offered her salutations in reverence or irony or both. It was good to hear the sharp thrust-and-parry of their repartee. Tablas, veenas, fiddles stopped, fan women stood, transfixed. (Here Bade Chacha flung himself into mimicry. He enacted it all, the low bow, the sitting down with billowing trousers daintily gathered on the ottoman, the offering of paan.) "It is my good fortune that sire has crossed my humble threshold."

'"The good fortune is mine, Begum."

'"Your lordship has become for us as rare as the moon of Id."

'"I can no longer ride across as I was wont to do, Begum. That fall from the mare cost me four ribs and the ache never did repair."

'"A paltry loss, sire. Allah shall fashion of each rib a fair maiden for sire's paradise."

'"You jest, Begum. They say Mother Eve spent her leisure counting Father Adam's ribs to ensure that no new maiden trespassed into Eden. Mean you to do the same?"

'"Allah preserve us all, sire, finding a single rib in your gracious person would then be like seeking a pearl in the waters of the Jordan."

'The nawab probably swore—"Perdition take the woman!"—but

on the face of it he smiled. "God be praised, Begum, but your tongue is like the magic staff of Haroon, a fragrant flowering shrub one moment and a lashing serpent the next." Oh, she could reduce him to nought, he with his timid, dissipated face, his endless poor lusts, his elaborate forked moth-eaten beard. Oh, she knew how to use her voice and her face, to narrow her eyes or leave them veiled; she knew how to lift her haughty brows in disdain, to make the rage stand tall in her eyes and a fierce, black flame shake in the depths of the pupils; and she knew how to avert her face towards the filigreed screen, her lips atremble, her fine eyes fuming over, and ere the instant passed, they were veiled again and she played with the long, dangling emerald in her ear-lobe. A most mobile and splendid face, a noble work of great perfection though all her beauty was over. And she knew how to clinch an argument and bring the blush to the nawab's florid cheek with a choice quatrain or a couplet like—"Grey pigeon, for thee the still minaret, for thee the lonely sky. Leave to the bright bulbul the amorous flowers of paradise."

'Alone in his chamber with his minions he flew into his famous rages and declaimed upon his authority, his royal lineage, his prowess in love and in war. See, we whispered, the sun has set on them, these little three-copper sovereigns. Now even the *khidmatgars* do not bow quite so low when, earlier, a mere frown could set them ashiver like the twin minarets of Siddee Bashir.

'Do you know the ravenous rage of a king who is losing his kingdom, be it ever so petty? Or the power and the poison of a woman who has lost her beauty? Or the acrid lasciviousness of a man who has lost his manhood? For true, it was whispered, he was now no more a man, yet he did seek out the youngest, most delectable of maids, so subtle and strong was his lust, so deep his insight into the secrets and nuances of love. Such is the drama of decline and loss, Abdul Hamid, for can anything be more wondrous-strange than that which is laboured over with love and with art, that which is so fine and important, that which is cherished, polished and perfected, should perish without fail? And the mad *pir*, he that was ever loudly mediating betwixt God and the Devil, sang riotously beneath the banyan tree: "Dry, dry, dry, dry the well, hush! The empty pot doth hang upon its noose. And why did he fill a carcass with wine? To cool the street, ha?" And he roared gleefully and brought up the refrain: "He laughs, he laughs, he laughs, he laughs!" And no one dared ask him who laughed, God or the Devil or himself or all three, for he flung his wild locks back and piercingly demanded: "Tell me, doth the enchantment lie in the bottle? Why then doth not the bottle swagger and sing?"

'You want to know what happened? Can anything more remarkable have happened to me than that everyone I grew up with is dead? The nawab listened to his thumries. His beard grew darker with more henna, his brow more creased. He lost to those comic, pink-faced sahibs. He found new dancers. There was music for every season, for springtime, for the season of falling leaves, music for the day of lamentation when the procession sallied forth and men smote their breast and walked the fire and wept and wept in an ecstasy of grief. O Hazrat Ali, O noble martyred one, O brave, loyal ones, alas, cheated of all, duped, done to death, treacherously, treacherously, killed, killed! I was one who composed the saddest songs, who wept the most burning tears. It was a skill, God given. Sorrow was with me an art par excellence, elegant, acclaimed, a lavish abstraction. Ah, woe, woe!—wept the men. Alas, alas!—groaned the women. Now with age I have lost that joy in weeping. Sorrow is but sorrow, without exaltation, without cure. The nawab in his balcony sat moist-eyed, till the season of mourning was over. One day he died and we musicians dispersed.

'Ah, Abdul Hamid, an old man carries many aches. Many were the gold mohurs I won from rai-bahadurs, khan-sahibs, khan-bahadurs, nawabs even. Courtesans came to me to be tutored in singing. Nobody wants a musician of that kind now, for an age has just died, don't you know? I am my own audience now. When I sing, each note thrills me and with a shock I realize that it has achieved its ultimate shine. It dangles, polished, like a gold mohur I give to myself. Sometimes Rahmatullah, my young nephew, begins laughing. "Bade Mian, your voice is cracked like a split bamboo and can barely hold a tune!" he scoffs.

Nobody asked him to sing but Bade Chacha Imam Bux closed his eyes and sang. A raga, so the classics say, that mourns for a wife of many years. He croaked horribly. At high notes his voice squeaked. Even our Afeera sings better. Ilyas and I counted his dirty teeth. At last he stopped. Ilyas nudged him impatiently. 'But where was the

Evil One, Bade Chacha? And the *pir* with the incantations and amulets and cures?'

'Only a maulvi can tell, child,' sighed Bade Chacha. 'Perhaps not even he.' He raised a feeble hand to his throat. 'My Evil One lurks here,' said he. 'I once heard the maestro Faiyaz Khan say— "When one's art has attained exquisite youth, one's voice is reduced to a wretched ruin because seldom the twain do meet."'

MAJOR EVENT

For the first time in years, Vasant Panchami had fallen not only on 31 January but on a Tuesday as well, announced Badal Kaka. We all roared and thumped grandfather on the back. And when grandmother opened her mouth to speak Shubho popped a sondesh into her mouth.

'Fifty years of marriage, grandfather, and to such a spitfire, heavens!' gasped Probhat Kaka, putting an arm affectionately around grandmother's shoulder.

'But I dealt with her, ah yes,' chuckled the deaf old man, shouting fit to raise the dead.

'So we perceive, Baba,' said Bimol Kaka with a wicked grin and a wink at all of us. 'There's the eight of us standing evidence of how well you dealt with her.'

'Hush, you rascal,' hissed Aunt Bithika, pulling Bimol's ear. 'Take no notice of this young scapegrace, Baba. Times are different now.'

'No different!' roared grandfather, mishearing again. 'It was Saraswati puja day and no different.'

In those days we lived in a distant suburb of Calcutta which lay within the 24 Parganas. The vast city hummed in the background but where we lived the sea-breeze came thrashing in, bending the palm trees low. All the shadows which stood still in the green ponds went sliding across the mirror-dark water. And in the twisting lanes a dark young woman went balancing her pitcher with a plaintive melody of Bengal on her lips:

> Tree like I catch my fingers in your clouds.
> Undo these bones, unfasten these thoughts,
> For my heart is full; ah, do not touch me, lord,
> Lest a shock of tears shakes out of me . . .

The areca nut trees thrummed their dry green leaves like taut, vibrating strings under the chilly wash of wind.

Do you know what Saraswati puja day meant to us in those days? We awoke and saw the pale fumes of light collected in a corner of the sky. For half an hour the day seemed dazed by that dazzling fuzz of light and the morning was a shimmering fabric blown across the land. Then a sharp, crisp sunlight came and thawed the masses of cloud. Out in the open in the little tents, the slim white goddess sat on her swan, her long fingers curled upon a celestial raga. Little girls and boys, clad in yellow, learnt their first alphabets at the feet of the goddess and the bare-chested old priest lifted aloft the bowl of smoking incense. On such a day there was music everywhere.

And on that Saraswati puja day the eight sons and daughters, the sons-in-law and daughters-in-law and we nineteen grandchildren assembled to celebrate the golden jubilee of our grandparents' marriage. Nobody enjoyed the pantomime more than the old couple themselves. Grandfather sat on the old canopied four-poster dressed in his crinkled white dhoti and white *panjabi* with gold studs, eating sweet rice paste. And Aunt Bithika draped her rich Benarasi silk round grandmother's portly form, laughing at her protests. The treasure box was unlocked, the gold peacock pendant hung round grandmother's neck and the heavy bangles forced into her dried-up wrists. Then young Mita ran and fetched the blue gauze veil from her dance costume, never mind if it did not match. And Aunt Minoti rubbed sandal paste and drew a pretty ceremonial pattern on grandfather's creased forehead. Grandmother scolded and laughed in confusion, hustled about by the crowd of rollicking youngsters. Nobody listened to her. But grandfather sat with a twinkle in his eye, his hearing aid plugged into his ear. Only the headgear was missing. And Probhat Kaka ran and got down the dusty white, conical *topor* and matching coronet from the kitchen loft, left over from Bithika's wedding.

'A little crooked, but it'll do,' he said, blowing on it as he placed it carefully on grandfather's bald head. A roar of cheers and laughter went up. Somebody produced a marigold garland. Somebody thrust a box of sacred vermilion powder into grandmother's hands. Somebody blew on the conch and in unison, rolling their tongues in their mouths, the women burst into the shrill *uloodhvani*, laughing. Sondesh was passed round and even the two dogs got one each. 'Camera!' shouted Badal and old Mr Roy, our neighbour, appeared with the battered box camera.

'Not so far apart!' he shouted. 'A little closer, a little coy, now smile.'

And the old man put his arm around grandmother's shoulder.

'That's the spirit!' cried young Mita, clapping. 'Now another one.'

Little Sumana wanted to sit in the middle, near grandfather.

'Hush, child, people will get confused as to who the real bride is. They'll think Sumana has married an ugly old man.'

'Ho, grandmother, don't let him hear you!'

She smiled, her mottled face puckering up in impish glee.

'He can't. That's the fun of having a stone-deaf husband.'

'Speech! Speech!'

By a miracle the old man heard. 'Why do you shout, young fools? Nineteen twenty-two!' he roared. 'I drew my salary from the British exchequer,' he glared round importantly.

'Stop him,' someone groaned, '—before he launches into Burke's speech at the trial of Warren Hastings again.'

'Our Collector sahib said at a wedding, "Marriages are made in heaven."'

'And broken on earth, Baba?' piped up Mithu. The aunts shushed him and he subsided.

'Marriages,' continued the old man pompously, '—are made in heaven.' We asked our Collector-sahib, "What, Sir, is the secret of your happy marriage?" "Listen, gentlemen," he replied. "I shall let you in on a secret. On our wedding day we decided, memsahib and I, that all major events were to be in my charge and all minor events in her charge. The secret, gentlemen, is that not a single major event has occurred in our life!"'

A commotion of merriment filled the room. 'In my own case I have been, alas, in the same unenviable situation as our revered Collector-sahib. Not a single major event has occurred in my life.'

Shibu Kaka rolled his eyes at his brothers. 'Well, here we are anyway, baba, your eight minor events!' And everyone rocked with laughter, grandmother loudest.

'Marriage,' said the old man, '—is the everlasting companionship, the imperishable tie. Whom god hath joined together none can draw asunder.'

'Oh, oh . . .' said someone faintly.

Grandfather went off into a long rumbling Sanskrit passage. 'Amid the most transient things,' he translated, '—a happy marriage is proof of the permanent. On this day we thank you, my wife and I, for being present and celebrating this day with us. Thank you.' And he looked grave and sombre, quite edified by his speech.

That Saraswati puja day is vivid in my mind. Its pellucid laughter throws into bold relief the stark drama of the following day.

In the grey light of dawn Aunt Bithika went slowly up the dark staircase with a mug of tea and softly pushed open grandfather's door.

'Your tea, Baba.' The old man slept with his back to the door. By his pillow lay his string of prayer beads and a closed book. 'Baba,' called Bithika and then a strange terror leapt into her voice. She swiftly crossed the room. The old man lay with his eyes wide open, staring in amazement at the far corner of the room.

She shook him and shook him, then ran calling 'Badal, Badal!' down the stairs. Her husband stirred in his bed. 'Badal, come! Baba!' She burst into the room.

They stood by the old man and Badal closed the eyes with trembling hands. 'All that excitement yesterday . . .' he murmured. He looked up at his wife. 'Let us wake them up . . . tell them baba's major event has occurred at last . . .'

'Oh, Badal . . . Ma! How shall we tell her?' And they thought of grandmother asleep peacefully downstairs, an arm round the youngest grandchild, rising and falling gently with the child's living breath.

Bithika looked at her husband and clutched him by the shoulders as though assuring herself that he was there with her. And as they gazed at the old man, then at one another, the first terrible tears began shining in their eyes.

SONG OF INNOCENCE AND EXPERIENCE

Fifteenth of August is the day of flags and a fortnight later is God's birthday—both holidays and no lessons to recite, no tests, no homework, for fancy doing sums on God's birthday!

So Bittu and his friends spent the morning sprawled upon the floor with their Camel paints and brushes, dabbing large sheets of paper with saffron and white and green, throwing in the blue-spoked Ashoka wheel in the middle, plastering one end with glue and sticking it fast to long brown sticks stolen out of Dularibua's coconut broomstick. Five big, beautiful flags to hang outside the balcony or wave at passers-by, accompanied by joyous cries of 'Vande Mataram!' as those men on TV do. And, when Dularibua comes mopping the floor and sends you fleeing for life onto the terrace at the back of the house, you can line yourselves up, four-abreast, and one leader ahead, and snap out crisp, military orders, your face a stern unyielding mask, and march up and down the terrace, left and right, left and right and round and round and round. But, everyone wants to be leader so the flags go crashing down, forgotten, and what began as a dignified and glorious military parade ends as a free-for-all with punched noses and scraped knees and blubbering voices.

'What now?' laughs Mother, mopping the tear-streaked face. 'So they wouldn't make you General, the bad ones?' She combs the shock of hair out of his eyes. 'Never mind, never mind, there's custard and jelly after lunch today and a nice film for you. But do look at your poor flags, all torn and crumpled in the dustbin! And all that morning's hard work, painting them and pasting them up.'

'Aw,' grimaces Bittu. 'I'm sick of them.' Who on earth could play with a rotten old flag all day!

They are assembled upon the balcony now, Mother and Father and the shrill, blousy aunt and the slow, stylish, scary aunt and the two uncles from Delhi, all upon their cane chairs and the trolley going round, the tea circulating, the knitting needles, the cards! A few boats drifted lazily on the surface of the green lake beneath and across the giant boulder towered, gloomy, disinterested, into the clouds. Nainital had few tourists this year, remarked the aunts. The rains have been heavy, remarked Mother. Nainital was sinking, announced one of the uncles and Bittu held his breath. How very thrilling? And, when was it going to be swallowed up into the bowels of the earth?—he was impatient to ask. He couldn't wait for it to happen. The fifteenth of August is a jolly holiday with wonderful inspiring songs in the air, flags in the windows, special pakodas on the balcony. And, the stylish aunt came dressed in a saree that everybody exclaimed over, though Bittu didn't know what was special. 'It's made with thread that Nana spun in jail,' explained mother. Bittu is horrified. Nana in jail. Lurid visions of Nana as a criminal, race about in his head. His respect for Nana grows. 'Why was Nana in jail?' He tugs at his Mother's saree. But the fat aunt is lamenting: 'Fancy, someone stole our water pump this morning. We were out on our walk. We returned and my God!—it was gone! So, there's an acute water shortage at our place today . . . ! Bittu's attention had wandered from Nana as a jail-bird to the tea trolley. That trolley could be used to ride on, couldn't it? Perhaps harnessed to the dog and let loose upon the terrace. What an absolute winner! One could be an Eskimo any time one liked. Some day when the family was asleep in the afternoon . . .

'But won't you show Nana your lovely new flags?'

'They're torn.'

'Never mind. He'll love them, I promise.' They all laugh. 'His poor old brain, Anoop. That freedom-fighter's allowance won't even pay for his pills and tests now. But a flag may still bring back the roses in his cheeks!'

'Medicines have suddenly shot up in the market. Twenty-two rupees a pill—that's what I was on. And, there's no knowing if they're fake or genuine.'

In his old deck-chair beside the shuttered window slept the old one, slumped over like a slack old garment.

'Nana, I made a flag today.'

'Eh?' The old one opened his watery eyes and gazed uncomprehendingly at the four-year-old and the piece of coloured paper, torn and muddy, in his hands. Then, he turned away with a snort which may have signified indignation or weariness or sheer lack of interest.

And, meanwhile there is God's birthday on the twenty-sixth to be celebrated with another holiday. Oh, to be born in a jail and out of a cucumber! Bittu's fascination with jails has grown ever since he learnt of Nana's jail stay. And God himself, he now learns, was born in a jail. How wonderful! There's a little argument with the madam in school who insists that God was born in a stable but one cannot take everything she utters seriously. What is certain is that God seems to like sheep and cows and cowherds. Why wasn't he, Bittu, born in prison and out of a cool, green cucumber? The river in full flood outside, the tyrant king, the sentries, all spellbound in slumber, the gates of the prison falling open, one by one, *clang, clang*, just like that. To lie in a basket and have Father carry me across the wild river with a huge horrible black snake opening its hood upon my head like a vast, curly umbrella. Then to grow up eating butter, playing pranks and dancing with pretty ladies. How lovely! Does this God have a cake like mine on his birthday, Mother?

'Why, nobody said he couldn't. I'm sure he'd love it,' says she with a smile. 'But you see, child, we don't eat eggs on holy days so I can't bake you one today.'

'I want a cake!'

'This is an Indian god, child. Why not make him an Indian cake? Set some halwa in a box? I can even put beads on it and flowery icing. You can even put candles or tiny deepaks around it and get God to cut it for you after the arti, no? You can even sing him a nice birthday song.'

'When we were kids, Bittu beta, we made lovely toy villages on the floor, yes, the jail and the Jamuna, the serpent and the groves, swings, milk maids, cow sheds, ponds, kadamba trees, all Vrindavan upon the floor.'

'Wait, Mother, can't you make a halwa-cake with Vrindavan upon it?'

'It'll be tough but I can try. I'll have to spread it out on a large tray.' Mother is quite taken up with the thought. This is Janamashtami with a difference! Just suppose it worked out and its photograph appeared in her Ladies' Club journal. What a stir it would make. A modern Janamashtami with deepaks lit all around.

'How many candles, that is the question?' she brooded.

'How old is God today, Mother?'

'But he's just been born, Bittu beta.'

'He was born last year too.'

'Each birthday we are born,' declared Father didactically.

But, that scarcely solved the essential question. 'Your God obviously is as old as you are,' said Father. That brought one back to the primary enquiry. The ignominy, the enormity of that pain. 'This child here hasn't got a birthday!' cried the urchins at school.

'I do!' he had cried in shame and in fury, his eyes smarting with angry tears.

'Oh, naw, you don't. Last year you brought sweets on the twenty-eighth of February, and this year it was the first of March. You're lying!'

'I'm not.'

'If you ask me, you haven't got a birthday at all! You're just pretending.'

That your face should swell with crying and flame a furious beetroot, that you should become the centre of such an immense tragedy for no fault of yours, that you should be condemned to be always, always different, solitary and apart from humankind, frail, lonely and exiled. Why me?—you ask a dozen times. Maybe, the ugly thought occurs to you for the first time, maybe I wasn't born at all and ah, how terrible that would be, and now everybody suspects and some know. 'Mother, why wasn't I born?' asks Bittu, tense and tragic.

'What now?' exclaims she. And when she hears it all, all that she and Father do (and those detested aunts and uncles and the entire neighbourhood), is laugh, laugh and laugh and repeat the shameful story over and over again. Calendars are brought out and many complex explanations made.

'Your real birthday came when you were born. Believe me, child, you were born like all your friends, only it was on a rare and valuable day. So it comes once in four years, for you are a rare and valuable child. The next birthday shall come when you are five, that's next year, and then when you're nine. The twenty-ninth of February is a great day, you know. Not everyone can be born on that day . . .'

And, a lot more in that sugary voice to the same effect. It's that sugary voice that renders it all suspect. 'Every fourth year Bittu shall have not one birthday but two,'—the elders decide by common consensus. But, nothing, nothing can make up for that shameful secret one nurses. A grave barrier lies between Bittu and all other people. They are aware of his problem. One fake birthday they took him to Agra to see the Taj Mahal. In the dark vault one naturally produced one's new toy car and raced it across the king's grave where they said he was still sleeping, and the old guide was so cross!

'Nana, do you have a birthday too?' Bittu posed the anxious question. The old man grinned in languid merriment. He sometimes did seem to understand when Bittu spoke. He shook his head slowly.

'No?' asks Bittu, edging closer to him. 'You, too, don't have one? Nana, how old are you?' All that the old one did was smile and rock and wag his large head and roll his musty eyes.

'Nana is ninety years old,' said Mother, coming in. 'But, he doesn't know it any more.'

'And I,' calculated Bittu, 'am either four years old or else just one. With only one real birthday so far, how can I be four?'

This question never found an answer. It's made Bittu sit alone in corners. It's made him stand on the tips of his toes before the window, watching other children play, scorning their society and playing games alone, saying boo to his shadow, chasing himself around and round the house, divided into two, he one and himself the other. And that Holi when the colony rang out with shouts and squeals and the walls turned rainbow splattered, then all he did was plunge his hands into his mother's red vermilion powder and angrily smear his own face with it.

'Oh-ho-ho-ho!' appeared the old crone Dularibua with her ladle. 'Wait till your Ma sees you. Turning yourself into a goblin! Just you come and wash up.'

But before she could come and grab him he is off, dodging this way and that, under the table and behind the bedstead and out of the room and into Nana's and the door safely slammed behind him!

And Nana turns his sleepy eyes upon his hobgoblin face, incredulous, fascinated, then his collapsed jaws part in a wide, silent, toothless laugh. He shakes and shakes and his laughter is endless, tremendous. He can't ask why but Bittu tells him why:

'I was playing Holi with myself, Nana. I have no friends now.' Hugging him, he leaves his parched face looking like a goblin's too and he laughs more and more until a loud rapping on the door frightens both of them out of their mirth. Timorously Bittu unbolts the door, expecting the worst and heroically resigned thereunto. But, when Father enters and sees them, he explodes into his huge, huge laugh, calls out to Mother, the aunts, the servant. And, besieged and blessed by all, a mirror is held up, a camera appears out of the cupboard and a blinding flash goes off in their faces.

'And now, off with your clothes!' says Mother, laughing. 'The siren's just begun wailing and its bathing time now. Come, let's clean you up, there's a good boy.'

Off with my shirt! Off with my shorts! (Shame, shame!) Off with my boots, off with my vest, off with my socks! There comes that flash of illumination—a brand new possibility! He is firm, stubborn. 'Take off my feet too,' he insists and sits down on the floor.

Mother is exasperated now and her eyes snap dangerously as they always do before he is dealt a resounding slap. But, he is fixed and unbending. She coaxes: 'It can't be done, child. See, Papa and I, have you ever seen us with our feet off?'

'I've seen you with your shorties off. But, why don't you take your feet off too?'

Mother looks too confused and embarrassed. 'You can't just put yourself on and pull yourself off, child,' she says angrily.

'Why not?'

'Bittu!' There is now peril in the air. Vanquished and undressed, he is led off to his bath. But, the idea must be discussed with Nana when they two are alone.

'Nana, I'd love to take off both my feet.'

His watery eyes, his drooling mouth draw together in sudden intelligent unity and he chortles, extending a stick-like arm feebly to his cropped hair.

'My hands too. I'd hang them up on the peg. Then maybe my shoulders and my stomach. They'd have to go on hangers into the wardrobe like the clothes Dularibua irons out.'

Oh, he understands perfectly what is meant. 'And then,' he brooded tensely, 'I'd run away and they would never find me. They'd shout and shout, what fun!'

There exists between the two of them such natural fellowship and such burning rivalry. When Bittu got a smaller bowl of kheer he minded very much and there took place many sulks, many truces.

'Look, Nana,' he says excitedly, 'I've made rain!' And he dabs milk out of the glass in pretty round droplets upon the floor with the spoon. 'White rain. Now you do the same.' So they play all afternoon, alone, while everybody is away and the old ogress Dularibua snores upon the mat, until the clock sings out upon the wall and strikes four times and the old fiend awakes with an oath.

That clock is far better than all the toys put together. No circling helicopter or dancing bear can ever match it. It mutters on like a chirping cricket, *kit-kat, kit-kat,* all the slow afternoon through and then, without warning, it clears its throat, churrs, swells and then bursts into peal after peal of shrill squeals. And, one day after listening intently to its squeals, Nana signals to Bittu and points to the wall. It's what Bittu wants to do too—investigate, once and for all, that intriguing toy. So, he pulls a chair, scrambles upon the cabinet and carefully, very carefully, brings it down and sets it on Nana's knee. Together they study it in delight. Nana, it was evident to Bittu, had never learnt to count but Bittu had and he strokes the golden numbers and recites them aloud, feels the two unequal whiskers and puts his ear to the *kit-kat,* muttering. It wouldn't chime when they wanted it to. They shook it and slapped it but it would neither sing nor strike and then the old demon on the mat awoke and descended upon them and snatched it away, their curiosity unrequited. 'You! Cursed be this half wit and cursed be this brat—they'll drive me crazy between them!'

'But, Dularibua dear,' says Bittu in honeyed tones, '—why won't it strike and sing?'

The monster hung it back upon the wall. 'It will when it wants.' was the grim rejoinder.

'Why won't it sing when we want it to?' persists Bittu.

'Patience,' says the crone. 'It can't because it can't.'

'Why?'

'A clock won't strike, a baby won't get born and a man won't die before its time, Baba,' expounded the old hag discursively.

'But, I want to hear it sing now,' Bittu insists pitifully.

'There's nothing for it, Baba, you'll have to wait.'

'Another question,' continues Bittu gravely. 'Does eight o'clock in the morning and eight o'clock in the evening mean the same thing?'

The monster now clutches her head, clenches her fists and batters her forehead with them. 'Drat this boy and his questions!' she shouts, 'Be off now and none of your chatter!'

Nana and Bittu hated her so much, so much for her speeches, her smacks, her stern supervision of meals, her commands to go to sleep or to wake up and wash the face. No mutiny against her ever worked. Bittu felt burning hate smouldering in his heart. Oh, he could bite her, box her ears and kick her in the tummy when she slapped Nana the day he pissed in his chair. The piss collected in a big pool under the chair and Nana looked this way and that and his eyes grew disconcerted and his mouth fell open in surprise and the monster swept down from the kitchen and swore and scolded and slapped him in a rage and Nana hung his big head and cried, and Bittu hid behind the door and cried and wished she'd eat snails! She always slapped Bittu when he used to piss in his clothes and now she was doing it with Nana too. Bittu hugged Nana as he shivered in the dusk and the two of them hid silently from the world in shame until Mother returned home but nobody said a word.

But, Bittu is worried about Nana now after that incident. Especially when they tell Bittu that he is now to go to a big school. There is to be a test and so his hair is combed and his shoes are polished. 'There'll be a tall man in a long white gown and he'll ask you things. He may have a very loud and scary voice but don't be frightened. He'll speak to you in simple words. Answer him. If you don't know, say so.' All this, Father spoke down from several miles above Bittu's head. That's how it goes. 'How many fingers do I hold up here?' asks the white-clad wizard. And Bittu shakes and manages to mutter—'Four.' And the apparition booms 'Good.' And, now Bittu goes to a big school and gets sums to work out and things to write out. He sits beside Nana in the afternoons, writing away. Nana for his part strives to write his own name on a shred of paper and keeps getting it wrong and laughs slowly in those long-drawn, secret laughs that seem to give him so much pleasure. The monster sits muttering, counting piles of coins upon the mat.

'What are these for?' asks Bittu seriously.

'To buy sweets,' says she archly. 'Don't you wish you had some to buy toffees with and "logense" and "chaaklayt"?'

'Pooh!' spurns Bittu, scornful. 'I don't need to buy sweets.'

'Oh, yes?' asks she tauntingly. 'And where is the tree which grows sweets for you, baba? Not in our garden for sure.'

'Uncle Shiv brings them for me,' answers Bittu loftily as one who has friends in high places.

'Oho!' says the crone, flashing massive gapped teeth.

'Yes. Sometimes there are four, sometimes six. I find them near my pillow. Sometimes gems and five stars too.'

'Oho!' barks the crone again and a nasty look creeps into her brown face.

'When I'm falling asleep I say loudly: "Uncle Shiv, bring me four lollies tonight." And he always does. Mother says he comes riding a bull. She often makes coffee for him in the dead of night'

'That she does,' mutters the nasty old hag. 'But, what's this about the bull? He comes in a red Maruti and always when your Papa is away in Delhi.'

'Yes,' says Bittu calmly. 'He comes to protect us from harm when Papa is away.'

'Oh, Shiva protect this child!' exclaims the hag. 'Oh, God have pity on him!'

'Why haven't you seen him, Dularibua? Look, I'll draw him for you.'

'Oh, oh,' says Dularibua, rocking herself, half in malice and half in piety. Superstitiously she breaks into a cracked song in her raucous village voice: 'He has a blue face. He has the river in his locks. He has the moon, the young moon, asitting upon his temple, and a trident in his hand and the serpent about his blue, blue throat . . .'

'Look, here is the bull,' Bittu held up a sheet. 'He dresses only in tiger skin. Mother says he powders his face with ash. The bull likes coffee too.'

Nana loved to doodle with a pencil too, so he often amuses Bittu with his lovely elephants and horses. Bittu kneels beside his chair and puts his pencil in his hand and the drawing upon his knee. And Nana suddenly, carefully, draws a loop in Shiva's hand, like a lasso, and colours the white bull black and gives it huge, huge horns and draws out a long, long tail.

'Oh, oh!' cried Dularibua in a frightened voice, '—Bade Sahibji, you are still wise though you have lost all your thoughts. Oh, God have mercy on us all, the Goddess have mercy, the God of Death shall not come yet for you, master, may you live a thousand years!'

'Who?' persists Bittu.

'Get out!' she barks. 'You'll find a sweet under your pillow, but please get out now.'

'Two sweets,' bargains Bittu shrewdly.

'Out!' shrieks the crone and Bittu dodges out in the nick of time. Only to bounce back in a frenzy of excitement: 'Look, Dularibua, look outside the window! Look at these two dogs. Someone's tied their tails together and they can't get away now! Look, Nana! Come out, come out!' And dragged her out to see the strange sight.

'It's two dogs, Nana. They can't get away from one another—someone's tied their tails together—!' And throwing open the window, pointing out the quaint spectacle to Nana who must not miss it for anything in the world.

Dularibua's coffee-coloured skin cannot possibly go red but her scowl is fearful to behold. And Nana's great, slack mouth falls open and closes, opens and closes, and his eyes get shaded and, neck craned, he peers out of the latticed window in perplexity. Then he turns away and there is a tic in his jaw and his brows are working fiercely in a terrifying frown, the ragged, beetling brows contorting upon his parched forehead. Dularibua shuts the window, muttering. To Bittu a brand new query has suggested itself : 'Why are dogs naked, Nana? I mean, why don't they wear clothes like the rest of us?'

There were many, many questions. To lie awake, lost in thought, is usual with Bittu; to sit up till midnight, as the gate jangles and the doorbell tinkles faintly, and wonder if Shiva actually came in a red Maruti or on the old faithful bull is the occupation of an hour. Footsteps race down the corridor and it is prudent to shut the eyes fast and draw the sheet over the head and wait with baited breath for the tiger-clad, moon-bearing one to arrive. God puts man to sleep while he goes about his business, this Bittu knows well.

He awakes to find himself in the middle of a still, warm day, the sunlight floating in and lots of motes of dust smoking about in the broad beams that cut across the air, crickets chirping in the garden and only one measly toffee underneath his pillow. Of all the unspeakable, niggardly things.

'But I asked him for six and he only gave me one,' frets Bittu, outraged.

The house feels odd. The aunts, mother, nobody in sight. Father sits with a neighbour, a little folded and grim upon the balcony.

'Who?' intoned he.

'Uncle Shiva. I found only one sweet under my pillow and I asked him for six. He comes on a bull and sometimes in a red Maruti.'

Father raises his eyebrows. 'I'm sure I don't know what you're talking about. Nobody put any sweets under your pillow last night.'

'He did,' Bittu persists. 'See here.'

'It must be the old witch,' mutters Father to his friend in an undertone. 'Must have made it off the milk.'

'But why only one when I asked for six?'

'Oh, shut up. I've been up all night,' growled Father. That's when, looking about, Bittu vaguely notices that Nana's chair is empty.

There is no school today, as it happens. Two big white vans curve up the drive and all the doors in the world seem to slam at once. There are cars and cars. The neighbours begin pouring in, yes, even the nasty boy's parents, and everyone sits quietly here and there.

The big bundle turns out to be Nana. They don't bring him into the house. They put him on the floor in the porch. They take off his dhoti (shame, shame!). And nobody laughs. Nana seems to have dirtied his dhoti but nobody scolds. He sleeps through it all as Bittu does when he wets his bed and his pyjamas are changed in the night. Bittu wonders if Nana will take off his hands, take off his feet, take off his shoulders, his stomach and his hair and then run away, and nobody would be able to catch him . . . Bittu experiences a pang of jealousy at all this attention Nana is getting. 'If only I could have a few of those roses they are covering him up with. It must be lovely to lie beneath roses, but nobody will give me any.' Bittu steals a few and pockets them until he is spotted and chased away.

There is actually nothing to do except sit brooding quietly in front of the TV while Mother and Father and the aunts sit with sullen faces and the old ogress walks around with horrible bulbous, streaming eyes.

'Father couldn't think at all towards the end.' Mother is saying with her eyes fixed on the floor. 'But when our Mother was alive she specially desired you to have her old sarees as a token of her forgiveness. I remember her saying you should have received some of them thirty years ago but there was all that anger then. It's never too late. Now that he is gone, I guess all that is over and I feel I must honour her wishes.'

And the fat aunt bursts into funny hissing sobs and croaks: 'To think of it, to think of it! She gives me sarees I'm too old to wear, sarees too old to be worn!'

'The rocking chair is for you.' Mother tells the aunt who smells like a flower pot. 'Do you remember this chair? Every morning before he left for court, he sat, rocking in it and smoking, a fine man then. It is the chair Nehru sat on when he was here on a visit. I've heard Father say.' Mother sobs quietly. But the flower pot protests. 'What I'd really fancy is that porcelain collection that Ma brought in her dowry in 1914. There was a tiny Napoleon, I recall, and a little Pickwick. I rather hoped . . . I mean, I really appreciate such things and they cost a pile and they're only lying in a trunk here.'

'I'm sorry,' says Mother. 'But our Mother specifically left them for Bittu's little wife, when she comes. It is to be our Mother's gift to her granddaughter-in-law.'

The flower pot tinkles out a nasty laugh. 'If they manage to last that long, you mean. There were also some old teak cabinets Father had made and I'm sure you wouldn't mind . . .'

That's when Bittu spoke up, grave and decisive. 'What I want to know is where's Nana gone?'

They turned to him, shocked. Then Mother recovered and said: 'Nana has now gone to a bigger school. We got him admitted.' Bittu subsides but a fresh train of thoughts overwhelms the brain. 'Must have had a test too. Like, "How many fingers do I hold up here?" I wonder if he was afraid of the Father in the long white gown. And just suppose he didn't know the answers? Now he'll go to a big school and do new sums and write new words.'

'But why,' spoke he aloud, 'doesn't he come home in the evenings?'

'It's a boarding school,' said Father gravely.

Bittu stared at him sceptically. 'Oh, you mean he's dead,' said he nonchalantly. Everyone stopped speaking at once while he continued to worry his little car this way and that on the floor.

'How do you know?' asked Father.

Bittu shrugged. 'I know,' was all he said mysteriously.

And, the old hag shook her huge head at Mother and said in her rustic tongue: 'Ah, Babuji, how does a child grow wise and know everything inside his head, and how does a man grow old and die, only the God above knows for sure!'

A GIFT FOR PRINCE CHARLES

He is marrying at last, the goddess be praised! They ought to have found a suitable girl for him long ago. But no, he was always too choosy. Girls came, girls went. He was not to be trusted, the philanderer!

Hush, what do you know of it? Girls these days are very calculating. Hard as nails. And he was such a good catch. Little wonder, then, that he had to pick and choose carefully.

So we sat on the wattle mat through the dark, humid evening. Mother waved her palm-fan in the air. The lantern burned, throwing huddled shadows on the wall. Mohini and Mitali, those inseparables, sat together, whispering and giggling against the wall, and Shonali, the odd one out, the angry one, the perverse one, sat opposite, disagreeing with everyone. Often Aunt Maya and her daughter, Sneho, would stroll across the lane and join us. Sometimes the old ladies, who sang prayer songs next door, grew weary of the Lord's name and dropped in for a bit of reviving gossip. There was so much to narrate and so much to speculate on—jobs, marriages, rumours, shops. The mosquitoes hummed. The breeze came in, faintly rancid from the gutter. Outside among the thin palm fronds a cluster of stars clung together in a black, steamy sky. That summer the power cuts often lasted ten hours at a time. Sweat beaded our faces. Eight o'clock and our father, Prafulya Dutta still hadn't returned from office.

Shonali banged her knuckles on the floor in a passion of rage. I hate it! I hate it! I hate this city! I shall not live in it any more! There was a burst of laughter. Where will you go, my little hussy? A Calcuttan cannot breathe the air of lesser cities. Or maybe a Prince will marry our Shonali and take her away to London, sisters. A

150

Prince with a long face like a horse's and thirty years old too.

He does not look like a horse! And what is thirty years?

Father was forty-two when he married Ma—and she only fifteen years old.

Do you know, sister Maya, he is marrying at last. We were just talking about it when you came in. My son, Shubroto, read it out to us from the *Amrit Bazaar Patrika*.

And, who is he marrying this time? Aunt Maya was satiric, disbelieving. There they marry many times. One of their kings married six times . . .

This is his very first marriage, aunt. A girl of nineteen, the daughter of a lord. Her name is Diana.

Aunt Maya frowns. Not so grand sounding as Bhictoria, no? Is she of Bhictoria's kin?

Her parents are divorced. Her mother has a new husband, announced Shonali who loved uttering things like that for the joy of teasing the old ones.

Aunt Maya's hearing isn't all it should be. Bhictoria a new husband? Nonsense, she looks so old and fat, sitting on her marble throne outside the Bhictoria Memorial. And besides, she's dead.

She is not Bhictoria's daughter, Aunt. You have it all mixed up. But, she is the daughter of an aristocrat.

All the old ladies nodded. This they understood perfectly. Brahmin must marry Brahmin. We upper castes have our rules to uphold. Why, fifty years ago in Kulti, if a Brahmin was so much as seen buying garlic or onions at the marketplace, everybody pointed fingers at him and ten years later nobody came for his son's thread ceremony or his daughter's marriage or his mother's thirteen-day death-feast. No, not till he had shaved his head and done penance and publicly begged pardon of the community did the village forgive him. Once an aristocrat, always an aristocrat.

All over a silly onion!—sneered that Shonali. What did they season their fish with, anyway?

Keep quiet, miss, and don't be impertinent. Now, the landowner, Phatik Chandra's son had a fling with just about every young woman in our village. But when it came to marriage, it was a girl who had five generations of landowners behind her on both sides.

What does he see in her?—mused Mohini. I don't like her hair, said Mitali. I wish she'd part it in the middle and tie it in a knot, perhaps put a circlet of jasmines round it.

She might for the wedding. Collyrium for the eyes and sandalpaste for the forehead.

Mother, you know nothing! There they wear long white frocks when they marry.

But they cover their heads same as we do. I suppose she will give up her job in that nursery school. Daughters-in-law may not work, for what will people say?

I suppose, sister, the invitation shall be in the name of the Queen.

No, the Queen mother is still alive. It will be large and red, gold-embossed, with a tassel of red silk, like the Kidderpore Choudhurys had. With a large white conch on top and the words 'Auspicious Wedding'—and it shall begin 'Om, humbly we beg, our son Charles's sacred conjugal knot tying ceremony has been fixed for the fifteenth day of the month of *sravan* . . .' By the way, has the date been fixed?

It hasn't been announced yet.

Then a dash of turmeric on the envelope. In north India, sister, the family barber carries the invitation card along with a few lumps of turmeric! My brother maintains that for the wedding fish, there's no place to match Farakka across the Bangladesh border.

Postmaster babu, can you help me?

Oh, Prafulya da, is it? Come in, come in. Pray be seated. And how is your colitis? And how is your arthritis? Your daughters? Your wife?

All well, by the grace of God. Postmaster babu, I want to send a present—by post. A wedding present.

Where to? To your home in Krishnanagar?

Er—no. To—to London.

To London! I didn't know you had people there.

I don't. All my people, all my friends, foes, all, all are here in Bengal. I haven't even been to Patna or Banaras or Delhi.

Then, plucking up courage, Prafulya Dutta speaks in a rush: I wish to send a wedding gift to Prince Charles. You know, the son of the Queen of England.

Postmaster Das Gupta looked at Prafulya Dutta as though he thought him unhinged. His dark lips twitched and his eyes shone gleefully.

And what, dada, do you propose to send? A box of kumkum powder and a white shell bangle?

Prafulya Dutta shook his head. I know old Kalyan Haldar well. Surely you have heard of him, brother. The same Kalyan Haldar who can inscribe a grain of Burdwan rice with the most intricate, the most microscopic Bengali calligraphy. A single grain of rice.

Postmaster Das Gupta's face broke into a grin. His large, yellow teeth flashed. Say, dada, and what would the sahib-log there do with your grain of rice? Cook it for the wedding banquet and belch heartily afterwards as Lord Krishna did?

Prafulya Dutta, annoyed, searched for the right words in which to express the fineness of his feelings.

A gesture—he explained vaguely. Just a matter of sentiment. I shall ask Kalyan to inscribe a beautiful dedication on it. A—a local art, you understand. Bound to be appreciated.

Ah, said Postmaster Das Gupta satirically. Their appreciation means a lot to you still, does it?

I—I feel that I owe it to them, said Prafulya Dutta. Her son's wedding, imagine! Why, it might be my own nephew. She, Elizabeth, the daughter of George the Fifth, whose face adorned my mother's prized golden guineas, granddaughter of Edward the Seventh, great-granddaughter of Maharani Bhictoria, great-great-granddaughter of William the Fourth . . .

All right, all right, interrupted Postmaster Das Gupta in vain.

She, Elizabeth, of the blue sash and the long gloves!—went on Prafulya Dutta in a rapture. When I was young I often thought she looked like one of the little porcelain dolls that sat in my mother's China cabinet. Tell me, Postmaster babu, how shall I send my present by post?

But Prafulya Dutta had not reckoned with his son, Avinash. Avinash was his name but we called him Sarvanash Dutta— Destruction Dutta—so fierce was his rage, so deep his pledge of general devastation. No sooner had word gone round that Prafulya Dutta was planning a grand sentimental gift for the Prince on the occasion of his wedding, than Avinash came storming in, in a fit of rage.

He's done it again!—he shouted. Gone and disgraced me before the whole *para*. Made of me the laughing stock!

Who has, you firebrand?—asked his mother while the sisters nudged one another and giggled.

He has!—raged Destruction, pointing an accusing finger at the old fourposter where Prafulya Dutta sat, bent over his paper. Prafulya Dutta trembled inwardly. His son, Avinash in one of his fits was not a pleasant debating partner.

Stop him, Ma!—shouted the lad. D'you know what he plans to do? Send a grain of rice with a ridiculous message or some such thing all the way to Buckingham Palace to Charles, care of Elizabeth, Queen of England! A wedding present! Hah!

And Avinash sank, speechless with fury, on to the old divan and glowered balefully at his father. Prafulya Dutta lowered his eyes.

Baba, spoke the young man at last. Each escapade of yours is worse than the last. I never knew senility could be this bad.

Enough! said Ma, striding up, our domestic Goddess Protectress. Shame on you for speaking to your father like that!

The young man bristled. D'you know what the boys of the Party said to me, Ma? Can you imagine my position? The son of an imperialist's foot licker! The son of a toady!

Keep quiet! hissed Ma. A lot of airs you Party boys give yourselves, that's what. All you do is paint hammers and sickles on the walls of buildings and beat up law abiding citizens at the football matches.

The boy became sententious. Ma, please. What do you understand of these things? It's no use explaining to you. Haven't you read history? Baba, do listen to me. D'you realize what you're doing? You're sending a grain of our Bengal rice to our former oppressors. And your own mother died in the Bengal famine? A grain of rice to those imperialists! Why, if it weren't for them you'd still be living in Dhaka and a lot better off than you're now. Sentiment, hah!

Oh, go and write a book or stand on a tea chest in the Maidan and shout! declared Ma scornfully. Big words!

I shan't let him do it, said the boy, his face settling into stubborn, childish lines. Not if I've got to lock him in the house for it. I won't have them laughing at me. I shall drop out of the B.A. exam. I shall go down for every morcha and get thrown into jail.

Avinash looked challengingly across the mat at his father. Prafulya Dutta looked away, dejected, and tiredly drew out his snuffbox.

But the boy was loving his rhetoric. Why, in South America, they dashed the brains of little babes against the rocks. And think of the Red Indians massacred in their hundreds, think of the slave traders, the countless Zulus gunned down. In our own land . . .

Prafulya Dutta was partial to stirring speeches himself. He drew himself up and addressed his erring son in stiff Queen's English, the sort that can only be heard now in certain pockets of Bengal. The women paled. English upon the master's lips signified domestic disaster.

Sit down, sir, intoned Prafulya Dutta. It is with insurmountable anguish that I behold the impropriety of your speech and your conduct. Long have I contemplated reprimanding you upon it but I did trust that some natural probity and filial sentiment would prevail upon your unripe judgement.

The boy's lip curled and a dangerous stillness of pent up fury froze his frame. Prafulya Dutta resumed his address: This apostrophe, sir, is to bring home to you my unshakeable resolve to adhere, without further debate, to my original intention of despatching my wedding gift to London, a decision that you, sir, have neither the authority nor the wisdom to call in question . . .

It was a fine speech. When imperialist and comrade match words, there is no poverty of eloquence, for sure. But horror of horrors! Before our very eyes, the lad gave vent to a sort of spasm, a shudder of revulsion, and gods above! rushed upon his old father, grabbed him by the shoulders and shook him and shook him in loud, lunatic passion. Never, never, have we witnessed as shocking a spectacle in our circle. Mother threw herself down upon the pair, shrieking aloud, and the two girls, hysterical, grabbed their brother by the wrist and dragged him away, shouting for shame, for shame!

Nor was that all. The lad's blood was aflame. We say here, to tether a young calf or to pen up a young lad is to provoke the rage of the elements. That Avinash went stark mad and lived up to his nick-name, none in our *para* will ever dispute. For he snatched up the tiny box which held the tiny grain of rice, raced out and hurled it into the still green *pukur* beneath the palm trees like one possessed; raced back like the monsoon whirlwind, caught sight of his father's hookah and aimed at it a furious kick, threw the old string cots acrash across the veranda, stamped upon the platters and the ladles, ran down the steps into the courtyard and viciously, crazily uprooted the old holy tulsi plant, hurling it into the gutter, and finally the worst of all, raced into the prayer place and attacked the sacred shelf, sending Krishna falling askew, and Shiva topsy-turvy, Ganesh asmash, and, for some reason, pocketing the tiny gold Lakshmi, he raced up the steps and through our two rooms and veranda, down, down, down, down the long, dim lane and was gone. Oh, what a revolution broke out in our small home that day! Mother wept loud into her saree fringe, the girls lamented and in his corner old Prafulya Dutta sobbed loudest of all. It is always a great shock to see our elders weep as helplessly as the young. It happens but seldom in a lifetime but it is enough to wipe out that artificial staircase of relationships, norms and forms of respect that are so rigorously maintained in our old families. You may say that something irrevocable happened in our home that day. Never again did Prafulya Dutta's children regard him as an object of veneration and dread. We were, as one in our horror and shock, equal in hurt and classless in our confusion.

We shall never forget that day though Father recovered his dignity and Mother dried her tears and the girls went quietly about their business, picking up the crushed tulsi plant, setting the little gods aright upon the shelf, washing up the trodden platters. But Baba's beautiful inscribed grain of rice—who could recover that from the pond? We did not speak of Avinash though word reached us that he was in north Calcutta. See how a light story has turned into a serious one. That is just what happened in our home. I don't know if we forgave him but I rather think we did, for, after all, Avinash felt more strongly about our poverty than we did and he truly believed in his earnestness, poor lad, that the anger of a few could undo the ways of history and that happiness could always be distributed equally.

Meanwhile we cooked our meals and read our papers. Some things don't ever change in life. The Prince of Wales and Lady Diana Spencer were married at St Paul's Cathedral on 29 July. The photograph on this page shows the couple on their way back to Buckingham Palace after the ceremony . . . Look, Ma, what a strange dress! exclaims Mitali, looking up from the *Amrit Bazaar Patrika*. It sweeps behind her for yards and yards and takes half a dozen people to hold it up. It says—'lace and mother o' pearl' and it cost a fortune. The great west door was thrown open and the principal guests were greeted by the Lord Mayor of London, by the Dean of St Paul's the Very Reverend Alan Webster, the Bishop of London, the Right Reverend Graham Leonard, and the Arch-Bishop of Canterbury, the Most Reverend Robert Runcie . . .

Ah, village elders—observed Ma wisely.

More like pundits, ma—said the enlightened Shonali.

The bride's arrival at the cathedral was greeted by a fanfare by the State Trumpeteers of the Household Cavalry. And . . . and Ma, it says that they followed some new-fangled ceremony and the bride undertook to love and honour but not to obey her husband!

Not to obey? exclaimed Ma, outraged. Not to obey your husband! Not to obey your father, ah, these times were bad and worse times were to come.

That's what it says. And when they left the cathedral, people threw handfuls of rice after them, same as we do. See, here it is, strewing the steps beneath their feet . . . Oh, please, do be quiet; think of Baba, snapped Mohini. And, placing a finger on her lips, she pointed silently at Prafulya Dutta's cot. The old man looked dejected. Bhictoria's kin married and no participation from him, Prafulya Dutta of Krishnanagar.

Last summer our Avinash returned after an absence of nearly nine years. He stole into the room as Mother bent over the vegetables and many tears there were, many embraces and exclamations.

What fine clothes, my lad! What shoes and what slicked down hair! Why, you've even grown these whiskers! Oh, my moon! sobbed Ma, star of my eye, why did you go? Where did you go? Your old father wept and would not eat; look, look at your old father, boy! And Prafulya Dutta drifted in, now retired, carefully supporting his hernia. Oh, that a man must grow old and bear his errant entrails in his hand thus from place to place, afraid that they may slip. That he must go from clinic to clinic, carrying his poor sordid excrement in bottles to be tested, diagnosed and dealt his destiny! Prafulya Dutta was a sick man now and most of all he was sick at heart. Avinash stared and understood all, though he did not speak a word, did not move a muscle.

And now that he actually has a job in a furniture shop, no less, we must get him married, announced Ma. A royal wedding it shall be. Neither the old man spoke his terrifying English, nor did the young man deliver his dogmas. Instead what we all noticed was this new openness between the two, sitting on their charpoys beneath the areca nut tree. Yes, something was rebuilt between the two. It could never be the same again but maybe it was better. So I say to my friends at the tea-shop: when father and son quarrel, do not despair, for something new shall be born of this clash. Why, we even jest over that day of revolution in our family now.

He has two sons now, Father, says Avinash gravely. The old man turns suspicious. Who? he asked guardedly.

Why, Bhictoria's great-great-grandson. Baba. Why not send that gift now?

The old man smiles solemnly. What do you suggest? Some toy hammers and sickles, would that be right?

NOTES AND CHAPTERS

In the introduction to this study we outlined the subject and the scope of this dissertation, viz., the history of five lesser known Oudh havelis that suffered destruction during the upheaval of 1857. In the present chapter it is proposed to take up, for historical investigation, a particular mansion known as Vishnu Kutir, situated in the riot torn zone between Lucknow and Cawnpore and approximately fifteen kilometres south-east of Unnao.

Built circa 1800, Vishnu Kutir formed the home of a family of *taluqdars*. The Virendra Pratap Singhs were ancestral landowners, Rajput in origin. They had settled in Oudh during the reign of Akbar, it is surmised. No reference to the family, however, occurs in any historical manuscript other than their own chronicles, dating before 1800.

The *taluqdars*, as has been earlier elucidated, were a special feature of misgovernment in Oudh during the period in its history as a protected feudatory state with full internal independence that dates from Lord Wellesley's famous treaty of 1801. The *taluqdars* were landowners, in many ways comparable to the barons of medieval England, who, in their fortified strongholds, resisted the officers and chaotic armies of the king and exploited the hapless ryots and the weaker members of their own class. At the end of the 1857 revolt, Lord Canning made an injudicious proclamation declaring the lands of these *taluqdars* forfeit to the British Government, except for the six specifically mentioned. The British Government's intention was, undoubtedly, to restore most of these estates after careful enquiry. But the situation was misunderstood by the *taluqdars* who, in large numbers, renounced their former neutrality and engaged in active guerrilla warfare against the hard pressed British forces. Many of the fortified homesteads associated with this period bear marks of military devastation and Vishnu Kutir is no exception. What confers upon Vishnu Kutir a special significance and human interest is the strangeness of its history and the quixotic character of its Rai Bahadur as is manifest from his memoirs, letters and other obscure documents of the time. Of the five houses under consideration, this one, though the smallest in size, has the distinction of owning a formal, fairly comprehensive chronicle of its history, a feature of no small merit to the interested scholar. Certain mysteries however, persist.

November 28

Spent another day pottering about in VK. I do not know what it is about this place . . . one is absolutely overpowered by the past. Insistent, fanciful scenes enact themselves before the eye. I come here to observe architectural styles and investigate historical spots and all I do is dream. It isn't just a place, its become for me a quality of mind. Everything so deathly still, everything vibrating inwardly. A lofty archway with mouldering lotus and elephant carvings. Two grim lion guardians by the side of the heavy, studded gates. There must be ancient owls upon the eaves. (What is the average life span of owls?) A long, pillared court, then numerous mildewed stairs. Beyond the orchards a ruined Shiva shrine. A tall, dark staircase. Three outer walls have collapsed and two are badly shelled. If one speaks, the words shall swing from wall to wall. If one sings the notes shall go spinning up into the sun-smoking air. Over the twin mango trees, that watch upon the shrine, sequins of sunlight tinker in through the branches. There are thirty-six chambers. I think of the births, the wedding-nights, the death agonies that have occurred beneath this roof of blackened beams. Men have been laid out in death and wedding drums have droned. The cook houses were behind the cow sheds; the walls are still blackened by woodfires. One thinks of copper cauldrons, hookahs, old chests of locked brocades. In the vast yard the grass is almost knee high. There are squirrels and flocks of insolent parrots. There must be snakes. A broken stone bench. This is where I sit, non-participating eyewitness, alien scribe, working dimly to time's dictation.

A cart comes round the shoulder of the hill, stealing along a long red sky. The two old bulls sway their dewlaps, gaze fixedly out from under dusty lashes and their four pairs of hoofs trace a long waddling trail down the arid slope. At the well across the Vishnu Kutir grove the bulls have to be watered. The cartman throws a contemptuous glance at his strange passenger, a woman, veiled and subdued. His faded eyes wear a piercing expression of outrage. In his rusty voice he rasps out a call to the girl at the well, jerking his thumb at the silent woman in his cart. The girl almost drops her pitcher. She stares hard at the woman. Then, recovering, she beckons grudgingly and the woman alights, clutching her bundle.

Munnawwar Bi is shown into one of the dim lower chambers to rest till such time as the lady of the house deems fit to meet her. The decision to invite Munnawwar Bi to share the haveli has taken the inmates by storm. Whoever heard of a Rai Bahadur's widow unabashedly inviting her husband's mistress to share valued property? Munnawwar Bi has aged. Dark, watchful eyes swoop down upon her, devouring every detail. Not beautiful, is the women's verdict. Her face is too frayed. Her eyes come too slowly to life. It is wondered if she too has a share in the late Rai Bahadur's famous will.

It is difficult for a 'native' historian to be in accord with the stance that 'the government in which they (the Company) have borne a part has . . . been . . . one of the purest in intention (and) one of the most beneficent in act ever known among mankind.' (*Report to the General Court of Proprietors*, 1858, p.2.) Howsoever much the sentiment be announced that 'the honourable British Company cannot allow its subjects in the native states to be downtrodden', however loud may be the emphasis upon 'the abuses to which native rule is so fatally liable' it cannot be denied that along with the professed purity of motives there was a real desire for self aggrandizement which, as events establish, came to constitute a great breach of national faith. Speaking of the Doctrine of Lapse, Lord Dalhousie has gone on record as stating: 'The government is bound, in duty as well as in policy, to act on every such occasion with the purest integrity and in the most scrupulous observance of good faith.' (*The Life of The Marquis of Dalhousie*; Sir W. Lee Warner; Vol. ii, p. 116.) Against this protestation we may place the general overriding of native feeling and native susceptibilities which marked every step in his career and which on higher political grounds proved extremely impolitic. Between ideal—and what is more, retrospectively ideal policy—and its enactment, as between act and intent, there is to be found, not only in regard to British practice in India but in relation to most historical reconstructions, a wide breach. An elementary lesson that the student of history learns is that history lies. Events are both less and more than they are accounted to be.

Nor can the impartial critic of the 1857 revolt hold that the event was honourable in execution on the part of the Indian armies as partisan historians would have us believe. That the valiant Rani of Jhansi, who died a soldier's death in her battle with the forces of Sir Hugh Rose in the second phase of the mutiny, had, prior to her gallant combat, massacred every European who fell into her hands, is no secret. That under the guidance of Nana Saheb from his estate in Bithur, innocent Europeans at Cawnpore, who had surrendered on promise of honourable treatment, were subjected to a hideous carnage, is also one of the unsavoury details of the revolt. It is recorded that only four Europeans escaped the massacre and their subsequent fate forms part of the peripheral hypotheses of this dissertation. One hundred and twenty-five women and children were dragged ashore and along with other prisoners, were foully murdered and their bodies flung into the infamous well of Cawnpore. To examine the revolt from an amoral angle is not possible. History witnesses the overthrow of most so-called moral norms and yet historians employ moral yardsticks to judge history. The status of moral ideals in history clearly indicates that many of our values are interpretatory and not substantive. Or that there are, as the Gnostics suggested, two parallel, interwoven worlds and two sets of laws operative in all things, linked but disparate.

November 30

I don't know where this story is taking me. It's leading me as at the end of a leash and I sense my own failure to resist its pull. History has a plot above and beyond our unities. We do not know where our own plots are heading. I am trying to construct in this chapter my own version of an integrated narrative. There are accounts I read, theses I construct and lengthy analytical chapters I churn out.

Out of it all I select what seems to possess truth to my sense, whether it is factual truth or fictional truth. There are notes I jot down, odd significances I notice which hang loose and unrelated but which surely cannot be unmeaningful in some elusive context. There are imaginings I surrender to and surely they are the remnants of some real event which my fancy retrieves from the air. 'Do you know why everything appears incomplete in the world?' asked my teacher and then went on to answer. 'Because this is just a fragment of the real world, maybe half, maybe less. Everything we observe, everything we state or imagine or know is unfinished. We have to look for its corresponding parts intelligently. They've got to be around, here or maybe in some other epoch because time and history aren't linear. You can't plot events out geometrically—an old fallacy.'

The sixteen-mile circuit is overgrown with tall, dense trees. Every four or five miles or so the mood of the landscape alters. Behind a lofty mildewed monument which looks like the gateway to a mosque, lie scattered eleven Muslim graves. The land rises in smooth, green hillocks, then hollows out in gentle undulations to form an extensive mango plantation where still some koels may be heard, most miraculously. And in late spring and early summer, the scent of the white mango blossom pervades the groves. The air is shiny blue and above the bird cries is a crystal sky afloat with sunny breezes. Somebody still tends the Shiva temple. The bells look as though they still ring out. A steep turn of the path makes me step into a miniature English park. There are remains of what must have been a gravel path, rusted iron benches, a broken pavilion, an imitation forest and even what must surely have been a rose garden; and suddenly, surprisingly, a European grave with a black marble tombstone. What amazes me enormously is that there are dry garlands upon the graves, Muslim and Christian alike. On Fridays there is ash from incense sticks and in the grass, wrapping paper and discarded cardboard incense stick cartons. There are silver edged sheets upon the Muslim graves. Somebody comes up from the city of Unnao every week and performs these graceful courtesies to the dead. I track him down after a patient wait. It is an old man in filthy clothes and mud caked sandals and an unexact, simian face. 'Why do you perform this ritual? You, a Hindu? What are these dead ones to you?' 'Nobody,' answers he. 'It is a duty given to me and my family by our masters who lived in the haveli. My father did it and my grandfather before him and I do it now. It is auspicious for us.' What a courtly gesture—wellbefitting the temper of the dead Rai Bahadur. I find much in this chronicle that is fine and sensitive; much that struggles and aspires to be understood. But where are these things ever recorded? Beneath the outer crust of history there is another layer of anonymous events. I wish it were possible to write the history of every creature that ever lived and aspired—there I go again. I really must be severe with myself but this place stimulates such imaginings. There is still so much to do—the Rai Bahadur's chronicles, his diaries, the legend of the will and the country fair, the myths of this derelict old mansion. Three weeks is too little and I must pack two visits to Lucknow in between.

December 1

The Rai Bahadur purportedly left a treasure and set forth its distribution in a legendary will. I am suspicious about this will. Knowing the Rai Bahadur, there's bound to be a catch somewhere. After all, this was the man who constructed a tomb for himself, yes, and he a pure-bred Rajput. He was never buried in that tomb but he had it constructed upon a whim. I do not trust this Rai Bahadur. Everything was a joke and a gesture with him. I have come to recognize his special touch, as it were. That the will is a legend he himself concocted and the fake tomb in the grounds somehow a key to the entire mystery is a hunch I have—a touch of paradox only he was capable of.

'Excellent, Imroze, for that pretty piece of poesy you become master of a hundred gold mohurs. Wait till you see my will.'

'Fair one, for as many bells as tinkle in your ankles, so many pearls will I leave you.'

The late lamented Rai Bahadur Virendra Pratap Singh had a way of promising people a place in his will long before he died. Which was why, as local legend has it, Vishnu Kutir was besieged by numerous hopeful claimants—brothers, half brothers, crazy bewhiskered musicians, stone carvers, courtly punsters and poets, ivory, silver and miniature specialists; ancient nautch girls with waists grown thick and ankles grown lumpy. They came with their rolls of bedding and were given string cots in the vast outer verandas. That was a little after Havelock and Outram's armies, on the famous march from Cawnpore to Lucknow, between 19 and 25 September 1857, shelled the mansion, mortally wounding the Rai Bahadur, who had come under suspicion for his correspondence both with Bahadur Shah Zafar at Delhi and with Nana Saheb at Bithur. There is proof that the dying Rai Bahadur was tended by a British doctor, a Cawnpore fugitive and a guest at Vishnu Kutir long after the Rai Bahadur's death. No sooner had the Rai Bahadur's obsequies been performed than expectant guests began clamouring for the will. It was strange that Rai Bahadur's formidable widow took so long to disclose the contents of the will. It was also strange that a minor riot broke out when, following the disclosures, a futile attempt was made to set the mansion alight, an attempt foiled, so the stories go, by Munnawwar Bi, the Rai Bahadur's erstwhile mistress, who came in response to the widow's summons all the way from riot torn Lucknow. Did Munnawwar Bi's late arrival, what with the chaos of the mutiny and the disturbance on the roads, have any relation to the mystery of the will? Despite all my efforts I have not been able to lay my hands on this mysterious will that so provoked the Rai Bahadur's dependants. My curiosity deepened as I combed the diaries, letters and legends of this place.

It was not until dusk that the mistress of Vishnu Kutir chose to meet her guest. Cool shadows streaked the balustrades when she finally summoned Munnawwar Bi to her chamber. In a little arching niche an oil lamp burned, its thin thread of flame tapering up and stroking the wall with its gold-black tip. Munnawar Bi smiled her watery, uncertain smile and bowed her head in deferential greeting. She saw before her a tall, cleanly carved woman, cold and still, who turned the battery of her powerful eyes upon her. There was a long silence.

'He died,' she spoke at last. Her voice was toneless and she held Munnawwar Bi trapped in her fixed gaze. Munnawwar Bi nodded mutely. The strong grip of the eyes that held her did not relent. Fixed on her, they slowly darkened.

'God bless his soul,' whispered Munnawwar Bi and her voice

was low and sweet, dark, dulcet. 'Did . . . did he at all remember me, lady?'

Chandravati Devi's face tightened. 'He did not recognize even me.' She rendered her account in stiff, formal utterances. 'It was,' she went on impulsively, '—so like drunkenness. Death is but an intoxication, Bi. Drunk on death he had trouble remembering himself, as so often happened before in his cups. How then could he remember me—or you?'

The hard gleam shone for a moment in the Hindu wife's eyes.

'The times are ill and I am alone among strangers, therefore, I have summoned you. There is much between us, Bi, though we have not had peace before . . .' All the while she cast upon Munnawwar Bi a long, measuring glance. 'Why,' she was thinking, '—she's just an ordinary old woman and her face and hands are those of a peasant's.' For Munnawwar Bi's face had lost all it soft contours, whittled down now to its bony essentials. Where was that sylph-like creature conjured up by the Rai Bahadur's lyrics, poetry that Chandravati Devi had read secretly with a burning heart? For the Rai Bahadur, while always noisily insistent on reciting his unwelcome poetry to reluctant audiences, had been strangely secretive about this poetry. Some words came slipping back from oblivion: "You have no beauty, but what is it in you that seems like beauty, O moon-cold one?" The words came unbidden into her mind, paled by time but still intact. That this was the great hate of her life, this Muslim woman. And that now, in her hour of solitude she should call upon her and that she should come across the troubled miles in her bullock cart, never failed to astonish her. Yet this was the only being in the world who understood the unspoken past, the man dead, and now the only possible companion for the dark years ahead. The lyrics to this woman were delicate, with a reticence, an agony of unutterable tenderness; a refinement that he was rarely capable of in verse though he was the soul of fineness in life. There was that smile playing about his lips as he slept, the mysterious gentleness that came into his voice and a silence new to him. And the Rajput wife knew that some woman was filling him with a maturity unknown to him. There were questions to be asked of this woman. She was different from those other common, flashy women of the frolicsome eyes and the honeyed voices and the swift, tinkling ankles that the Rai Bahadur usually patronized. But old hatred meant that there could be no trespassing on the unsayable. Her face was bitter and set.

'He has left a will,' she spoke stiffly. 'But what of it? What is a man's real will? What does he leave of himself?'

Her voice lost colour as she spoke. She looked away; over across the balustrades.

'I would that he was here to share these thoughts with me. Yet, I feel he is here. He seems to speak up in my thoughts. I feel his words, his whimsical verses in the air. I feel ideas not my own, on which I can lay no claim, coming down to me. Everything native to him. Yes, he is a presence encased in my presence and it is now my belief that a man, when dead, apportions himself out among those that love him. That which is gone is now in me, speaking up as me. That which is gone must also be in you and your place is here now.' She fell into an impersonal silence.

Munnawwar Bi looked up quickly at the slightly trembling woman before her, excited by her own fluency.

'The death that God gave him was strange. Most of the time he was not there in the process. I tended him, stanching his deadly wound, disbelieving it all, playacting, still sharing words with him in silent conversation, everything so lucid. Our existence that day was odd. My living seemed a pretence. His dying seemed a playact. We both marvelled over it in a higher dialogue, even as we performed the little details of a physical event, even as a man and a woman may continue to speak of ordinary things at the peak of intimacy . . . Ah, he choked and choked for breath. All I understood was that an important change occurred for him without in any way ending him. A new chapter of his history commenced— for him and for me. Why, even as I performed the funeral rituals I was recording the details in my memory, storing them up to tell him later. Thus did you look, my lord, thus did you breathe, and thus did you breathe no more. Ah, Bi, he was afraid he would die. I was afraid he would die. Death haunted us both for years and years. Do you know, Bi, we achieved it, we achieved it together at last—successfully!'

A mad light was flaring in her eyes, a strange, exalted smile upon her face, her hands clenched upon the arms of her chair.

'And I too,' murmured Munnawwar Bi, overcome, '—I too heard the Voice and it told me the Master was in pain. And I called upon Our Gharib Nawaz of Ajmer, our compassionate saint, in the dead of night. I called and called in my special prayer.'

'I know,' answered Chandravati Devi quietly. 'He spoke but once—and of the white sheet that came floating down from the heavens like a feather to rest upon him and the love that flowed all about in an eddy of pale light.'

'I knew it,' cried Munnawwar Bi. 'Oh, the Saint be praised! And . . . and you burnt him!' She wept into her veil. 'Oh, how could you? How can you burn one that was held so dear, O you barbarous ones!'

'How,' demanded the other scathingly, 'can you lie cramped, rotting slowly away, in a dark grave?'

They looked at one another silently. There could be no agreement on certain things, this they both realized. There could be no forgiveness too.

December 5

All this never happened. These words were never uttered. I sensed them hanging about in the air, ripening, waiting to be plucked in season, and if I didn't pluck them, they would, like so much else, fall and wither away. I used them up—I freely helped myself to what was lying potential in the air. I saw two charcoal sketches, one of Chandravati Devi and one of Munnawwar Bi, the two stubborn women who ran the haveli after the master's death. I cannot believe that they have left. Records establish that they lived in peace, sharing the haveli until they died; both survived the Rai Bahadur by many years. It is strange to realize that everybody one is dealing with is dead. More men are dead in the history of the world than are living. The living are immeasurably outnumbered! We who presume to breathe and to judge! History seems a study of collective death. I, stepping alone in this wreckage, come to doubt my own effective presence. Jotting notes, constructing possible dialogues, fantasies, referring to books, creating coherences— all by my own questionable scale. I am dealing with dead people who are not dead at all. Death is not the physical event we witness from the outside. I'm convinced it's only the physical result of some great positive change that occurs outside the body and that the body only obeys. All those beings are present here in a further fullness. I went over the Rai Bahadur's diaries and it is uncanny going over the living thoughts of a dead man, just as it is sinister going over the living significance of dead events. History is the past encased in the present— 'encased in the present' is a phrase which has obviously hung about me for some time, offering itself, prompting me to grow wise of it.

On no account is it true to history that the Revolt of 1857 was a united venture in which Hindus and Muslims were at one with each other in their opposition of the British. Sir James Outram was of the opinion that it was the result of a Muslim conspiracy taking advantage of Hindu grievances. That there was sharp division between the insurrectionists in matters of objectives is on record. Those that assumed direction of the revolt in its first phase sought to revive the vanished glory of the Mughal Empire—the traditional enemy of all Hindu states—and with this end in view, replaced Bahadur Shah Zafar on the throne. This was enough to estrange a large portion of the Hindu subjects who espoused the cause of Nana Saheb, the son of Baji Rao, and an attempt was made to re-establish Maratha supremacy—the old foe of Mughal imperialism. The effort, however, came too late for success. The slashing of Nana Saheb's pension by the British was deeply resented by all Hindu subjects. Sir John Lawrence held that the revolt was a purely military affair and founded solely on the cartridge business. Records prove that animal fat had actually been used in the ammunition factories at Woolwich; but the use had been purely incidental and no offence to Hindu or Muslim susceptibilities had been intended or foreseen. The above two, apparently unconnected facts, have been mentioned to demonstrate the point that misunderstanding and misplaced suspicion and offence lay behind a historical upheaval widely represented as a glorious chapter in the history of a nation.

But what lends special interest to the history of Vishnu Kutir is that out of the four Europeans who escaped at Cawnpore, at least one lived as a guest of the Rai Bahadur for the better part of the year. The grave in the forest bears no epitaph. It is also believed with reason that Nana Saheb spent a few days at Vishnu Kutir, recovering from a minor illness. How the Rai Bahadur managed to accommodate his diverse guests is a question that merits the scholar's respect and curiosity. More, he was in correspondence with Bahadur Shah Zafar, albeit on subjects poetic and personal

rather than political. Glancing through his case history, it is hard
to determine whether he was a dilettante; a conscious, cynical joker
and given to no loyalty or following, or a man of rare catholicity
and breadth of vision. Or are we to hazard the hypothesis that
human and historical processes frequently diverge and that the
former are temporarily dominated by the latter but never really
cease to operate and in that there is scope for hope. It is, however,
a matter of no small wonder that Vishnu Kutir suffered damage at
the hands of both insurrectionists and British forces. True to his
record, the Rai Bahadur, it is believed, continued to extend his
hospitality to runaway rebels and Europeans refugees both, a
feature that lends support to the contention that alongside our
official history runs a counter-history which must not be neglected
if we are to employ the past to understand and better the present.

Chandravati Devi's eyes began to snap fire. 'You too believe in that
will!' she scorned. 'I tell you, a man's only will is his continuing
presence in the people he has left.' Her voice cracked across the
inflexion. 'But they want gold and they shall get what they deserve,
the scum.' Munnawwar Bi shrank into her corner, frightened by
this diamond-hard woman whose temper was as changeable as
quicksilver.

'Vishnu Kutir is infested by vermin,' she spoke slowly in a calm,
dangerous voice. 'A race of curs who sit on their haunches with
lollopping tongues, fawning on me till my back is turned. You
have met them all, I daresay, those haggard vixens with rumps as
thick as cows, those creaking songsters who squeak like beardless
youths just turned four years and ten. I shall tell you of this treasure,
woman. Wait, I shall tell you all.' She laughed venomously. Her
eyes beat upon Munnawwar Bi's shrinking form, a faint mockery
warming into a cruel merriment. 'I shall tell you all,' she repeated
and her eyes were now screaming with dark laughter. 'But before
I do, there are some things of your past that I must know or die.
About him and you.' Now the eyes were steadfast, empty of
emotion. 'Where did you meet him? Tell me. I must know. What
was he like then? Was he tender? Was he demanding? What did
he share with you? What did he say the last time you met? I must
know all—the truth, the complete truth.'

Munnawwar Bi controlled her emotions. The only words she

could reach out and claim were bare, limp ones. He slipped out of their meshes, magnificent and indescribable.

'I do not remember,' she said quietly.

Their looks met in dire confrontation, one compelling, the other relentless.

Then Chandravati Devi laughed her acrid laugh 'You do not wish to tell. There are things I shall never know of him.'

'I have forgotten,' persisted Munnawwar Bi quietly.

December 7

The deeper I get into this stuff the more interested I am in this quixotic Rai Bahadur's nature. Its the less important details—his love life, his vile jokes, his quarrels, his tantrums—that intrigue me most. But there is more that is forgotten than is remembered. It leads me to wonder what happens to all those collective memories that just go off. Where do those thoughts go, the decisions, the conflicts within, the stanzas of poetry, the phrases of love? When history says—'I have forgotten'—where is it all actually, in which Overmind, in what essential, subtle form, ingredient of a further system? And what of that which is lost to all memory?

'I shall tell you all about this will, though you do deny me,' said Chandravati Devi maliciously. 'I shall tell you what nobody knows. He spent everything he had, yes, the very last piece of gold, on his audacious dancing fillies, on ungrateful curs, shabby little poets, foolish daubers, scheming kinsmen. He thought himself a great patron of the arts and letters and a great philanthropist, the fool! You should see the objects of his generosity and his patronage. A worse rabble of tuneless, witless knaves I have never seen. Do you know what he did. God is merciful that he saw through them all. It was too late to recover a fortune but he had his style and he planned revenge. He kept hope alive for many years, made them live on promises. He used the deadliest of all weapons, hope, on those that used him all his life. You have guessed? The treasury was empty at his death. There is no gold to give away. And yet a will, yes, a magnificent document and a list of names of harlots and flatterers with tender presents for each. Wait till you see it. This is his last vile joke, his last perverse laugh.'

She studied the woman before her reflectively. She could not understand the mixed feelings in her heart. This was the only being in the world with whom she could sort him out and resolve him into a coherent memory. She rose and crossed the chamber, uncovered and unlocked the massive, studded chest that stood at the far end of the chamber.

'I feel I must tell you this,' she spoke tonelessly. 'You and I alone has he excluded from his laughter—our names find no mention in this will.' She read over the unrolled sheet with a nonchalant face. "On Sharad Purnima day," she went on, "the secret shall be known." I bid you to read this—as a mark of my friendship.'

Silence fell in the chamber as Munnawwar Bi read in amazement and disbelief. That he could jest brilliantly she well knew, but that a jest could extend thus far, even those that knew him intimately could scarce believe.

'Mark the artful innocence, the absolute craft,' prompted Chandravati Devi. 'How sad he sounds when he speaks of the loneliness of the grave, the sorrowful separation from loved friends, loyal retainers, how true he sounds when he writes of the vanity of gold and of clay. And notice that grotesque list of tokens he bestows upon his beloved mourners, gifts of the soul and not of the purse, as he calls them!' Munnawwar Bi read on. Close behind her her cynical hostess spoke soft words of irony, drawing her attention to many singular and outrageous turns of phrase and of whim. 'Mark the wicked glee, Bi. I should love to watch Imroze's face when he receives the kerchief!—"which holds my tears upon hearing your poem". And Jauhar Jaan surely isn't expecting a cockatoo "tuneful with playsome speech and song as thee". Singer Madhav Prasad won't like his dead patron's portrait though it "keep him company full many a year". Nor shall punster Rasheed Rehman welcome that sermon in verse though it prove ever so well "that your master laugheth with you still". And fail not to see the others. Fifty-one gifts in all—"gifts of the soul and as enduring as your love!" And that is not all, Bi. Mark the end. "My real wealth" he proclaims, "—lies in the land of the unliving, beyond the five elements and the three essences. That awaits those friends of my heart that will lift up, upon this instant, their swords, and lay down their lives for their love of me. So come, my beloveds, and all my wealth be yours. To him that shall come unto me first do I leave half my treasure. To him that cometh after him do I leave a fourth. And to him that cometh after him do I leave an eighth. I bid you welcome, sirs, and await you there in the land of the shadows. Be sure, sirs, not to let your master languish alone ere you come unto him. And great inheritance be yours God willing!" Tell me, Bi, another man that could play that jest and half so well!'

Munnawwar Bi handed the will back in silence.

'To you and to me,' continued Chandravati Devi slowly. 'He has left another jest. We are to read it together. We cannot read it alone.'

'I do not understand,' whispered Munnawwar Bi.

'A book of his composition,' explained the other. 'A strange and demanding book. Half in Sanskrit and half in Persian. I know no Persian. You know no Sanskrit. Yet each sentence of my book finds its other half in yours. Each poem in yours continues in mine. Two interlocking books. Only he could think of that, Munnawwar Bi. But why, I often ask, did he have this taste for the strange, the unimaginable? This book, says he, shall be friend of our solitary hours but there's no choice for us save to sit ourselves down together, place our books side by side and seek him in their pages, await his voice and his mind to speak to us again . . .'

December 15

Interlocking books! I'm terribly excited over this discovery. My work is behind schedule but these three days in the museum were well worth it. Whoever thought of interlocking books in Sanskrit and in Persian! There are poems, insights, essays, personal addresses, jests, songs, all beautifully inscribed in flowing calligraphy, all quite obviously the product of a brilliant and accomplished mind. Some poems commence in one volume and continue in the other. Some run across from one volume to the other, alternate lines occurring in the two volumes. Ideas dovetail, piquant narrations overlap. The books are a comprehensive cultural get-together between three persons, one dead but still active, the others alive and responsive. A very strange experiment in continuity, really. The dead Rai Bahadur seems to sit at the head of the table, as it were, explaining, mediating, negotiating, translating, and a great sense of present interaction, of the here and now, pervades the contents. On some pages there are even riddles and nought and cross games with diverse artful arrangements possible. Going over the two volumes, one gets the feeling that the author is there, present and participating, living, directing the game, bringing two women close together, defying death and history.

December 20

All this time spent and just two sections worked out. Old Mr Usmani and Pandit Purushottam Misra just won't work together in peace. I never saw such bickering old fogeys, each trying to flourish the sophistication, the fineness, the grace, the infinite superiority of his own language before the crudity, the limitedness of the other! There is no way of confirming whether the will was ever announced and the kind of reception it got from the hopeful claimants. A copy of the will—perhaps the only one—lies tucked into the pages of the Rai Bahadur's 'conversations with his ladies'. I chanced upon it suddenly and my amusement and delight even infected the two venerable old guys. As we pore over the writings, paragraph by paragraph, the Rai Bahadur himself seems to be in our midst, a fourth presence, a sort of chief. What makes my own position academically awkward is that this Rai Bahadur forms but a peripheral part of my dissertation and yet his personality overwhelms the rest of my study. Moreover, the man played no part in major history and therefore merits attention only proportionate to his role in the events of his time. But I am now quite obsessed by his presence. I see no harm in upsetting the entire symmetry of my thesis in the service of his memory. What began as the objective history of a period of time has fast turned into the history of an unimportant but very interesting personality. The history of one man has become more important for me than the history of an age.

December 24

My nerves are undoubtedly below par. Something happened, so strange, so unnerving that I can scarcely trust it to paper. It held up my work altogether. I couldn't bring myself to go to Vishnu Kutir for two whole days. And I don't know how to put it across, even to myself. The more I avoid facing the implications the more inevitable a confession becomes. And yet to confess my suspicions, my certainty, would be to topple the entire respectability of my work. I am terrified of the place. And there's no need to go down now. I have only the translations to work on. Old Mr Usmani and Misraji quarrelled bitterly the whole week through and an insinuation of Misraji's so upset Mr Usmani that he has stopped coming altogether. It's no use as far as they go. I shall ask Misraji most politely, to spare me his gracious assistance. I am now attempting to work on these translations all by myself! I know very little Sanskrit and absolutely no Persian but there it is! It happens all the time . . .

Neither sleep nor waking. A lucid region of recognition. There's something very real and familiar about this state. If a phrase be needed it's 'but of course'. It may all sound idiotic but it's a cool, gracious, friendly assistance, ready at hand and very reasonable. Lengthy passages in Sanskrit and in Persian relax in my hands and lay themselves, line by line, intelligible upon the page. There is such courteous chivalry, such obliging forethought in every little gesture. It is all too exciting, too mind-boggling, and frequently it gets scary. But fear is a reflex, nothing more, nothing less, an ancient, repeating error. I did not seek this relationship—and it is no less than that. Today, for example, I was stuck with a particular passage and I just laid my head upon my desk and rested my mind and soon afterwards the words began flowing fluently out of my brain and I could hardly keep pace with their speed: 'I have some of the disposition of an epic poet, my ladies, but scarcely the fortitude of one. There came to me in a dream the Sacred Muse, beseated upon Her swan, a most High and Holy Presence, and she said: "Wilt thou be a poet? Ask and it shall be granted." But I know the ways of the gods on high. "What shall it cost me?" quoth I. "Some tears." She made the reply. "Some suffering queries. Some instants of doubt and distress. A lot of travail. But no ordinary existence." "Too great a price to pay, O Muse," said I. "Let me remain a bad poet, such as I am. Let me remain a lover of verses and women. Let me stay an observer of history and not an actor therein." "So be it," said she and left. And thus did I decline to be the great poet I could be. And thus do I leave unto you this imperfect work. This work is infinitely perfectible and in its execution did my meagre life lapse and many real imperfections did pass me by that I took no note of and God be thanked for that. And be sure I shall be perfecting a further form of this very work in the neighbouring world, just across a slumber path, and in the next and the next; for our tasks be the same for ever and ever . . .

'And, most surprisingly, did the theme change and a Persian harangue came to displace it: "Witness this rabble of mine. Imposters all. You can appreciate art but it is affectation, not art, sirs; it is aberration, not art, sirs. Mockery comes easy to men of this kind and mockery they believe to be a higher form of wisdom. The times are ill and no man is a friend. Wherein are gone those great friendships of old, those reposeful relationships? We are on the verge of disaster and our world shall end. Of history to come nought be known—which way the platter shall tilt and the oil shall flow, or which way the camel shall beseat himself in the sand." And just as suddenly as before sprang an unexpected insight in Sanskrit: 'Well be it that several dead men comprise one living man and several lives one complete personality. So are the generations perfected in one form and so may God come to be a superlative rendering of man.'

It took me two months, working fitfully, to translate the two volumes. All the time I was aware of that courteous, civilized presence living within me, as it were, and an enormous sympathy and what I can only describe as affectionate interest seemed to inform my work. On at least two occasions I thought I saw him— well, 'saw' is the wrong word. I grew conscious of him somewhere within my own self, a distinct entity, quite clearly apprehended. A head of luxuriant hair, a fine, thoughtful face, bemused eyes, a sensuous mouth beneath a scimitar shaped moustache. Turban and tunic, cummerbund and ornamented toe-turned footwear. I shall never know who this presence was—I have no portraits of the Rai Bahadur—but how could my mind fashion the form of a being, quite unfamiliar and never seen before? It may well be that my absorption in my work made me savour the full flavour of a personality and my mind performed an act of creation. It may also be that contact with the mind of a long dead man opened up a channel of communication between two areas of the mind. Many inferences are possible but how do I account for the help I was graciously given with the translations, I who knew no Sanskrit and no Persian to speak of? And I still cannot translate, left to myself.

There is much that is collaborative in our human understanding and our partners are not known to us.

It is my theory that Vishnu Kutir finally fell with the death of Munnawwar Bi, a good two decades after 1857, Chandravati Devi having died some years earlier. The grounds and buildings were taken over by the government and Vishnu Kutir turned into a revenue office in 1894.

The end of a man is what is conventionally reckoned his physical death and the decay of his ideas. The end of an age is the downfall of governments, changes in ideas, transformations in styles. My history had of necessity reached the limits of conventional study. But history, as I saw it, is always a pathetically unfinished business. I accordingly hazarded a final chapter, based upon highly personal convictions, in which I advanced the opinion that human history is yet not large enough to entertain a more accurate history of man. I was interested in tracing the story of a man that was not terminated by the grave. The Rai Bahadur's mock grave which housed nobody became for me a symbol of great worth. The two incomplete books which dovetailed into one another led me to deduce a further analogy and suggest the existence of an atemporal history into which our orthodox, fact based histories fit. I posited other time-scales and personal histories that extended beyond our 'living' histories. I dedicated my study to all that is known and never written and all that continues to happen in its own time and beyond the remembrance and the reach of other minds in planes of continuity apart and above.

My dissertation was, not surprisingly, rejected as being undemonstrative of scholarly discernment, deficient in objectivity, incomplete in data and inadequate in conclusive evidence. Despite this setback I have continued my work on ideas and experiences brought to me by it and invite correspondence from like-minded persons who have any fresh insights to offer or facts capable of endorsing my theories.

The seventeenth of March promised to be more of a homecoming feast for his mother and a requiem service for his father than a birthday celebration for him, Edwin reflected. It was to be a grand symbolic event in the history of their family.

The Watkinses had been a more or less nomadic family for well over two decades now, building provisional homes in sundry small and large places across the length and breadth of northern India, from Cossimbazar in the east to Rawal Pindee in the west. When the late Colonel Vernon Agnew Watkins was alive it was places as diverse as Umbala and Meerut, Cawnpore and Allahabad, Dehra Doon and Sialkote, Jubbalpore and Fyzabad. After his death the memsahib, her two daughters and son drifted from one place to another in the north-west, Punjaub, Oude and Behar, sometimes staying with friends, sometimes setting up residence on their own. The memsahib dabbled in missionary activity for a while in the hamlets of Jounpore, Azimghur and Goruckpore, distributing Bibles, tending the old and the sick; but her efforts at converting the heathen, though conducted in a spirit of the utmost sympathy and well-directed industry, accorded ill with her general disposition and it was not long before it was amply clear to her that to be an ambassadoress of Christ was not her natural *métier* in life. Thereafter she took up schoolteaching and holding piano classes for young ladies of genteel families and finally—and most lamentably—going into the millinery business.

This loathsome party was to be his mother's greeting to Calcutta and her farewell to hard times. Now that he was shortly to come of age and the solicitors in London had released the papers, the memsahib looked forward to moving in superior circles again. If his mother's protracted planning was anything to go by, it was to be a sweet, uplifting, cheerful-tearful occasion for family and guests alike.

The Colonel Memsahib, as she was known to the native bearers, had spent twenty years in genteel deprivation, living on her late husband's military pension and her own meagre earnings, concealing her reduced means behind a mask of cool Christian austerity with the demeanour of one who espouses want rather from choice than from misfortune. But the great occasion to come was evidently designed to give free expression to any dormant cravings for pomp and splendour which may have lurked in her gentle bosom. Left to himself, Edwin would much rather have beguiled the day alone with Mr Dutt, talking poetry and philosophy and world affairs and matters fantastical and no fuss at all. But Colonel Memsahib and the two girls gave vent to such an outcry at this mild suggestion that he let the matter go.

'Fancy!' cried Rosalie pettishly. 'Our only big party and he says he'd rather not! And I've told the Parker girls all about it and the Kelly girls and the Rickettses. And I've lunched with them all and they'll soon be off to Simla and I may never set eyes on Major Norton again. And whatever for have I been practising my music till my fingers and thumbs were ready to drop off?'—she demanded plaintively.

'Rosa, Rosa,' murmured Colonel Memsahib reprovingly. 'Pray do not pout and frown so. And recollect—a lady doesn't ever allude to a gentleman—be he ever so much her senior—as though she cherished—er—expectations from him.'

'I beg your pardon, Mama!' shrilled Rosa tartly. 'Whatever do you mean? I have the impression—if you'll forgive my saying so—that the expectations have been entirely on your side . . .'

What a cosy family, reflected Edwin, and how delightfully chummy!

Shortly after her arrival in Calcutta the Colonel Memsahib had let herself go, stinting herself nothing. She rented a bungalow on Bentinck Street, Bungalow No. 11, lately occupied by Major Burney and consisting of six rooms and two bathrooms at the handsome rent of fifty rupees a month. She purchased, after much deliberation, a very handsome park phaeton with moveable coach box, beautiful English lamps, cushions and rug, polished steel driving rail, pole, bar, shafts, and, to complete the outfit, a very presentable grey mare of about fifteen hands, advertised as, 'quiet to ride or drive, guaranteed sound and hardworking and about nine years old.' All for the colossal sum of eight hundred rupees. Oak wood chests, bedsteads, teak bureaux and dressers, settees, rocking chairs with embroidered antimaccassars. A complete service of plate, a selection of the latest books and music, furnishings and drapes, punkah-protectors, fire-screens and paper shades, pots of geranium, verbena, fuschias and violets and, as final necessities for social acceptance, a handsome chandelier by Defries of London, fitted with three plated Argand lamps, and a Brodwood's grand, square piano, almost new, with tuning fork, hammer and tin-lined case. From a Signor S. Barsottelli she purchased a very choice collection of classical alabaster table ornaments, mosaic tables, marble vases and diverse fancy articles. Into her and the young ladies' wardrobes went a quantity of grenadine, muslin, organdie trimmed muslin garibaldis, Alexander sashes, lace Berthes, chiccon, cambric and lace, handkerchiefs, collars, cuffs, bonnets, shawls, wooden bustles, whale-bone stays, velvet knots with fancy combs, ribbons of different widths and colours, corsets, feather fans, steel skirts, hair pads and nets, parasols, hats, stockings and fancy boots. Into her sideboard went a dozen each of table forks and spoons, dessert forks, teaspoons, gravy spoons, fruit knives, fish knives, soup ladles, milk ladles, a pair of muffineers, decanter stands, knife rests, wine glasses, tumbler covers, butter pot, jugs, sugar urns, coffee mill, salting machine, ice machine. Upon her shelves went an array of the newest novels—*Beatrice* by Julia Kavangah, *Luttrell of Arran* by Charles Lever, *Mercedes* by Sir C.F. Wraxall, *Bart* (in three volumes), the fashionable *Behind the Curtains* (in three volumes). It was absolutely *de rigeur* to have also some illustrated books for dismal evenings, hence there was *Hyperion*, with twenty-four photographs of the Rhine, Switzerland and the Tyrol; *The Lake Country* with hundred illustrations; *The Stones of Palestine—Notes of a Ramble through the Holy Land* by Mrs Mentor Mott; and finally *The Life and Lessons of Our Lord*, unfolded and illustrated by the Reverend John Cumming. Upon the music rack went *The Standard Song Book* and *The Great Comic Volume of Songs*, *Moore's Melodies* and her old collection of Schumann, Schubert and Chopin. Into her cellar went the best brandy, port, sherry, champagne, moselle, claret, hock, gin, porter, noyeau and beer.

It is but just to suppose that consequent upon her stupendous refurbishments, the memsahib felt amply equipped for civilized and gracious company, the joys of human friendship with equals, the niceties of culture, high thinking and living. It was a pity, though, that culture relied so heavily on the purse and the esteem of equals depended greatly upon appearances; nevertheless the memsahib now deemed it opportune to front her old circle again in a spirit of graceful elegance.

There were the girls' prospects to consider too. There was such a surfeit of eligible bachelors now in Calcutta. Even her own excessive adherence to form and her often unreachable standards of breeding and family could not fault some of the aspirants. But what with the closure of the Company and the recent takeover by the Crown, there was a collateral influx of fresh young adventuresses from home to outweigh the advantages of having so many new ranks of young officers and civil servants. Now was the time to cast herself in a role that ill-beseemed her—that of an astute lady mother. The party would have to be on a large scale.

But the Colonel Memsahib had, in her own way, bestowed a touch of soul to the proceedings. For the lady had long learnt the fine art of commingling the banal and the beauteous in her two decades of strife to maintain a semblance of aristocracy in her straitened circumstances. It had to be conceded that she did it exceedingly well. The memsahib had retained her lavender fragrant presence, like an angel from heaven drifting about on an earthly mission of cleaning house, doing the flowers, giving music lessons and administering quinine to the servants with a gracious head perpetually bowed, if not in true subservience, at least in a token modesty which added a pleasing piece of artistry to her well-modulated person. Given to many excessive notions of form and propriety, situation and style, the gentle lady was a law unto herself and already something of an oddity in the city with her many little dated insistences and observances. To the two girls' little perplexities, to Edwin's unsure, protesting self, Colonel Memsahib had adopted a habitual air of gentle remonstrance and patient admonition. Speaking in a low, tuneful singsong with a mock-rational tone of balancing alternative propositions of unknown absurdities which it was her sad lot in life to quell, swaying her head from side to side, a vague, abstracted expression upon her face. Thus did her cultivated voice ascend and descend the complete musical scale from reprimand to reassurance, from reasoning to persuasion to command. Some day when the girls found husbands and Edwin a calling, she would be free in a lucid world of reason and music and crystalline propriety of word and gesture and act and that was the Colonel Memsahib's dream.

Edwin had only the vaguest inkling of the stupendous spiritual scale on which the evening was being planned. There was to be plenty of music. Valerie and Rosalie were at the newly purchased piano all day, one hammering insensitively away in thunderous passion, the other stroking the keys in an excess of syrupy sentiment until all his nerves were on edge. There were to be readings from the Bible by Father Basil and a brief, presumably ennobling sermon. There was to be the cutting of the cake and the toasts and then he, Edwin, was to be ceremonially presented with his father's watch and gun which had lain awaiting this day for many years. The watch was a fine gold, engine turned hunting piece by Barraud and Lund with a gold Albert chain and key and a gold guard chain to match. The gun was a highly finished single rifle by Henry of Edinburgh, bore 451, length of barrel thirty-one inches, in a fine case complete with Vernier match and a Rob Roy ammunition box. There was also a letter from the late Colonel, sealed with his ring and addressed in his unpolished, soldierly hand, which had rested these many years embalmed in a locker. Upon receipt of these ritual gifts, he, Edwin, was duly to retire into the morning room to unseal and read the letter. The guests were meanwhile to regale themselves with a fulsome repast followed by convivial conversation, songs and dancing—this last in view of the girls' prospects—after which Edwin, duly overwhelmed and uplifted, was expected to make an entry and utter a few charged words which would bring tears to many an eye. More dancing, more singing, more conversation and the guests were to leave in a mist of heartwarming emotion, gladdened and grateful to remember an exalting evening for evermore.

'We must have Christina and Lavinia Dithers,' said Colonel Memsahib drawing up the invitation list. 'And Mr and Mrs Courteney Rawlinson-Smith. The Pages, the Parkers, the Lawrences, the Philipses, the Hamiltons. Young Master Jacob, Major Norton, Majors Burnett and Hyde, Brigadier Daniels, Mr Morris and his friends at the Saturday club . . .'

'And Uncle Chris and Aunt Lucille,' prompted Valerie. 'And Father Basil, of course.'

'I'd like to ask Edwin if there's anyone he'd care to ask?' murmured Colonel Memsahib, more in a correct observance of domestic courtesy than any serious expectation of dissent from his quarter.

'Edwin, my love, is there anyone you'd like to call?'

Edwin shrugged. 'If you really wish to know, Mama, there's my friend, the poet, Mr Michael Madhusudan Dutt.'

'Oh dear!' sighed the memsahib.

'A local Bengalee!' cried Rosa.

'Edwin, dear, do be sensible. Your Mr Dutt, I grant, may be a very fine man but shall he be comfortable here?'

'Mr Dutt writes English poetry, Mama,' said Edwin stubbornly as though that fact alone were sufficient to waive aside all social unease. 'His poem was noticed by the *Athenaeum* which said that he was akin to Scott or Byron. And he's the best neo-Milton this side of England. His 'Captive Ladie' is like a piece of medieval minstrelry.'

'Dear me,' said Father Basil unimpressed. 'What did you say his name was?'

'Michael Madhusudan Dutt.'

'Michael—eh? The devil's own name,' muttered Father Basil. 'And Madhusoodun—that's no Christian name.'

'I suppose we'll have to call him if dear Edwin insists,' sighed Colonel Memsahib. 'And is there no one else?'

'No one else,' said Edwin shortly.

'That's the one that made the native Bengalee boys chant verses from the *Iliad* and the *Odyssey* in their heathen temples?' ventured Father Basil conversationally. 'And all that to-do about ham and beef?'

But Edwin was in an ill humour. 'That,' rejoined he curtly, '—was Derozio. Dead.'

There was a long uncomfortable silence.

Edwin had not seen his father, the Colonel, that hero of Sind, that military legend, the Colonel Sahib having died soon after Sind. But nowhere in the memsahib's allusions to him was the past tense ever used. The Colonel Sahib might have been out on campaign down south or up north-west. Or else he might have stepped out of a pleasant morning to the Golf Links or the polo ground or the club. The Colonel Sahib's opinions still guided all moral questions in the household. His axioms were law and his decrees unconditionally binding. The memsahib, it was clear, was merely biding her time while her lord and master was out of town, soon to return and handle things as of yore. Meanwhile, she wanted him to recognize, when next they met, the worth of her contribution to the home. Edwin retained no recollection of his celebrity father but had constructed his own version of his grandeur. He saw, in his mind's eye, a short, sprightly, bewhiskered being with a scrubbed and freshly laundered look about him, a man who seemed to sparkle in every fibre of his person—his glasses, his cuff links, his gold collar stud, his buttons and medals and decorations, his pen and watch and buckle, his diamond hard eyes, grey and cold, like a Scottish loch in mid winter, his crisp, blond hair, his robust cheeks and smooth, ironic brow. There was invincibility in the man and all the radiance of mythology—a man who seemed to go about on padded feet, specializing in stillness and the sudden spring. That was his style—in repartee, in wit, in battle and in love. Whether Edwin's personal picture of his father corresponded to his historic progenitor, Edwin had no means of confirming. Father was everywhere, like God, and no family occasion could dream of excluding him. Father was the ultimate arbiter, the final court of appeal, the maker of family norms and forms, relayed through the utterances of their mother. And that letter in the locker awaiting his attention was his recognizable voice, heroic and ineradicable in their midst, conferring solemnity on the occasion and a higher continuity to their small personal histories. The high moment of the evening was naturally the presentation of the letter and the rest of the evening had to be worthy of that instant. Thinking of it, Edwin felt a shiver of suspense and emotion as though an invaluable key to an emotional mystery was to be handed him.

So it was that the parlour was painted and the carpets sent for cleaning. Dust sheets removed, the furniture polished till it shone. The giant cake, ordered at Goolam's, a massive eight-pounder with twenty-one ornate keys iced upon it, and candles, buntings, streamers aplenty. The durzee was in all day, sitting cross-legged on the mat, busy with bales of mull and organdie and light summer worthy silks, sashes and tuckers and frills. His own camelhued suit of Russia Duck was ordered at Wazirully's.

From old habit, Edwin surrendered, living as he did in mortal dread of his two sisters. For years he had maintained a constant critical watch on all their little pretences and airs and graces, their polite jealousies and rivalries, their genteel gibes, their mutual hatreds and false amities.

Valerie was the family saint, a self-absorbed saint of trance-like passivity, eyes lifted and all conscious expressions operating upon a high plane of sublimity. Edwin could never resolve in his mind whether Val was a very fine being indeed or just a wonderfully gifted humbug. Everything she spoke or did was sweet and equivocal. She had sad eyes which she continually put to good use, but burning, suppressed, furtive eyes too which had been trained to look soulful while they took note of everything. She had a face like a jaded madonna's, with hollow cheeks, lank, chestnut hair and a too-thin form. Of it all she made ingenious use, maintaining a certain cultivated silence and promise of depth and mystery as her most attractive feature.

Against Rosalie's rash, buoyant charm Val advanced her patient, humility. Against her quick, sharp wit, she matched her mock refined, non-committal reserve. Nobody knew what Val ever really thought but Edwin suspected that an elaborate little manufactory of schemes and subterfuges, submissions and strategies was active within her, carefully rehearsing while she sat with pliant, pensive mien at the piano, ostensibly carried away upon a flood of soul stirring music.

Rosalie was flightly but very consciously so, specializing in a certain charming indiscretion, a flair for the rash and the unreasoned remark, the sudden, dimpled smile, the innocently hurtful, the naïve apologetic little schoolgirl memsahib who said all the wrong things of sheer unworldiness. For ten years the family had been obligingly laughing at Rosa's quips—she expected it of them. She was confirmed in the role of the talkative and bantering naughty little missybaba with the ringlets and bangs, the small ankles and waist and the ever jingling earrings.

'Have I said the wrong thing, Aunty Lucille? I mean, your silver locks do really become you and go with this silver-grey gown so elegantly. It wasn't so good some years back when the colours of the gown and the locks of hair were both stronger. Oh, oh, don't look like that. What have I said, oh, dear me?'

'You mean it well, I'm sure. Now go, there's a dear.' And Rosa, eyes wide in innocent astonishment and contrition, all ablush in shy, endearing confusion. 'That young lady,' one almost heard the late Colonel's voice, '—deserves a good wallopin's o'er her britches!'

And Valerie, the great actress, all the while marvelling at her baby sister's wit and charm. And with an insidious simultaneity enacting her own perfect little tableau of superior modesty, demure reserve and cultured humility. She, the shrinking, sensitive soul, the flower wasting its sweetness on the desert air, throwing into sharp relief all Rosalie's brash, graceless speech, her rough, flaunting ways, her loud laughter, her squeals and her swagger. What a sweet, vulnerable maid, thought Edwin dourly. Practising to perfection the fine art of ingratiation. There were two kinds of memsahibs, reflected Edwin. There was the loud, indomitable one, shrill and authoritative, ready to expound a point, ready to grab everyone's opinion as her own, ready to tell you what to do and how to do it. That would be Rosa in twenty years. There was the other type. Vague, wandering, evasive, with a feeble sort of sincerity and a wavering goodwill; a woman who fades gently away, degenerates, and whose opinions become more and more complicated and unsure. She has a sad, unstated accusation against someone, who? one never learns; she has been wrongfully sacrificed for someone else's happiness and a sterling modesty forbids her speech. In everything she does there is graceful self-denial, quiet service. That would be Val's performance in another twenty years and Edwin was sure she'd perform excellently.

How it happened so suddenly Edwin never knew. A whole month the dreadful party was being planned and then, here was he, confused, in its very centre, turned out in his fine new suit of Russia Duck with a gardenia in his buttonhole, and a constant twitter of voices about him and the dazzle of dozens of candles, the very air starched with frosty light and the fumes of flowers and perfumes, pomades and potpourri.

The gentlemen were all in good voice and in excellent spirits, to judge by the babel of conversations severally raging in the overcrowded chamber. A dark-brown thoroughbred, sir. He's called Charlie—sire Sir Hercules and dam Black Bess; fifteen—three tall, rising seven years, the very cut of an English horse, take it from me, sir! The vessel Saladin left London on the nineteenth of

December and with a hundred and seven days out you can expect her any time. Eunice arrived from Melbourne, God help us all, on the *Queen of Australia*—I received the foul news by this morning's dawk from the dawk-khana. It shall be my pleasure, Mr Bunting, to present you with a selection of the finest brandy—Exshaw No. I, and Todd and Heatley's champagne for Mrs Bunting. Or assorted French liqueurs if you prefer. Or Marcobrunner hock or Graham's Geneva gin. And, I may tell you, that I have received a consignment of numbers 1 and 2 Havana and Manila cheroots and tobacco of various kinds, cut and uncut. That's a very serviceable grey mare I got, sir, goes perfectly, in buggy, gharry and saddle and a set of Cawnpore-made plated harness as good as new—all for a hundred and forty rupees. Enough, say I! I sail next month. I've written to the Calcutta Shipping Intelligence and booked my passage on the *Aberdeen*. Allow me, then, good sir, to recommend that estimable volume on *Our Tropical Possessions in Malayan India* by John Cameroon, Esq.—I trust that it shall acquaint you with Singapore, Penang Province, Wellesley and Malacca, their peoples, products, commerce and government long ere you land. About four thousand acres of waste land, Mr Lawrence, in the district of Lukeempore close on Nynee Tal. It adjoins large villages of the Shahjehanpore District and the soil is good and at eight rupees an acre my mind is made up and I mean to write to Mr McBarnet of the Simla Bank Corporation by the next dawk.

The young maidens were meanwhile in a twitter over the words of the songs in *Christey's Minstrel Songs*, trying them out on the instrument or else in fits of laughter over the grotesque verses in the *Great Comic Volume of Songs* as sung by Sam Cowell and Co. or else in raptures over somebody's white embroidered muslin, somebody's trimmed organdie or somebody's fancy silver buttons.

Away in their corner the old ladies discussed heartburn, dyspepsia, pain in the right side and shoulder, blotches, habitual costiveness, depression of spirits, oppression after meals, nervous and general debility, and examined the medicinal virtues of Dr E. J. Lazarus's Essence of Chiretta, created by the baids and hukeems of Hindoostan for centuries and now being advertised in the papers. I strongly urge Gregory to adhere to magnesia water or seltzer or potash water but all he retorts is: 'Deuce take it, Mama, or do you actually see me tippling orangeade at the Club?' And have you seen my new fuschias and my new violets, Clara? This miserable climate kills my nasturtiums a month too soon but it can't be helped, can it? Toilet and smelling salts, pomades, otto of roses.

'Well, well, well, Martha Parker, I scarce knew you!' Charming Leslie smiles a challenging little smile, eyes narrowed in quizzical glee. 'Admit,' her eyes commanded, 'admit, Martha Parker, that time has been kinder on me than on you though we're fifty if a day. Admit that I have had a better deal in life, that fortune has favoured me with strange preference and you, ah you, poor thing, though you did happen to be a general's daughter . . .'

'Indeed?'—smiled Martha Parker. 'But I knew you at once, dear, and so little changed from the night of the Darjeeling Tea Planters' Ball back in '36. 'Let it go,' her resigned expression wearily surrendered—some are granted more than others, some that least deserve; and some are denied that may with justice claim their due. Too late to eat one's heart out—I have long consented.

'Dear Uncle Chris, and how may you be?' Going up to him with both hands extended was Valerie. Leaning forward on an impulse, she whispers something in his ear. 'Bless my soul, bless my soul!' rumbles the old gentleman, roaring with laughter. And Aunt Lucille saying; 'That girl o' yours needs awatching, Charlotte.' Catching Rosa's eye across the room, she bows and throws her a kiss, then sinks down upon the blue settee and watches with bitter eyes and deprecating mouth. 'Behave yourself, miss, the missus is awatchin!' reprimands Uncle Chris with a twinkle in his eye.

And the Colonel Memsahib bowing, bowing, smiling, extending her white gloved hand, a band playing in the lawn. Upon the chintz covered armchair nigh the piano sat Father Basil, that lumpy personage, quite bald, quite rotund, eyes habitually falling shut whenever he ruminated a point a long, long instant before he hazarded an answer, fingers entwined above his enormous middle. All the vases filled with tea roses, platters of potpourri on tables, clumps of late blossoms arrayed along the walls. The Parkers, the Lawrences, Matilda and Emilia O'Brien in light summer dresses of mauve and primrose. The bluff old army veterans bending gallantly to kiss the Colonel Memsahib's hand.

'What a rude, rude man!' frets Valerie, 'Oh, there you are, dear Major Norton!' The Major sank jocularly down upon one knee and Rosalie hid her face, the bashful belle behind her ostrich fan. And the Major's unstoppable flood of utterance, each full throated syllable pounding richly forth with an air of jocund and indisputable authority. What an apoplectic face had he, the Major, and the full eyes of yesterday's lover and today's drunkard.

Edwin was confused all through the evening. There were bursts of melody from the fiddles and trumpets in the lawn. The long drive was lined up with buggies, dogcarts, gharries, phaetons, barouches . . . The buzz of many voices, luminous swirls of muslin and of silk, smiles, smiles. Outside, the punkah-pullers swung and the large fans undulated slowly, lapping up a warm breeze above their heads. He was aware once of Mr Dutt's presence and remembered crossing the chamber quickly to welcome and show him in. He seemed to recall that nobody spoke much to Mr Dutt or looked at him. But Rosa gave vent to an utterly uncalled-for titter over something the Major muttered. And Valerie studied him cautiously with that measuring, surreptitious eye that old spinsters have. The Colonel Memsahib, on being presented with her new guest, gave him two fingers to shake, allowed a frosty smile to hover a second about her seraphic face, murmured scarce audibly: 'Mr Datt—er—to be sure—please to step into the parlour.'

And then he was aware that a profound silence had fallen and the Colonel Memsahib was beseated upon the piano stool. The Colonel Memsahib played well. She had a way of addressing the keys with reverential reserve, touching them gently and a rustle passed through the room as though an enchanted hand had made a magic pass above their heads. Her fingers yearned upon the strangest melodies, pausing with infinitely restful reluctance before deep spells of stillness. She commenced with selections from Schumann's *Nachstucke* and a troubled music filled the air. Dark feelings and images, sinister funereal fantasies, tumbled out of the instrument. She followed it up with portions from Schubert's *Moment Musicaux* and a limpid coolness swept in, becalming the earlier agitations.

The she took up Chopin's *Raindrop Prelude*. The rain fell softly as it falls unseen at some incalculable hour of darkness or of dawn, as it falls, drip by unheard drip, outside the marges of the deepest sleep, until one does not know if one dreamt of the rain or the rain dreamt of itself. Such rare restraint and delicacy had she and so unlike Valerie's rapturous emotional playing and Rosa's tempestuous rhapsodies.

The Colonel Memsahib held her back very straight as she played and her head uplifted and looked, unseeing, into the candlelit distance, with an indrawn face which brooded upon precious perceptions won with strife and in pain, which saw into clarities and visions that made it plain that happiness, too, was no answer to human suffering, that love and loneliness had their extent and also their limits and which chose, wisely, a glorious self-forgetfulness.

So now she was adrift, pennants flying upon a shoreless sea, carried without effort before a northern wind, working her intricate, unhurried way alone through Bach's straits and channels. Lofty transports of contemplation became renderings in notation, high seriousnesses, orders and hierarchies known to light and to earth, to sky and to water, uttering unpronounceable symbols and simpler, superior solutions; then, giving way, acceding to its own impersonal rejoicings with the serene composure of the most high. Then, interrogating itself again in new ways and answering itself in many celestial idioms, all uttering the same changeless thing. And the listening heart stopped in speechless recognition of an old reassurance with each repeating reply. And this interior dialogue, this absolute geometry, saved from being mere debate by the complete tenderness with which each feeling phrase of the divine argument was addressed.

Then she dipped her head, consulted the conclusive theme again, listened deeply, conferred with another octave, crumbled a few final bunches of notes and a flight of ultimate sounds fluttered up and scattered upon the carpet and lay still.

So profound was the hush that for a long while everyone forgot to clap. Then the applause burst, Mr Dutt clapping louder and longer than anybody else. She stood up and bowed gracefully. The way Valerie ran forward and kissed her mother's hands, Edwin was sure she was consumed with intense jealousy.

'But my dear Charlotte, this was absolutely marvellous!'

'Breathtaking, madam!'

'Perfectly ravishing, my dear!'

'Madam, allow me,' and the old Brigadier seized Colonel Memsahib's hand and languished his lips upon it.

'They're all Vernon's favourites,' said Colonel Memsahib abstractedly.

Nobody could quite define the unease but the awkwardness of the moment was sudden. A dead man was the recipient of that soul offering not a chamberful of living men and women. For they all realized they did not exist for her as she played. That music was for Vernon's ears who lay buried somewhere in the north-west.

Many of the guests felt that the Bible reading and the sermon was not of a piece with the rest of the evening and served to impose an unnecessary ecclesiastical tone upon the evening's gaieties. But the memsahib was adamant on this point This was more of a sacred occasion than a mere birthday celebration. Hence Father Basil and his New Testament, and on the whole the guests bore with it in good grace. Charlotte was known to be strange in some ways.

A special lectern had been placed in a corner of the parlour, betwixt two clumps of white chrysanthemums in painted pots and this was to be Father Basil's pulpit. Thither went Father Basil, plump and pontific, the picture of priestly poise. Long years on this subcontinent had brought out in Father Basil a native priestly strain, that of dining well on most of his spiritual and temporal excursions to the homes of his flock, and but for the uniform of his calling and the nature of his faith and the colour of his skin, he might have been a local Brahmin priest to judge from his form. His was a well-oiled, well dined and well wined voice, rolling rhetorically forth as though each phrase were a special tasty morsel he turned over in his mouth with relish and each period a good, soul-satisfying gulp.

' "And whither I go, ye know the way. Thomas saith to him, "Lord, we know not whither thou goest; how know we the way?" Jesus saith to him, "I am the way, and the truth, and the life. No one cometh to the Father except through me. If ye had recognized me, ye would know my Father also. From now ye are recognizing him and have seen him." Philip saith to him, "Lord, show us the Father, and it sufficeth us." Jesus saith to him, "So long a time have I been with you and hast thou not recognized me, Philip? He that hath seen me hath seen the Father. How dost thou say, 'Show us the Father?' Dost thou not believe that I am in the Father and the Father in me? The words that I say to you I speak not from myself, but the Father who abideth in me doeth his works. Believe me that I am in the Father and the Father in me; or else on account of the works themselves believe me." '

The text had been chosen by the Colonel Memsahib and Father Basil, eyes half-closed in his ruminative exertions, launched forth upon his discourse, drawing trails upon trails of theological niceties like magic ribbons out of the great cavern of his mouth: 'Brothers and sisters in Christ! The destination of man is unknown to him except in its formal accounts. We are told that the Christian must seek Heaven and perfect fellowship with our Father. But it is a Father we have never met and the phrases that describe him are beyond our faculties to grasp: "Things which eye saw not and ear heard not, and which entered not into the heart of man, whatsoever things that God prepared for them that love Him." But though the destination be not known and be unknowable, brothers and sisters in Christ, yet the Lord pronounces unto us that each of us knows whither we are bound. We are daunted. Like loyal and literalminded Thomas, we ask how this may be. But reflect, my brothers and sisters, we do not go to a coaching inn and ask the inn-keeper to recommend a direction and a coach—it is only because we know something before we commence the journey, because we know whither we mean to go, that we even ask how to begin. "Whither I go, ye know the way." "I am the way," saith the Lord. The way is well-known because the way is the Lord Himself. The Christian must pass through the veil, must pass through the flesh. We must eat the flesh of the Son of Man and drink His sacred blood so that our being becomes one with the substance of His divine nature, so that we are united with Him and discover the deity indwelling in it. We become "very members incorporate in His body" and come to the Father through Him and thus does He become the way.'

The punkahs lolled upon the still air hither and thither and the flame of four dozen candles shook and swayed with every pulsation; upon the pale walls faded shadows flapped in gentle waves as though the very room breathed softly to itself, inhaling the thoughts, the scents, the words that bred within.

Lizzie Lawrence yawned gently and whispered something to Rosa. And when Father Basil uttered the words 'eat the flesh of the Son of Man and drink His blood' his bulbous eyes dilated in such threatening emphasis and his jaws worked up such a peculiar chomping motion that it sent little Lucinda Parker helplessly agiggle despite the desperate pinching of her lady mother.

Edwin sought the room for Mr Dutt. There he was, sandwiched between old Mrs Page and Major Norton, nodding diligently, the picture of sympathetic catholicism.

'Truth is a personal being apprehended in the only way in

which personality is ever fully apprehended . . .' the venerable pastor was holding forth. 'This is the only way in which spiritual and divine reality can be expressed. What is personal can only be expressed in a person. I grant, brothers and sisters in Christ, that this invaluable truth is made use of by most heathen institutions which, if anything, are composed of hordes of barbarous personalities of monstrous and questionable divinity . . .'

'At the very earliest opportunity I must get to speak to him alone,' thought Edwin anxiously. There was a lot that Edwin had shyly saved up for this evening. Questions of great import awaited Mr Dutt's judgement. Poems of his own composition waited to be assessed by the great man's discerning eye. Bookshelves to be displayed. But when the pastor had finished, Brigadier Daniels it was, grating out one of his sensational stories. And Edwin blushed for him and wondered what on earth Mr Dutt thought of the bluff, beefy British company present. Even when the company stood up to sing 'God Save The Queen' the words inspired acute embarrassment in Edwin's heart. And when they came, roaring roundly down to the words:

> O Lord, our God, arise, scatter her enemies.
> And make them fall! Confound their politics,
> Frustrate their knavish tricks, on thee our
> Hopes we fix, God save us all . . .

Edwin did not know where to hide his face. It was obvious that the God being thus invoked, was an Anglo-Saxon god, down from the Norse seas in his Viking craft, winged helmet, hatchet, eyes of ice and nostrils breathing fire. Edwin would have given anything to divine what Mr Dutt was thinking even as he stood, head bowed, with the carolling crowd.

'Ladies and gen'lemun!' the Brigadier's voice ground the silence to dust and his tale trudged down the air on martial boots. 'We have just given voice to our estimable anthem, a song of ancient glory and renown, a song to o'erwhelm each true born Englishman, be he a languishin' in 'eathen barbary, beyond the wild ocean.'

The Brigadier's narrations—no matter what their literal content—were usually delivered in tones of macabre gloom.

'This song, dear ladies and gen'lemun, forms the subject of the experience I am about to narrate to you. I owe to it not only my position but my very life, such as it is, as sure as my name's Daniels, as sure as I am astanding before you now.

'I ask you, gen'lemun and ladies, to envision a small group of us, British officers, staunch, tried and tested men, scarce ten of us and two faithful Gurkhas, lost in the tortuous ravines nigh Jhansi, whither we had followed in the wake of the forces of Sir Hugh Rose. I ask you to envision the rebellion of fifty sepoys, men we had drilled and trained in battle craft and that now uprose 'gainst us in dastardly betrayal.

'It is but just to admit, in fairness to the poor devils, that they escorted us to a place of safety, yea, saluted us and all, ere they decamped with their arms to join the army of the militant Ranee.

'A pretty kettle of fish. But, as I always say, 'tis easy to bait a native. Play on their ruddy emotions, I say. Pat 'em and coddle 'em awhile. Call 'em by their nicknames. Ask after the missus and the brats and the tribe. Send him a gew-gaw for the bambino. Ten British officers and fifty sepoys turned rebel! On the very march to Jhansi! Sir Hugh would have the hide off our backs and no mistake. But we got 'em back, yessir, that we did and it was the brain of my bright young Gurkha lad, Man Bahadur Thapa. Egad! Did it please the feller-me-lad to be called 'Man' by me, for sure he had the countenance of a lemur and there was I, Robinson Crusoe!

'You don't know those ravines. God bless you, sirs, that's where those devils, those thugs, plied their trade. In next to no time the infernal noose'd be round your neck, without so much as a by your leave, and next thing you know, twang!—and you'd given up the ghost and pretty silly you're feelin' then!

'Well, here we were, lost, and the nearest settlement a village of former thugs that'd taken to farming. But, as I say, once a thug always a thug and not to be trusted! Six miles of tramping in the dark and there we were amongst crowds of thugs—a most unlovely situation, let me tell you.

' "Those're no perishin' thugs," said I to myself. "There's something regular in their march, their backs are too straight. Those, my lad," I said to my self, "—are rebels and no mistake, as sure as my name's Daniels or I'll eat my hat."

'They welcomed us, every man Jack of us, and gave us food and shelter; and no man amongst us but had his hand to his holster. Two hundred or so thugs and fifty of 'em our men. And how in the name of Mike were we to tell 'em in the dark? And how get 'em to return, much less show us the way? Any moment and the devils would decide that enough was enough and we'd be partin' company with our immortal souls.

'Twas Man Bahadur Thapa saved the day with that bright thought of his. And here's what we did, ladies and gen'lemun: we built a campfire and, beseated round it, we forthwith burst into song. Aye, yes, we sang fit to burst our vocal cords, fit to raise the dead. You wouldn't take me for a lusty carollin' choirmaster—hey? I give you my word for it, I'd ha' outdone the entire chorus at Canterbury Cathedral that night. We sang "Now Are We Met" and "Home, Sweet Home". And "The Soldier's Farewell" and "The Departure For Syria". Yea, and "Bonnie Dundee" and "Go Where Glory Waits Thee".

'There's no one to beat 'em natives for good, wholesome curiosity. All round the camp we grew sensible, presently, of waiting, listening figures, asquatting upon the rocky ground. Some of 'em, poor blighters, even beat time and one of 'em brought a little two-faced drum and beat his native tattoo 'pon it to speed our singing and we made a very pretty company indeed, very cosy and chummy, take it from me. Then when the singing and beating time was well under way and every man of 'em rocking and swayin' to our singin', we changed tune of a sudden in true defence strategy and commenced that most glorious anthem "God Save The Queen".

'You guessed it, fair ladies and gentlemen. That did it. Fifty men were 'pon their feet, saluting silently, quite, quite carried away, all thought of mutiny clean forgot. That's how I drilled my men, sirs. Fidelity and iron discipline. Why, they'd rise from the very grave to hear the anthem, but the poor blisters haven't any graves to speak of, curse 'em!

'In scarce an hour we were marching back through the wilds of Boondelcund to join Sir Hugh. So say I, my good sirs, the native's got his heart in the right place. He may get the heeby-jeebies and may up and rebel awhile and may work 'imself up into a fidget o'er ham and beef and the purdah o'er a woman's face and tripe like that but he knows what's good for him.

'"God Save The Queen!"—say I. God saved me that night and all for that song. You know the phrase 'bought for a song'? Our lives were bought for a song that night and no mistake!'

There was to the Brigadier's deductions on native psychology a general outcry, the subject being dear to every spirited English heart. The morality of the native, his maturity or absence thereof, his secret wiles and wishes, was something that most of the company present held strong opinions about.

A babel of voices rose into the air, a general hubbub of political discourse, all very familiar, all very predictable to Edwin. For six years now, when Englishmen met in India, they discussed the mutiny, the native atrocities, the take-over by the Crown. Every aspect of the epoch had to be religiously gone over upon each possible occasion. Whether Napier was the superior statesman or Dalhousie. 'Statesman?'—shouted an angry voice. 'I beg your pardon! Tradesmen! Mercenaries! Nay, sir, be not over heated. Neither statesmen nor mercenaries. The proper phrase to employ is 'strategic sportsmen' and strategies can oft run amuck. I appeal to your forbearance, sir, but Napier's missives bear scant vestige of strategy. Do but consider his brash memoranda. The Marquis of Dalhousie, contrariwise, seemed in absolute control of the situation until 1956. Had Parliament appreciated the import of his repeated requests for more European troops, history would have transpired otherwise. Deuce take it all, sir, not a single European officer to command our sepoy armies betwixt Allahabad and Calcutta. Scandalous! Why, what is it but asking for trouble? It's serving mutiny to them on a silver platter—only a dolt wouldn't help himself. And the native is no dolt, whatever some of us may be disposed to feel. The man of salt was Lawrence, gentlemen. He alone, if I may say so, had the vision and the political sensitivity to foresee the disaster. Witness the way he provisioned the Lucknow Residency in anticipation of a long siege. That was a man of a different stamp, yea, built of sterner stuff. We didn't have postmen then to run our affairs, sir. We had generals and men of mettle.'

Edwin thought it very bad form to attack poor Lord Canning for his past calling. 'Well, he was Postmaster General—that makes him general enough!'—scoffed the lively young voice. More laughter rocked the company. 'Poor Clemency Canning and his pettifogging policies, his pussy-footing pacifism, his endless pardons.' Pardon?—Shame, shame! The native has known no peace for fifteen centuries, sir. Pardon, freedom, peace, are things he cannot apprehend emotionally. Why, let 'em run the show for a year and see the godawful mess they'll get it into. You can't run a country on baksheesh, sir. The baboo had better stick to his baksheesh. Moreover the native philosophy of honour isn't the same as ours. Honour here is amoral. This country, sir, has never known a republic.' 'Nay,' uprose the youthful dissenter, 'I cannot concur with you, sir! Consider . . .'

It was time to draw Mr Dutt away, decided Edwin. He found Mr Dutt holding polite converse with old Mrs Page on, presumably, the breeding the roses in Indian climes.

'But, Mr Datt,' protested she. 'When you breed the English tea rose and the native variety, it is to be seen that the native strain often overwhelms the English strain. And what began as a warm, peachen blossom turns into a miserable tiny crimson bloom. The native strain,' she said acutely, '—is a nuisance.'

'Not entirely so, my lady,' was Mr Dutt's meek answer. 'For your potpourri, recollect, native petals are best.'

Edwin plucked at his sleeve. 'One moment, please,' he whispered.

'Mr Dutt, sir, I particularly desire that you behold my room. There's something I must sound you on and I'm afraid it isn't very congenial here.'

'As you wish, Mr Edwin,' readily agreed Mr Dutt.

'This way, please.' Why did Mr Dutt persist in addressing him as Mr Edwin—only servants did that! Edwin felt belittled by that tone of natural respect that stole into Mr Dutt's voice whenever he spoke to him.

'A very extraordinary room, in sooth, Mr Edwin,' observed Mr Dutt, looking around with interest. 'It is as though two men dwelt herein, not one.'

'It used to be Father's room when I was little,' explained Edwin, trying not to be amused by the other's quaint turn of speech. 'Those are two of his tigers.' Edwin pointed at the two striped pelts asprawl upon the far wall above the bookshelves. 'Yonder are his war trophies. He was the hero of Sind, you know. And that is his native sword collection.'

'And these books?' enquired Mr Dutt.

'Mine,' said Edwin bashfully.

'The chamber of a soldier and a man of letters! Remarkable!' pronounced Mr Dutt precisely in his too-careful English. 'Sophocles, Plato, Augustine, Hume, Spinoza. And this I perceive to be literature. The Complete Works of Shakespeare, the complete

Pope, Blake, Gray, Spenser. Scott and Mr Wordsworth. Even, dear me, the melodious Mr Tennyson's newest lyrics. This, Mr Edwin, is impressive. And you have read all these volumes?'

'All of them,' replied Edwin.

'And reflected upon them?'

'I have endeavoured to—in a modest way, of course.'

'You do not seek to be a soldier like your estimable father?'

'I believe I have a singular want of aptitude in that direction, Mr Dutt. There are other areas of usefulness in which I aspire to render such small service as I am capable of.'

'Such as?'

Edwin drew a deep breath. 'I wish to write, Mr Dutt.'

'Ah,' was the non-committal rejoinder. 'Poetry?'

'Well poetry . . . and . . . and things speculative. I . . . I have thought generally upon things a bit and put down my . . . my views.'

It sounded so preposterous, so presumptuous, that Edwin was constrained to blush. The words came in a rush. 'I am putting together my very first volume, sir. If . . . if you'd care to examine it . . . I'd be most obliged to you.'

'It would be a pleasure, Mr Edwin,' responded Mr Dutt suavely, beseating himself.

How that hour flew past Edwin scarce knew. Not all the questions he had accumulated in his mind found satisfactory answers. Some sounded downright silly.

'Mr Dutt,' he asked gravely. 'Why are poets unhappy men?'

'I don't believe they are, Mr Edwin,' replied Mr Dutt with a twinkle in his eye. 'Many of them, I find, have proved themselves singularly churlish and not one whit different from other men. Much of the unhappiness, I'm disposed to believe, comes from a formal tone of voice. Men of thought and feeling, it is commonly presumed, must of necessity be of a melancholic disposition and the minor poet makes it a point of honour to be distressed and world-weary. I beg your pardon, Mr Edwin, have I uttered aught that is amiss?'

'How do you tell a minor from a major talent?'

Mr Dutt smiled disarmingly. 'In me, Mr Edwin, stands before you an example of a contented minor poet. And I pray that I may ever stay so and never have too big a price to pay the Muse for what she may choose to bestow upon me.'

'I do not altogether understand.'

'I'd rather have bread and peace than poetry, Mr Edwin.'

'But the . . . the search, Mr Dutt? The prophetic mission, the special destiny? To utter, to know, to show the way, to find words for things?'

Mr Dutt shrugged and said with a very straight face, 'Allow me to offer an opinion, Mr Edwin. Actually there are no words for things. The only language is analogy. There are only roughly similar resonances. The poet strives to reconstruct a similar vibration, that's all.'

'But there is the simple truth in a line—like the cut of a knife, like the taste of water . . .'

'There you are,' smiled Mr Dutt. 'Analogy again.'

'You think my compositions lack complexity?'

Mr Dutt reflected. 'On the contrary, Mr Edwin, they abound in compound visions. Where they fall short of ideal expression, if I may be excused for saying so, are the places where a natural simplicity is deliberately avoided in preference of a tortuous complexity.'

He picked up Edwin's leather bound notebook.

'I see that you are indeed a good nature poet,' pronounced he kindly. 'Consider this line—"the tipsied, twinkled tremor in the trees" and "the white sky streaked with silver scales". Excellent alliteration. A very vivid flash of observation, a very arresting expression. And this image of the world blowing out of the sun in a broad, smoking beam. Very striking. And this phrase about "a wisp of a river folded up in sky". And "the heavens crumbling up into creased clouds". Very moving. But, Mr Edwin, the stanza I like most is the one about the birds. You speak of their "long discourse, long, shrill narrations, long tuneful exclamations". And then there descends this lovely rain of words—"bat, soar and flit, dip, twit and quip", followed by that sudden brake to the speed with this beautiful visual image of the single raven marooned upon a pole in a grey sky! This is indeed well expressed. Yet, say I, the vision you beheld was simple, and the expression you construed of it is compound. Truth moves in one direction, these lovely phrases move in another.'

'But don't they meet in some real images, sir?' asked Edwin anxiously.

'That they do, but whither are they bound? Are these pictures ends in themselves? If so, there is no more to be written or said? Or do they correspond to some state in you which you must infer? Some phrases go round in a circle and meet at the far end of the circumference, as it were; the sense must wait for the picture to form. Which is why you must use natural metaphors, not conceits, Mr Edwin.'

'And this one entitled "Hymn"—' went on the great man. '"Lord, cool my soul with showering rain. All nature trapped in a dewy net. Swarms of trees, streams of breeze; shoals of cloud, flowers wading wet." In despite of the questionable grammar and the confused movement of the lines, I find a general freshness, a monsoon wetness, a washness—and the idea of fluid mobility is put well across. A little cleaning up and it shall be a fine verse yet.'

'I . . . I rather believe that the first two lines are bad ones and sort of . . . stumble into the next two lines which are reasonably good . . .' Edwin endeavoured to expound his personal assessment of a verse which had troubled him much.

'If you are inclined to consider it that way, yes. There is a distinct rise and fall of inspiration, as it were. Excellent expression and bathos. To speak of trees afrisk in the sun and tricked out in trickets of the sun is surely pretty phrasing but to the punctilious maker of phrases it may well appear an overdone alliteration, if I may say so. In inspiration too there are alternating pulses of action and rest. Actually I don't think one may speak so simply of good lines and bad lines, Mr Edwin. There are lines which follow the contour of observed and felt reality and lines which stray and lose themselves. In a poem, as in battle, one trusts to the unknown accident.'

It was at this point in the dialogue that tripping footfalls sounded just outside the door and a mirthful voice shrilled wickedly in the corridor without:

> *Follow my Bangalorey man*
> *Follow my Bangalorey man.*
> *I'll do all that ever I can*
> *To follow my Bangalorey man!*

Edwin knew the rest of that absurd ditty: We'll borrow a horse, and steal a gig, and round the world we'll do a jig, and I'll do all that ever I can, to follow my Bangalorey man!

The rhyme ended on a high, affected operatic tremolo and

Edwin rose hastily and threw open the door.

'Oh, there you are, Edwin dear! Its naughty of you to hide yourself so, Mr Datt. We're going to sing and you must promise to give us a song,' dimpled Rosa with mischief in her eye.

'I . . . I'm afraid I don't know any English songs, Miss Rosa,' said poor Mr Dutt, confused.

'Oh, come, come,' twinkled the charming young miss. 'You can surely give us a Bangalorey song—or a Bengalee song!'

Edwin gave her a savage, scorching frown which she blithely took no note of. 'And you're not to run off again, Edwin dear. Matilda O'Brien's pining to sing a duet with you and she simply won't let you off.'

The grand Brodwood piano was now thrown open to the guests, more candles brought and everybody seemed in good voice from ancient Mrs Page and Brigadier Daniels to wee Emilia O'Brien. Chairs were pulled up and cake and fruits passed round, the native bearers moving hither, thither and yonder like mute, impersonal puppets.

Majors Norton and Perkins led the singing with a gruff, hearty rendering of "Before All Lands In East or West", with Brigadier Daniels adding his rusty baritone to the snatches which pleased him most.

> Be-fore all lands in East or West, I love my na-tive land
> $\qquad$ the best,
> With God's best gifts 'tis teem-ing.
> No gold or jewels here are found, yet men of no-ble
> $\qquad$ soul abound,
> And eyes of joy are gleam-ing
> And eyes of joy are gleam-ing.
> Be-fore all peo-ple East or West, I love my coun-try-men
> $\qquad$ the best
> A race of no-ble spi-rit.
> A so-ber mind, a gen'rous heart, to virtue trained, yet
> $\qquad$ free from art,
> They from their sires in-her-it!

Then followed a long, lank, listless lament by the old and young Mrs Pages—"On The Banks Of Allan Water" which retold the tragedy of the dead miller's daughter. Then another patriotic effusion in the form of "The Red, White and Blue" rendered by the three rollicking Lawrences:

> *Bri-tan-nia, the pride of the o-cean,*
> *The home of the brave and the free,*
> *The shrine of each pa-triot's de-vo-tion,*
> *The world of-fers hom-age to thee,*
> *At thy man-dates he-roes as-sem-ble,*
> *When Li-ber-ty's form stands in view,*
> *Thy banners make ty-ran-ny trem-ble,*
> *When borne by the Red, White and Blue!*
> *When war spread its wide des-o-la-tion,*
> *And threat-en'd our land to de-form,*
> *The ark then of free-dom's foun-da-tion,*
> *Bri-tan-nia rode safe through the storm.*
> *With her gar-lands of vic-t'ry a-round her,*
> *When so no-bly she bore her brave crew,*
> *With her flag float-ing proud-ly be-fore her,*
> *The boast of the Red, White and Blue!*

So catching was the melody, so well harmonized, that all the guests joined in and the chamber rang with the glad throb of many voices. A deep, charged silence fell as the last bars died away and it was now the Colonel Memsahib's turn to sing. True to her general strangeness the lady chose an old Scotch air, "Wae's Me For Prince Charlie". She rendered that old Jacobite lament with such intense sadness, such personal meaning, her lone, fluting voice seeking old resonances, that many a lace kerchief was applied to the dewy eyes of the auditors and many a manly throat cleared in nostalgic memory. A great wrong, an ineradicable sin still commanded penance and expiation. And when she came to the final words:

> *Bonnie, bonnie bird, The tears cam' drap-pin' rare-ly,*
> *I took my bon-net aff my heid, for weel I lo'ed Prince Charlie.*

and then

> *O this is no'a land for me,*
> *I'll tar-ry here nae lan-ger . . .*

a distinct sniff from the old Brigadier drew the attention of all, young and old, to an indefinable misery they all felt. A loud encore received the closing bars and this time the memsahib rendered two choice old pieces composed by Sir Thomas Moore, "Silent, Oh Moyle" and "Oh! Breathe Not His Name". And yet again the sheer poetry of the haunting words was pregnant with that curious evocation to a personal lover:

> *Si-lent, oh Moyle, be the roar of thy wa-ter,*
> *Break not, ye bree-zes your chain of re-pose,*
> *While mur-mur-ing mourn-ful-ly, Lir's lone-ly daugh-ter*
> *Tells to the night-star her tale of woes . . .*

And as she slowly sang the last words it was as though an ultimate human sorrow, so simple as to be unutterable in the history of human emotion, had at last found musical relief.

> *Oh! breathe not his name, let it sleep in the shade*
> *Where cold and un-hon-ured his re-lics are laid!*
> *Sad, si-lent and dark be the tears that we shed*
> *As the night-dew that falls on the grass o'er his head.*

The lady had an ineffable air of profound tragedy and immense refinement blended together in a strangely striking aristocratic brew. The awed silence which received her words, her playing or her singing was an extension of her powerful presence. She had a masterful sense of volume and time and pitch. And yet it could scarce be overlooked that this tremendous, tragic, tuneful eloquence served to oppress the spirits of the light-hearted. Some of the younger guests essayed to enliven the spirits of the company with that lively old air: "Come, Let Us A-Maying Go" and the popular ballad "How Should I Your True Love Know".

Suddenly Rosa, laughing mischievously, all atwinkle and asparkle, with a dangerous shine in her smile, pranced upto the piano stool, flounced down upon it, struck a few random bars and playfully announced a duet.

'And for my partner,' she proclaimed gleefully, clapping her little hands, '—I must have our Mr Datt and no other. Come, Mr Datt, be a pet. I absolutely insist and I won't take 'no' for an answer.'

Mr Dutt's brown face all aflush with embarrassment, he half rose out of his chair, vainly striving to preserve his composure.

'Oh, but Miss Rosa, I told you I know no English songs. I beg you, let me off.'

'Dear me, how very ungracious,' retorted she. 'In our parties everyone does as we do and we brook no excuses and no exceptions.'

'Oh well,' sighed poor Mr Dutt. 'I must look a fool then before all the company. I appeal to you, ladies and gentlemen, to bear with my singing. I know no English songs and I can't read music, but the lady insists and gallantry demands . . .' He made a feeble bow, and charming Rosa struck a comic pose. This was to be the comic sequence of the evening. Edwin sat, glowering and incensed, in his armchair, truly alarmed at Rosa's frivolous malice.

By some curious stroke of chance Rosa began 'Hark, The Lark', glancing wickedly out of the corner of her eye, with a dimple in her cheek, at poor, awkward Mr Dutt. But, to Edwin's immense astonishment, Mr Dutt was proving neither poor nor awkward. No sooner had Rosa given melodious utterance to the first two lines:

Hark! Hark! The lark at heav'n's gate sings!
Hark! Hark! The lark at heav'n's gate sings!

than did the surprising Mr Dutt nimbly follow with the next two lines:

And Phoebus 'gins a-rise his steeds
To water at these springs.

Nobody could help remark this extraordinary situation and everyone stopped speaking all at once. True, Mr Dutt sang a melody all his own but he had a rich, bass voice and the strange tune he improvised, while nowhere near the original melody, was by no means wanting in pleasing notes or surprising contrasts and was, moreover, a just and appropriate development of the first two lines. More amazing was his obvious knowledge of the words of which even Edwin retained but a faint recollection. He wasn't reading them in Rosa's song book for he stood by the side of the piano, looking away at some potted ferns to the left. And such an expression of delight seemed to play upon his swarthy face. And when they came to 'My lady sweet, arise, arise, my lady sweet, arise . . .' he chanced to smile upon his young tormenter with such comic meaning in his face, pulling such an expression of tender distress and woe that the tension relaxed of a sudden and laughter filled the room, and clapping, and many cheers, whereupon Rosa, suddenly aflame, pounded a loud, discordant chord upon the instrument, rose sharply, and closing the lid with a bang, strode haughtily away, leaving poor Mr Dutt in mid-bar, looking astonished, dejected and injured.

Never had Edwin applauded his mother more. The Colonel Memsahib stepped smoothly forward, and, taking Mr Dutt's arm, smiled coolly upon the company.

'But what a pleasant surprise, Mr Datt! That was an impressive rendering, Mr Datt. How do you know the words so well?'

Mr Dutt blushed. 'That was Shakespeare, madam,' he replied simply as though he were speaking of an old friend. 'Miss Rosalie happened to pick up the serenade to Imogen in *Cymbeline* . . .'

'Ah, so it was, so it was,' murmured the memsahib.

She turned to her guests. 'Gentlemen and ladies,' spoke she in her clear, soft voice. 'Will it please you to move into the dining room? Dinner is laid and the time has now come to present dear Edwin with our gifts. And,' she added, smiling, 'Mr Datt being our Edwin's chosen friend at this gathering, it is only meet that he join me in offering my late husband's gifts to Edwin upon this happy occasion. Mr Datt?' And still lending him her arm, she conducted him regally into the dining room. Good form and grace saved the day for Edwin and it was with relief that the company rose to accompany their hostess to the dining chamber.

'Gracious Heaven!' he heard Rosa tell Matilda O'Brien as, arm-in-arm, they trooped into the dining-room. 'Whatever can Mother be thinking of! And who would've thought the Bangalorey man could sing our songs?'

'But doesn't it come out all funny?' was the whispered observation. 'I mean, doesn't it?'

In the sombre dining-room three extra tables had been accommodated to extend the length of the one massive mahogany and the guests, beseated at the four tables, drank Edwin's health, the late Colonel's, the memsahib's and lastly, the glorious Empire which had occasioned their presence together upon this glorious evening.

'Honoured ladies and gentlemen!' Mr Dutt apostrophized the assembled company in his best ceremonial manner. 'I stand before you tonight charged with a right sacred duty for which I am much beholden to my gracious hostess.' Here he made a stiff little bow in the memsahib's direction. 'Dare I express my appreciation for the immense honour that your hospitality, trust and fellowship have conferred upon me this evening, an honour I can with certitude say I shall never efface from my memory in all the years to come. In bestowing upon Mr Edwin, on his twenty-first birth anniversary, this missive from his late father, the heroic Colonel Vernon Agnew Watkins may I prove the bearer of messages bringing good cheer and solace to his young heart and hope and meaningful commitment to his young years. This invaluable gift do I, in the presence of this august company, offer unto Mr Edwin in the name of our Maker and as Mrs Watkins's humble agent and friend, now and evermore.'

'Hear, hear!' cried Major Norton as Edwin rose to receive the sealed paper packet.

'Hear, hear!' cried the young ladies and clapped their gentle hands. And Mr Dutt made his odd little bow again, smiling all over his face, touched, confused and quite, quite overwhelmed.

An abrupt silence fell as the Colonel Memsahib rose to her feet, bearing a well wrapped and oddly shaped parcel.

'On this happy occasion I have pleasure in presenting the gun used by my beloved husband in his numerous military engagements. It bore him company full many a year and with my best wishes I do hereby confer it upon his son and heir, Edwin Reginald Braithwaite Watkins and express the hope that, as of yore, it may be used well in the service of his country and the service of his fellow men with justice and honour.'

With this short address she turned to Edwin and laid the heavy inheritance in his awkward hands.

'Give um a big hand, gentlemun!' roared the old Brigadier and the next moment, as though by clockwork, everyone was on their feet, singing 'Happy Birthday, dear Edwin!' raising their glasses, smiling warmly, and two bearers, sashed and turbanned, slid in, bearing the large twenty-one key cake and the beribboned silver knife upon a salver.

The younger guests had every intention of dancing all night, the older ones, of sitting over horrific dawk-bungalow tales. The hall was cleared and the band installed behind a screen of potted ferns. Dinner over, the music struck up, anon and away floated the young ladies in the arms of the young officers and even the gallant old Brigadier sought out old Mrs Page and offered her his hand with a deep, old fashioned bow.

The door slid to, muting the music of the band, and Edwin was alone with his father. The seal gave way with a reproachful crackle and Edwin found himself confronting what appeared to him a curiously familiar countenance beheld in a crowd.

He had the impression of knocking upon a door which opened to admit him into a stern, military chamber. Behind the green baize covered table, beseated magisterially betwixt the maps and the globe and the almanac, was a man. A stiff, formal voice accosted him: 'Major Vernon Agnew Watkins,' said the man, rising cordially and his grip was firm and staunch upon the hand. 'The fifty-eighth regiment under General Napier. Elevated to Colonel after the takeover of Sind, having rendered gallant service in the engagement of Imangarh.'

The ink upon the yellowed sheets had paled with the years. A small, impersonal hand and a distant, unimaginable voice addressed him. Yet there was a ring in certain lines and a real person it was that uttered those careful words into the formless future. And a strange thought occurred to Edwin: just as this father, this voice out of the past, was a myth for him, so must he, Edwin, a babe in arms, a future auditor, be a myth for this father.

'My dear Edwin Reginald Braithwaite Watkins,'—the handwriting addressed him by his complete name, as one man apostrophizing another. They were confronting one another, man to man, save that one man sat upon a chair and the other stood to attention. It may well have been 'My dear Sergeant' or 'My dear Corporal'.

My dear Edwin Reginald Braithwaite Watkins,

It is with the utmost affection and pleasure that I take up my pen to greet you, this day of the future, 17 March 1865, upon the twenty-first anniversary of your nativity.

Endeavour as I might, I find it beyond my powers of conjuration to envision you, though you do stand before me, a phantom of my brain. I undertake this extraordinary enterprise of writing to you in person because it is my apprehension that I may not outlast this melancholy year, Labouring as I do under sentence of death from a tribe of Afghans which, in no uncertain terms, has spelt the fate in store for me. To Napier I owed a debt of gratitude and duty which I have abundantly fulfilled. To you I am accountable as is a father unto his son, as is the past unto the future. And to my Maker am I responsible for the honour of my actions and the truthfulness of my confessions, so help me GOD.

Edwin felt the unaccountable command in the air, as though he were obeying the fantasy of another man, twenty years in the past. It was the voice of a self-conscious stranger, choosing his words with care. Large spaces of self-debate and deliberation divided the phrases; the laboured sentences tentatively offered up their arduous clauses, eked out the formal niceties with genteel caution. There was unease in the lines of this uncomfortable monologue wherein the speaker sought to measure the response upon a phantom countenance ere he ventured further. What was it that one generation had to tell the next about itself, wondered Edwin, searching the lines. What was it that it could not bring itself to utter despite the pleasing formalities, the many parentheses, digressions and deletions. The half-truths were articulated in the lines, the whole truth hid somewhere in the deletions and pleaded for understanding and absolution.

Now the tone was grandiose, self-congratulatory, twisting moral meanings this way and that to uphold a personal assertion. Now it was pompous, vainglorious, officious, false.

'My place in history,' wrote the myth,

is of necessity tied up with the province of Sind, the name given to the country lying on both sides of the Indus south of the Panjaub and extending to the sea. The river gives it life and fruitfulness. On the west and east are barren deserts. This was the cradle of the most ancient civilization, this the route taken by the venturesome invaders of history, the Aryans, the Macedonians, Mahmoud of Ghazni, the Huns, the Mongols, the Turko-Afghans, the Moguls. Sind accepted the supremacy of the Great Moguls and submitted to the plunderers Tamerlane and Nadir Shah. Against the design of history, it was but meet that Sind be claimed by British conquest. History demanded it; the natives foresaw it. 'Alas,' wrote a Sindee native, 'Sind is now lost to us since the English have seen the river!'

It may justly be asseverated that our policies in Sind were nobly in accord with the traditions of British rule in India and that any lapse on our part may ethically be indicated to our complete satisfaction by reason of our disinterested intent and by our earnest aspirations of extending the incalculable blessings of British administration upon a province unremarkable for any native ability of government. If it be charged by posterity that our action in Sind did not err on the side of indulgence to the susceptibilities of the native population, and if, unfortunately for our national credit, British performance in India fell to a lower level of unscrupulousness than ever before, I have this to advance: that there is for me no insurmountable necessity of seeking for any moral justification, the peace and progress of the state achieved by the talents, the energy and the ability of Sir Charles Napier, our general, being altogether admirable and deserving of the approbation of history. Indeed, it is my conviction that our conduct in Sind was ever marked by a strict observance of propriety and fair play, the previous Governor- General having justly refused to consider the proposal of the Maharaja of Panjaub, Ranjit Singh, that Sind be partitioned betwixt himself and the Company . . .'

Edwin read on, scanning through several pages in the self-same style of narration. It could not be mere suspicion. There was, he thought, some confusion in that military tone. Halfway through the epistle he met a new, unbecoming, ingratiating tone of voice, almost appealing, almost imploring, a crop of phrases alien to the style: 'It is in a moment of the utmost trepidation', 'the forbearance and forgiveness of the years to come', 'endure my words with patience and fortitude . . . !' 'You,' wrote the myth, '—are young and possibly enjoy the privilege of not having yet been vouchsaved

opportunities for misconduct.' 'You,' mused the voice,'—may yet
be innocent of the discord betwixt intention and act . . .'

The Colonel was no longer sitting. He stood up, ceremonially
peeled off some of his decorations and met him as a man, older
and weaker, And on his side were youth and judgement. Centrally
dividing the letter was a dissent of voices, a contest betwixt
conscience and convention.

'There are occasions,' wrote the voice,

> —when I am disposed to entertain the speculation that
> the treatment of Sind, however expedient politically,
> is somehow personally disconcerting to me. There are
> times when I am prone to review it as indefensible—the
> flagrant violations of treaty, the formal announcements
> unto the weaker foe that we honourably intended to
> violate such provisions of the treaty as suited us. 'The
> article,' wrote we in the utmost courtesy that language
> is capable of, '—must necessarily, regrettably be
> suspended.' We benevolently warned our enemy, in
> all justice and fairness, that neither the ready power
> to crush and annihilate them nor the will to call it
> into action were wanting if it ever appeared requisite,
> however remotely, for the safety and integrity of the
> Anglo- Indian Empire or frontiers. I recollect the sums
> of money exacted under threat of advance, the use of
> intimidation, the astonishing course of marching upon
> the desert fortress of Imangah—literally 'citadel of
> honesty'—without any declaration of war and razing
> it to the ground. No one shall ever deny Napier's
> brilliant generalship and the valour and devotion of our
> soldiers. With a small force of 3000 we utterly routed,
> against tremendous odds, a large army of 30,000. If
> Napier alone made 70,000 pounds from the plunder of
> Hyderabad, well be it known that he deserved every
> penny of it for his estimable artifice, endurance and
> strategy. Of his benevolent intentions he alone is the
> best judge, though his words to the effect that we had
> no right to seize Sind and yet we did so and made of
> it all 'a very advantageous, useful, humane piece of
> rascality' has occasioned me no little disquietude . . .

It fell to me to plant the British colours upon the ruins
of Imangarh, a duty of no mean honour and credit.
The recollections of that spirited triumph are none
too distinct. Suffice that Davis and I led the uphill
assault, cheek by jowl, and Davis it was held the British
standard. And Davis it was fell, shot from behind and
mine was the hand that planted the British flag. Only
one other man did witness how my comrade Davis fell,
Captain Andrewes, and he lived not long enough to
give tongue. No one knows how Davis fell. I do, my
son. Imangarh made of me a war-hero, a Colonel, and
Davis my friend a dead man . . .

Edwin was conscious of a curious breathlessness and panic, a
constriction of throat, a dryness of mouth. The words struggled
out of the yellow pages, gracefully overstepping the hurtful truths,
but leaving a bizarre welter of possibilities to the imagination.

'Pir Muhammad,' went on another paragraph,

—was more than a bearer. He was a devoted admirer,
a fervent follower, staunch and true, a man in whose
eyes I could do no wrong. I ask myself ever and anon:
what else was there for me to choose? Invaluable
information was promised forth and all I had to give
up was the native spy. I sent up Pir Muhammad, my
servant, my friend, the only native in my camp that
night. A hostage for a day, I assured him. The British
army would not permit the barbarous Baluchs to injure
a hair on his head. Pir Muhammad would not doubt his
master to save his soul. We decamped that night under
cover of darkness, carrying back with us the secrets
Napier needed. No one ever found out what happened
to Pir Muhammad. They gave him, I presume, a horrific
end when news of the flight of the British regiment
got abroad. Imangarh fell and then Hyderabad. But I
beheld, one evening, a carrier pigeon a-hover above the
eaves of the homestead wherein we were billeted. The
note was brief. "We punish dishonour with death." I can
no longer pretend ignorance of the act alluded to. The
vengeance of the barbarous tribes of these hills is well

beknown. My soul is now reconciled to the unknown end in store for me. I entrust unto you the truth, my son: not upon a field of battle did the hero fall, nay. Mayhap in the dead of night shall the coward be felled, the hero of Sind, stabbed in the back with a poisoned dagger, as is the way of vengeance in these parts, the code of honour among the hillmen here. For my part, my son, I have long learnt that the world is not run on principles such as we believe. The world is run on principles other than honour, my son, and wisdom comes with this dire knowledge. Yet one who is raised upon a tradition of honour can but seek to guide himself by a rough imitation thereof in a dishonourable world. Honour is not dead. Honour has just never existed, my son. And if it does exist, whither is one to look for it? I must search my soul for an answer and herein do I find it: witness the honourable confessions of a dishonourable man. My disconcert disproves me. I rejoice in my fall for it proveth me wrong. You have heard of the parable of the Prodigal Son. I bring unto you the parable of a prodigal father . . .

The exigency of self-vindication dictated such enormous feats of adaptation, the old yardsticks being twisted and tormented into new applications. Suddenly there was naked sincerity, raw appeal, confession of wrong done and waiting to be expiated. Suddenly Edwin had the impression of being down there in the chair with a troubled, shabby man across the table, a man with a care-worn, anxious face, with a shrinking eye, a question in its expression, a plea for merciful judgment writ upon his countenance. No decorations, no medals, no epaulets, no sparkle or rasp or repartee, no bark in his voice, no sting in his words.

Many cancellations occurred upon the troubled pages, crossed out but evidently meant to be read as though they were the dictate of a conscience not weak enough for silence and not strong enough for speech. The personality founded upon the cancellations alone was a full-bodied one, consistent and convincing. This was not the picture he had constructed of a hero but a dark negative image. Edwin read on, read over and over again times without number, until the account wound up with the ultimate words:

> With which words the author of this missive humbly
> solicits that he be compassionately remembered and
> that his name, however unworthy, be not omitted in the
> prayers of his son, Edwin Braithwaite Reginald Watkins
> in whose safekeeping be entrusted the legacy of truth
> herein recounted and that the mercy of his progeny be
> vouch-saved, commending the soul of their sire, Vernon
> Agnew Watkins unto Jesus Christ, Our Lord, Amen.

Edwin never knew how long he lay thus, head down upon the table, weary beyond words. Many a time he looked, uncomprehending, from the gun to the faded sheets before him. Only two truths struck him as conclusive—violence and words. Edwin had the sensation of being somehow edged, weightless, in an inverted world at an awkward slant, of looking down from a great height upon a curious, oblique landscape of tree tops, the geography of which had not been plotted out and for which the old cardinal directions were useless. And winding betwixt them a thin white trail of a path that was not composed of land but was a shred of empty sky. A panic seized him that he might never find his footing again, overstep the safe confines of firm land and step into that insubstantial space that led nowhere beyond itself, that dissembled as solid earth but was composed of treacherous perspectives of nothing. Nobody, resolved Edwin vaguely, must see that letter. And yet its contents awaited his evaluation. His judgement had to be framed and privately pronounced, his face set in a decisive expression ere he left the chamber and met them all without. A great fatigue overcame him. In what way, other than physical, was he connected with that man? Why should his judgment matter at all? Why was it assumed by that long dead man that some moral continuity was necessary and natural, that errors long ago committed merited assessment and allowance, that confessions conferred integrity and release from guilt? That man had fallen in his own eyes and he now waited to be reinstated in dignity by an act of emotional surrender, twenty years late. Suppose, reflected Edwin, I were to decline this honour, deny this responsibility? However could one resume one's own continuity bereft of so many favourite ideas ? Too much had to be redefined before he could look another human being in the face unashamed. What an ungracious birthday gift to confer—a lexicon gone suddenly bankrupt!

A bonfire had formed no part of the memsahib's plans for the evening, yet she was presently amazed to behold a glorious bonfire ablaze on the drive with Edwin rallying up the visitors to partake of the pleasures of the night air with an elation altogether out of accord with his sombre cast of mind. And when, led by an aghast Colonel Memsahib, the guests assembled in a confounded bunch upon the porch, Edwin lurched out a piece of hectic oratory, the merriment of which was absolutely at odds with the senselessness of its words. Only a smattering of phrases reaches the ear in a grand, garbled delivery:

'Gentlemen and ladies!' cried Edwin. 'As part of this evening's delights I am required to make a speech upon perusing the memoirs of the late Vernon Agnew Watkins, unhappily my father. I wish to bring to your kind notice, ladies and gentlemen, that the posthumous confidences which the late Colonel thought fit to repose in me this evening of evenings, lie rightly reduced to cinders at the bottom of yonder bonfire and I defy any to induce me to utter a word respecting them now and evermore! I wish to draw your attention, ladies and gentlemen, that this is no ordinary bonfire. Into its making have gone the thoughts of Spinoza, the sonnets of Shakespeare, the reflections of Marcus Aurelius, yes, all the prized books of my library, all the prized preoccupations of my brain. Into it have gone my petty compositions, my shabby speculations . . .'

'Edwin!' cried the Colonel Memsahib, aghast, hastening forward and laying an arm upon his. 'What's all this, Edwin? Speak up, my son. Pull yourself together. Compose yourself, do.' She stared up in shock and dismay at his strange, glazed eyes, his working jaw.

Edwin shook her off. 'Farewell!' cried he in derision. 'Goodnight, gentlemen. I have now come of age and enjoy the privilege of granting you leave to tread the measure all this lovely night through, I, for my part, shall advert to my chamber, alas, empty of all I cherished, and leave you to your joys!'

Oh, heavens, the scandal! Rosalie was in tears and the memsahib tight-lipped, took in the situation. Already there were delighted whispers being exchanged. However would they ever live it down? All Calcutta would hear . . .

Commotion reigned in the ballroom, cries and exclamations, queries and bewildered exchanges. The servants peered from behind curtains, their black eyes shining in excitement. Nothing like this had ever happened before—a sahib gone berserk and without a drop inside him!

Knocking on Edwin's door, calling out and pleading having proved of no avail, it was Mr Dutt the hostess quietly sought out.

'Please, Mr Dutt, we shall be infinitely beholden to you if you endeavour to exercise your influence upon Edwin. . . remonstrate with him to behave himself . . .'

'I shall endeavour, madam,' said he.

And when the gentle knock sounded upon Edwin's door and Mr Dutt's low voice responded from without, the guests were intrigued to behold the door slide open, admit Mr Dutt's slight form and close behind him.

'Mr Edwin,' ventured Mr Dutt quietly. '—why was all this necessary?'

The boy raised tired eyes into his face and an expression of shame and misery filled his countenance.

'I don't know,' stammered he. 'I had to do something. An act . . . a gesture . . . to mark the break.'

Mr Dutt nodded. 'May I sit down awhile?'

'I earnestly ask you to,' cried Edwin.

Mr Dutt complied. 'That letter upset you?' asked he simply.

Edwin looked away. 'I cannot speak of it,' said he, sullen.

'I do not ask you to,' said Mr Dutt. 'But one thing intrigues me, Mr Edwin. What were Shakespeare and Spinoza paying for?'

Edwin hung his head.

'You must needs make your spiritual fathers pay for whatever you hold your fleshly father guilty of?'

'Please,' begged the boy irritably. '—don't ask me anything. I know nothing now save that everything is wrong. Everything is different. It's always been so—and I never knew it. Somebody has been wrong about things. Has ever been wrong. A—a chronic error somewhere. A most godawful misconstruction!'

Mr Dutt let him speak. Edwin rose and walked the half-dozen short steps to his now empty bookshelves.

'All these years,' he spoke up with some difficulty, finding himself slowly as he uttered. 'All these years I've been teaching myself, preparing—for what? There's nothing to say and nobody to speak to. No more words for me, I say. No more expression . . .'

'But one who is trained to render in words will go on doing so, speaking, if necessary to the vacant air,' put in Mr Dutt. 'You shall go on doing what your soul is trained for, God alone knows why. The spirit has its habits as much as the body.'

'You saw this terrible evening, sir. People, music, singing, sermons, speeches, stories, natter! Do you know how much money my mother squandered—to make herself estimable in the eyes of these . . . these fakes, these boors, this empty, unkind lot. What are they capable of even at their best and brightest? Did you hear them speak? Buying, selling, conquering and imposing! Did you notice the manner in which they meet old friends? What haste they are in to render an account—their station, their emoluments, the number of baboos they command! They judge of fineness by a chandelier or a dinner service. They judge of a man by his rank, his decorations. I would I could ask some of them: "But where are you now, sir? Whither have you reached? In yourself?" I daresay they shall answer: "I began as a grocer's boy and look at me, I am the Viceroy's bootblack now and wear the livery of the Government House!" Oh God, Oh God, I'm through with it all, I say. That's why I burnt it all up—let them squeal! Men aren't creatures of such excellence that their approval should matter any more to me! I hate these successful people! I love the world's great failures—I wish I knew 'em all!'

He sank into the chair, clasping his head, overwrought. 'My head aches. My head aches with it all! I'm through with this natter, this cunning speech, these crafty ideas. I would I could cross 'em all out of my heart—as one crosses out a wrong line of verse! I will not play this lying game. I . . . I decline. I . . . resign my membership of humankind. I shall never read or write again. I shall not pay for my term on earth in counterfeit coins. I want a . . . a real language, or no speech at all!'

'Wait,' interposed Mr Dutt. 'You are uttering a real language, son. And if you have not noticed it so far, let me make you wise of the fact that you are speaking the stuff of philosophy even when you do deny it. And were you to write it down you would realize that this is your first real poem . . .'

'No, no, no, no!' burst out Edwin. 'To trim lines again with garden shears! Never, never again! I'd rather be a cook or a carpenter!'

'I often wonder,' said Mr Dutt, ignoring his companion's ravings, '—what life would be like to those who need not utter anything about it, who need no language. But you, my son, are one who must ever render things constantly to himself? Even when you abuse it. You shall never be free from the imperative to express. Some day you shall write it down—in a different form maybe. . .'

'Some day!' said Edwin bitterly. 'And meanwhile I am left clutching a gun and a story of deception. General falsehood, death. The whole pattern is wrong and why were we wrong?'

'Not the whole pattern,' said Mr Dutt 'But a few parts thereof . . .'

'But if,' argued Edwin. '—if a single part seems right, do you accept it with equal force?'

'If you piece it out, son, you are disposed to notice that there are more things that seem right than seem wrong.' He fell silent, reflecting. 'One excellent line of verse can save an entire poem. And recollect: one man's blood expiated for the sins of generations

Edwin looked up, confused.

'The good thief, recollect, was exalted to heaven on the strength of one act. It's a mixed world—a game of noughts and crosses. You must needs plot it out as you see fit, make it work as you deem right, let the noughts overwhelm the crosses or the crosses overwhelm the noughts—but for every nought there is a cross. I suspect that every wrong has a corresponding right somewhere in the world.'

'And honour?' asked Edwin. '"The world is run on principles other than honour." That's what he wrote.'

'Edwin Reginald Braithwaite Watkins,' spoke Mr Dutt and there was a note of paternal command in his voice that made Edwin look up in slow comprehension. 'I ask you to believe me. Honour is never dead, my son. Human honour may yet be found among the world's fools and failures, spread invisibly all over the world and usually anonymous. Look for it still. Look where you least expect to find it. Be not misled by birth or breeding or speech or style. Fineness occurs oft in the most unrefined. Even when we act in utmost dishonour we know full well what honour is. Even when we do lie most flagrantly we know in our souls what the truth is. That's how goodness continues even in the foulest of acts.'

'Ineffectually,' said Edwin.

Mr Dutt shrugged. 'I wonder,' said he.

'"These are the honourable confessions of a dishonourable man,"' thought Edwin. 'He wrote that too. He knew all along. And one good line of verse can redeem an entire . . .' There were now no clear definitions, no cut and dried solutions, no straight causes there were complexities, qualified situations, flexible yardsticks. But still the old words existed, if no longer absolute at least adaptable and living, still living.

'And, Mr Edwin,' said Mr Dutt, smiling, '—when you order a fresh stock of books for your shelves, dare I hope that I may be present? You shall, I am sure, read the old books again, once you have refurbished your library.'

Edwin rose sheepishly, still confused, but nodded.

'And now come, my son,' said Mr Dutt. 'They await you.' And Edwin followed.

'Your son, madam,' said Mr Dutt.

'Where is the letter? Oh, you burnt it! How could you? What did Papa write?' cried Rosa.

'Hush!' warned the Colonel Memsahib. 'Don't speak of it. He is a little disturbed. It's all been very trying for him.'

'Nay,' said Mr Dutt. 'Edwin has come of age. Some claret for Mr Edwin, madam.'

'Who in heaven's name is he?' sniffed Miss Parker. 'The life and soul of the party, bless us all!'

'Some sort of a native English poet,' whispered Rosa.

'Nay, Miss Rosalie,' smiled Mr Dutt, hearing. 'A Bengalee poet is what I am now. Like Mr Edwin here I have—how do you say?—come of age.'

Emilia O'Brien came and led Edwin away. He strove to remember the steps of the waltz. And did. The band began playing "Leezie Lindsay". The empty floor began filling up again.